The Wolfstone Curse

JUSTIN RICHARDS

templar

For Alison, Julian, & Chris –
may the wolves never find you

A TEMPLAR BOOK

First published in the UK in 2013
by Templar Publishing,
an imprint of The Templar Company Limited,
Deepdene Lodge, Deepdene Avenue,
Dorking, Surrey, RH5 4AT, UK

www.templarco.co.uk

Cover illustration by the-parish.com

First UK edition

ISBN 978-1-84877-551-0

Printed and bound by CPI Group (UK) Ltd, Croydon, CR0 4YY

If Death Were an animal,
she would be a Wolf

(Medieval proverb, thought to originate in the Cotswolds)

Operation Velvet Claw

It's what you don't know that kills you.

But I do know this: the next 24 hours could change the course of the war.

Am I exaggerating? I certainly feel like I have the whole future of the world in my hands. Not just me of course - Acer is in charge. And Boffin's the man who first discovered the terrible secrets of Castle Wolfenburg.

I keep this journal to take my mind off little things like that.

Boffin has briefed us on the background – the why. He told us about the Nazi experiments – as much as he knows, as much as his colleagues in the Special Operations Executive have managed to discover. It sounds incredible – incredible but grotesque. Inhuman. Devilish.

Acer then told us the plan. We all have codenames taken from trees for some reason. I'm Copper – as in Copper Beech. At least I'm not Elm or Gum. Not that real trees could survive in this stifling, claustrophobic underwater world. I'm not cut out for life in a submarine; I don't know how the normal crew copes.

It's a relief to me we're only on-board for a few days.

But that's a small enough sacrifice compared with what the people have been through where we're going. I guess if you don't have a child of your own you can't really imagine it. The loss. Not knowing. The terror of what might have been, what could have happened in the night – when your teenage son just vanished. Hoping that if you do ever see him again it will be as a pale, emaciated corpse ripped to shreds by the wild animals in the forest. By <u>something</u>.

Knowing that fate must be better than what else might have happened.

I can't imagine cradling the broken remains of my child in the shade of the medieval fortress that looms over this whole landscape. I can't imagine living in that shadow. Afraid of the darkest nights and what they might bring. Dreading the moonlight even more...

It's time. Acer is ready. Time to venture into the dark forest. Time to face our fears.

Mercifully, there was no moon.

It took Copper, Acer, and three other commandos the best part of half an hour to reach the high stone wall surrounding the castle grounds. It was a difficult journey, in the dark and trying to stay silent, clambering over the rocky escarpment on which the castle was built. All the time, it loomed above them – forbidding and implacable.

Grass gave way to stone as they approached the main castle. Copper felt the cold biting through the thick rubber soles of his boots. Looking up, he saw dark shadows moving slowly round the battlements. The stone head of a wolf jutted out from the wall at the apex of an arched window. A reminder of where they were: Schloss Wolfenburg.

A dark shape detached itself from the wall in front of them – a figure.

"Who's there?" it called out, in German. "Hans?"

He never knew if he was right. A young commando rose up from the ground silently beside the approaching soldier. His hand moved so fast the knife was barely a glint in the pale glow of a distant searchlight. The guard didn't even have time to cry out before the soldier was lowering his body gently and quietly to the ground.

The young man's hand was shaking as he wiped the knife clean.

"First time you've slit a throat?" Copper wondered.

"I wish." His voice was trembling too. "You remember them all, don't you? Every single one."

Acer was checking his watch. He nodded with satisfaction, and gestured for them to stay close to the wall and wait for the diversion.

They didn't have to wait long.

The castle was silhouetted against the sudden flashes of orange and red. The percussive thump of the explosions followed a second later, but the fading noise was quickly drowned out by the alarm klaxon. The first thought of the German commanders must have been of an air raid, Copper decided. But it wouldn't take them long to realise they were actually under attack from other commandos on the ground.

Machine-gun fire split the night. The *crump* of grenades. It was a gamble, but Acer's plan was that a small force could penetrate the castle when it was left relatively undefended as the guards hurried to help their besieged comrades.

Acer led the way to the end of the wall. Peering round, Copper saw a line of storm troopers running out of the gates, machine guns glinting metallically in the light of the fires and explosions. Their distinctive coal-scuttle helmets masked their features.

Timing was everything. Too soon, and they'd run into more troops. Too late, and the castle gates would be slammed shut. But Acer judged it almost perfectly.

Almost.

The five commandos charged towards the gatehouse. Two sentries were pulling the heavy wooden doors closed. Bullets from Acer's machine pistol stitched a line across the gates, ending at one sentry's chest. He was slammed back into the castle. The sound of Copper's own gun was loud even against the noise of the battle. He opted for single shots, the first going wide and chiselling into the stone wall. His next shot found its mark and the second sentry collapsed in a lifeless heap.

As he leaped over the body, Copper spared the man a glance. If you could call him a man.

The young commando who'd killed the sentry jammed a grenade between one of the gates and its main hinge. He flicked out the pin. It took him scant seconds.

But that was too long. Three SS troopers were sprinting towards them across the courtyard. Late to the main battle, but horribly punctual for this one. They fired as they ran.

The first burst of gunfire lifted the young soldier and threw him backwards. Copper saw enough blood to know the man was already dead.

"Back – back!" Acer shouted.

"Then we'll never get in," one of the other commandos yelled.

Acer didn't reply. He grabbed the man's shoulder and shoved him roughly aside. The ground at the man's feet erupted in a flurry of gunfire.

The SS men paused in the gateway. The searchlight from the top of one of the castle towers picked out Copper and his three colleagues as they stood helplessly exposed outside the main gatehouse.

Then the grenade wedged between the huge wooden door and the castle wall went off. The blast engulfed the nearest soldier. His uniform caught fire and he cartwheeled away, a screaming mass of flames and flailing limbs.

His fellows turned in shock and surprise. The blast hadn't caught them. But the massive wooden door did – tearing free of its fractured hinge and crashing down.

They raced across the courtyard, bullets whipping past them. The searchlight struggled to keep up. The commando next to Copper hit the ground, his body jumping and convulsing as more bullets ripped into it.

Three of them reached the tower and dived through the doorway. Copper barely had time to note the stone wolves staring down at him from the ornate doorframe. They were echoed in the carved stone lamp holders on the walls inside the tower.

Acer was firing up the spiral staircase. They heard the sounds of bodies tumbling and falling above them, blocking the stairway. Copper, Acer and Elm ran down the other way. The only light was flickering torches held in the mouths of the stone wolves.

"We'll split up," Acer decided at the bottom of the stairway. He handed them each explosive charges. They were small but powerful. Enough to rupture the castle's foundations and bring the whole structure crashing down. "Find the laboratories and let's end this madness."

Elm stuffed several charges inside his tunic, and hurried off down the corridor.

"With me," Acer ordered.

"Where to?" Copper demanded. "Shouldn't we–"

Acer cut him off. "This way."

From above and behind them came the clatter of heavy boots down the stairs. With an almost casual gesture, Acer set the timer on one of the small charges, and lobbed it back towards the stairway. He and Copper both broke into an immediate run.

Behind them, the whole corridor erupted with sound and flame. Stonework crashed down, blocking the bottom of the stairs with a heap of rubble.

"We won't be getting out that way," Copper said, coughing away the dust and smoke.

Acer didn't answer.

He strode purposefully through the smoke-filled stone

corridor. A man appeared through the grey air – not in uniform, but wearing a suit. Acer knocked him down with the butt of his gun – a sudden, swift, brutal movement. Copper stepped over the prone body and followed.

The corridor ended in large double doors. Acer flung them open, spraying machine-gun fire into the room. Two more men in suits were caught in the hail of bullets. A woman in a white coat was slammed backwards across one of the beds. The syringe she was holding fell to the floor and shattered.

It looked like a hospital ward. Metal-framed beds with patients stretched out unmoving. Fluid tubes fed into their forearms. Artificial lungs wheezed and groaned. Chests rose and fell in a steady, almost lazy rhythm. Eyelids blinked open to reveal rheumy eyes. A hand clawed at the sheets, ripping through them.

Similar double doors led from the ward – the laboratory – into another room.

It was like walking into a cathedral. The high-vaulted roof extended into the upper floors of the castle. Leaded glass windows shone with the flashes and bursts of the fire-fight in the woods outside. A stone altar stood on a dais in the centre of the chamber. From each corner of the altar a carved wolf's head stared out. Where the stone arches met the upright pillars, more wolves watched impassively as Acer strode towards the altar to place his explosives.

"It's like a shrine," Copper said. His voice echoed eerily.

There was an atmosphere, a sense of foreboding. Copper did his best to ignore it, setting his own explosive charge at the base of each of the main supporting pillars. He was bending to place the third one when a bullet hammered into the pillar above his head. Splinters of stone stung his face as he whipped round, bringing up his own machine gun.

He was in time to see a black-clad figure step back behind a pillar on the opposite side of the chamber.

Acer had ducked down behind the stone altar. He gestured for Copper to edge his way round – to get a line of sight on the soldier.

The figure reappeared. Another shot – worryingly close. Copper saw enough to know he was facing an SS officer. A colonel.

"*Standartenführer*." Acer called out the man's rank, trying to distract him. "You're outnumbered. Surrender now and we might all get out of here alive."

Copper eased further round the edge of the room. But still he didn't have a shot. The end of a handgun – a Luger – appeared round the pillar. It spat flame, and a bullet chipped the altar close to where Acer was sheltering.

Copper leaped sideways, firing a long continuous burst. The area behind the pillar misted with dust and fragments of stone. The noise was deafening as it echoed round the chamber.

But the SS man was already gone – sprinting for another door at the back of the chamber. Acer fired after him. A light shone out from the doorway. Then the door slammed shut, the wood immediately ripped open by the shots from both men.

Copper's gun clicked on empty. He pulled out the magazine and reached for another.

He didn't have one.

"I'm out too," Acer said grimly.

"Leave him?" Copper suggested.

"Charges are set. Stairs are blocked – but he might know another way out."

Copper nodded. "Worth a try."

Acer heaved the door open. They both ducked back as three more shots rang out. Then, together, they hurled themselves through the doorway.

Copper rolled to one side, leaping back to his feet. He held his gun like a club. More shots, then the staccato click as the Luger fired on empty.

But Copper couldn't see. He was dazzled by the light. He blinked, desperately trying to get his eyes to adjust. He shielded his face, but the light wasn't coming from a single source. It was all around them.

He heard Acer gasp in surprise, maybe in pain. And as his vision finally, gradually returned, he could see why.

The room was made of glass.

The walls, ceiling, even the floor were polished glass or crystal. It had a strange milky quality, like quartz. The light of the candles positioned in glass-shelved alcoves was magnified and echoed all round the room, and the whole place seemed to shimmer. Only one of the many alcoves didn't contain a candle. Instead, a sword handle projected from the glowing wall, the blade visible as a shadow thrusting deep into the crystal.

In the centre of the room stood the SS officer – the only dark shadow in a world of shining crystal. The light threw his gaunt features into stark relief. His jutting chin, thin nose, the arrogant set of his jaw. His eyes were dark, set deep within hollow sockets. His hair was cut short and swept sideways.

The man's voice was a deep rasp – full of hate and anger. It was a voice used to giving orders.

"Welcome to my lair."

It took Copper a moment to realise he had said it in English.

The man's next utterance wasn't in any language. He threw his head back and roared – a tremendous, guttural burst of sound. Saliva dripped from his mouth. His whole face seemed to shimmer and crawl in the glowing light.

Like something was trapped under his skin, and trying to rip its way out. The man's eyes had taken on a red tinge. The gun clattered to the floor and the man spread his arms, his hands clenched like claws. His teeth glinting and yellow. The death's-head emblem on his lapel glowing angrily.

Claws.

Teeth.

Death.

Another roar. The creature in the SS uniform hurled itself at Copper, snarling with rage and anticipation. Claws raked down towards him. Elongated jaws snapped hungrily at his throat. The pervasive glow of the crystal was blotted out by darkness – by black uniform, dark fur and death.

SEVENTY YEARS LATER...

She lost count of the days she spent in her room.

She lacked for nothing. She could have whatever she wanted – with just one exception. The view from her window made it worse – seeing what she could never have. Freedom.

She could see the woods. If she opened the heavy casement, and squeezed her head and one shoulder through, she could lean out far enough to see along the side of the house and catch the smallest glimpse of the edge of the circle.

She had thought about jumping. But the window was too narrow and the drop was too far. Mr Edward could do it. Her friend from earliest childhood would fit easily through the window, and the drop would be as nothing.

Mr Edward watched her across the room through glassy, unfeeling eyes. He sat on the bed, close to her pillow – impassive and silent. But she loved him, even after all these years. She loved his warmth, loved how soft and yielding he felt when she hugged him tight. She didn't mind the roughness of his snout, or the way his hairy face scratched at her own pale cheeks. And he didn't mind that her tears soaked into his fur. All the better to comfort you with, he might have said – if he could speak.

Mr Edward was not part of her plan, but when she heard the man at the door, she was clutching him in a tight embrace. She lacked for nothing, but Mr Edward was all she had.

She didn't know the man's name. He had a broken ear, and he spoke almost as little as Mr Edward. Sometimes he had questions for her – questions that were not his own. Usually he just brought her food, and took away the empty plates. The first few times, she'd thrown it back at him. He didn't seem to care, and she had gone hungry.

He came less often now, so she was always hungry. He'd watch, amused, as she wolfed down the food. But not this time. She stood behind the door, holding tight to Mr Edward, whispering to him that they would be all right. Just like when she was a child. If they had put him here to stop her growing up, then it had worked.

The man's eyes narrowed when she pulled the door further open. He suspected something, watching her closely. Ignoring Mr Edward, which annoyed her. But it pleased her too because Mr Edward had now become a part of her plan. She smiled at the man's frown, and stepped back from the door.

"That's better," the man growled. He put down the

tray on the floor just inside the door like he always did. He never came far into the room.

"When's he coming?" she demanded as he let go of the tray.

"Who?"

"You know who. My father – when is he coming to see me?"

"Soon." The man began to straighten up.

"How soon?"

The man sighed. He was slightly off balance as he stood up – that was when she did it.

She hurled Mr Edward at the tray of food, as if in anger. The glass was knocked sideways – milk spattering over the man's shoes.

"*When*?" she yelled – for the noise and surprise as much as because she wanted to know.

The man was staring at the mess – at the teddy bear lying in the spilled milk and ruined food. He was caught halfway between crouching and standing. She pulled the skirt of her long white dress up above her knees and kicked out as hard as she could.

She wasn't allowed shoes. But her anger and desperation gave her strength, and her bare foot connected with the man's chin. His head snapped up and he grunted in pain and surprise, falling backwards. There was no time to get his keys, but she knew the door had a bolt as well as the lock. She leaped over his fallen body. Felt his sharp nails scratch down her leg as he grabbed for her. Heard his growl of anger.

Then she was past him, slamming the door shut in his snarling face and ramming the bolt across.

"Sorry, Mr Edward," she murmured. But she wouldn't come back for him. She was far too old for toys.

And she had to get away.

Night was drawing in and the house was in near darkness. There was no light except in her room. It took a moment to get used to the dark. To get used to the contrast between her well-lit room with the patterned wallpaper and soft carpet, and this twilight world of bare, dusty boards.

Something heavy thumped into the door, shaking it in its frame and shocking her into movement.

The dust was slippery under her feet. She cried out as a cobweb swept across her face. She brushed it away, shook her long, fair hair out of her eyes, and kept running.

The stairs creaked. Her ancestors watched her accusingly, staring down from their gloomy, age-darkened portraits. How long since any of them had lived here? How long since *anyone* had lived here apart from herself, and the man with the broken ear?

Across the hall. More cobwebs. Her foot scratched on a

splintered floorboard, but she scarcely noticed.

The night air was fresh and chill, and she gulped it in hungrily. She stood for a moment, looking round, getting her bearings. Which way was the village?

She kept to the shadows, close to the walls of the house. Past the broken and boarded windows, along the cracked and uneven paving.

A single light shone out from a high window, in a tower at the end of the house. Her room. She must have run all the way round to the back of the house. But that was good – she knew where she was. She could remember the view. She glanced up at the light.

There was a dark shape in the window, silhouetted against the light. Eyes stared glassily down, and for a moment she thought Mr Edward had somehow clambered up to watch.

The shape forced its way lithely through the window. Forelegs scrabbled at the edge of the sill. Fur bristled and ruffled in the breeze as the blood-red eyes sought her out. Then it leaped – out from the window, into space, legs still scrabbling in the air. The night split by its howl.

It landed on all fours, snarling and snapping. The animal's broken ear was a mass of matted fur and tissue that scarred one side of its head. The eyes caught the moonlight so they seemed to flash and glow. It took only a moment to gather itself, then the creature was running – bounding towards her.

She turned, her long white dress billowing out as she moved. Her feet pawed urgently at the grass as she ran from the house. The blood was pounding in her ears, like the thump of the predator's feet behind her. Ragged gasps of breath, the wind in her hair, her dress pressed tight round her as she ran.

If she could reach the hedge, maybe she could lose him in the maze. How well did her pursuer know it? She'd played there as a child – laughing and hiding from her brother. Racing him to the centre to find the statue. If she could find it now, would she be safe?

She didn't dare look back. She could feel the animal's hot breath on her neck. Could smell the musky scent of its body – the same smell that accompanied the man into the room when he brought her food. When he brought her milk and raw steak.

A wall of green. The moonlight filtered through, casting shadows like the pattern on her wallpaper. She ran, turned a corner, pushed through a narrow gap between hedges.

Ahead of her, eyes glinted in the night. She doubled back.

Close beside her, jaws snapped shut. A snarl of anger sent her off down another green corridor.

The next opening – even overgrown, even after all these years, she recognised it. She forced herself through the brambles and bindweed. Barely noticed the tiny purple flowers opening as the moonlight touched them. Something whipped at her face, like the cobwebs in the house. She cried out, wiping the back of her hand across. It came away smudged with blood.

She stared at the crimson stain for a moment, before licking it away. Like an animal licking its wounds. She felt the blood welling up again, and running down her cheek like tears.

But she was here now, she'd made it. She'd escaped from the room, from the man with the ragged ear. She'd made it to the centre of the maze, just like in her childhood games. Safe.

She let out a long, sighing breath. The wind riffled through her hair. She could feel the night through her flimsy dress. Her breathing settled into a gentle rhythm.

And now could she hear its echo. The low, rasping breath of the animal that was hunting her. That had found her.

Only now did she realise there was no other way out of the centre of the maze. She was just as trapped here as she was in her room.

She turned, just as the creature leaped out of the

darkness – paws out and claws extended. Its snarling face filled the night as the wolf slammed into her, knocking her down. Its jaws opened impossibly wide, and its roar of triumph echoed round the green prison.

CHAPTER 1

Welcome to Wolfstone

The Historic Village at the Heart of the 'Wolfstone Park' Luxury Development.

Historic Wolfstone lies in the midst of the Cotswolds. It is of course best known for the famous Wolfstone Circle – a set of standing stones close to the village. Wolfstone Manor is also of historical interest, although it has been neglected in recent years.

Away from main roads and railway lines, the village itself has generally been in decline since medieval times, when it served the local farming community.

But with the extensive Wolfstone Park development now well under construction by Forrest Homes, the village will be reborn as the prestige rural location for people working as far afield as Cheltenham and Evesham.

Wolfstone Park is being built on part of the ancient Wolfstone Manor Estate, saturated in local history and tradition. It will provide three, four and five-bedroom homes of distinction.

Call Trisha at Forrest Domestic Estates for an executive brochure and price list, and ask for estimated completion dates. Part exchange available.

The Red Fleece

The Red Fleece is a seventeenth-century coaching inn,
fully restored and oozing with period ambience.
It is a favourite of visitors to the area,
providing excellent bed and breakfast.

The bar is well stocked with a variety of real ales,
including Hook Norton, Theakstons,
and the locally brewed Claw-Toe.

As well as bar snacks, the fully licensed restaurant
offers an à la carte menu of locally sourced food,
including the Fleece's signature dish: *Huntsman's Pie*.

A shadow stalked the Range Rover. Peter saw it through the window as he glanced up from the leaflet. A glimpse, no more. Maybe it was the shadow of the vehicle itself – thrown across the edge of the wood beside the road, broken up by the trees and dancing up the slight incline.

Just a glimpse. When Peter turned to look properly, there was nothing but the patchy sunlight and the irregular shade under the trees. He put the leaflet back in the side pocket of the door.

"If I read for too long, I feel sick," he said, still looking out of the window.

"It's not that bad, surely," his dad said.

"No, I don't mean the leaflet. If I read *anything*..."

Peter's voice tailed off as he realised his dad was smiling. Professor Crichton glanced quickly at Peter before returning his attention to the driving.

They were on narrow country lanes now, the main roads far behind them. They emerged from the woodland, and the view suggested they had hardly climbed at all. At least the rain had stopped. The late afternoon sun was struggling unenthusiastically to escape from behind the clouds, bathing the rural landscape with pale yellow light.

Peter resisted the temptation to ask if they were nearly there yet. Instead, he said, "So what's it mean when it says the place has been 'in decline since medieval times'?"

"Oh they're exaggerating. 'In decline' is a very emotive phrase, and I seriously doubt if there's any real evidence for that."

It was a historian's answer. Or maybe an archaeologist's. Dad was both.

"You said there's loads going on," Peter reminded him. "You said I wouldn't get bored."

"Did I?" The Professor seemed to be concentrating more than ever on the road now.

"Yes, you did."

"Well, it's up to you whether you get bored, really, isn't it? You can help out on the dig. Lots going on there."

"You've got Mike and Abby for that," Peter pointed out.

"Could always use an extra hand."

Peter sighed. "If I don't like it," he said. "If I do get bored. If there really is nothing to do – can I go home?"

"You can do what you want. You're old enough. Off to university and everything. Course you can. But you'll get bored at home on your own and Mum's off lecturing for another month in America. *I'm* off digging up ancient stone circles, so ask yourself what your best option is." It was clear what Professor Matthew Crichton considered the best choice.

They were staying at the Red Fleece pub. It was built from Cotswold stone, weathered and grey. The window frames were painted black, so the only variation in tone came from the sign swinging gently above the door

It showed a sheep's skin. At least, Peter thought it did. Looking closer, he saw that the skin was draped over another animal – a wolf in sheep's clothing. The wolf's eyes shone from beneath the sheep's dead head. Although the pub was called the *Red* Fleece, mercifully the fleece on the sign was a dirty, flaking white.

"I bet there's some local story," his dad said, following Peter's gaze. "Come on – give me a hand with the bags."

Peter followed the professor round to the back of the Range Rover. He glanced up at movement from a window on the upper floor of the pub. The light was reflecting off it, so he couldn't be sure, but he thought someone was there, watching.

The door from the car park gave a choice of Lounge Bar and Restaurant one way, and Reception the other. Reception turned out to be little more than a hatch in the wall. There was an old-fashioned brass bell on the narrow counter, which the professor rang.

"You must be Professor Crichton," the woman said when she arrived at the other side of the hatch.

"I suppose I must," Crichton agreed. "This is Peter."

"Hello."

The woman seemed friendly enough. She was about the same age as Peter's mum – mid-forties. She looked older because she was wearing clothes that even Peter could see were out of date as well as old. A dark cardigan over a patterned blouse and a long black skirt. Her hair was fair, but streaked with white. She had a round face, with smiling eyes. A large silver locket dangled above the counter as she leaned forward.

"Sorry, I was pulling a pint for Dave Bennett. If he wants anything else, Mr Seymour can sort it out. Let me get the register."

Several metal bracelets jangled as she lifted the large book onto the counter. Every one of her fingers had at least one ring – most of them silver.

"If you could just sign in for me? And I'll need your car registration number. Then I'll show you to your rooms. Carys can help with your bags." She leaned across and rang the bell again. Several times. "I'm Faye Seymour," she went on without pause. "I think we spoke on the phone. But just call me Faye. And shout if you need anything."

"We can manage our bags. We've not got much," Crichton assured Mrs Seymour as she attacked the bell again.

"Could you? I'm so sorry, she's usually pretty good. But you know what teenagers are like."

Carys guessed it was Professor Crichton and his son. She heard the Range Rover, and saw them from her window as they got their bags out of the back of the vehicle. The boy glanced up at the window, and instinctively Carys took a step backwards. Silly – he probably couldn't see her anyway. And so what if he did? The boy was older than Carys had expected – about the same age as she was. But he obviously wasn't trapped at home like she was. Well, maybe 'trapped' was a bit strong, but there was no way she could leave Mum to cope on her own.

Carys heard the bell from her room. She'd been in the bar all through lunchtime, and this was the first chance she'd had for any time to herself. Not that serving at lunchtime was hard work, unless there was a coach party in on their way round the Cotswolds or en route to Cheltenham.

Besides, the boy and his dad didn't need her help. She'd seen them carry their bags across the car park, so they could manage a few stairs. Then again, it would be an excuse to meet the boy. She hadn't really mixed with many people her own age since finishing school. But what would they talk about? What could they have in common? He looked so confident and at ease, talking to his father.

So why would he want to talk to Carys – poor girl, stuck working in her mum's pub in the middle of nowhere? She flopped down on her bed and stared up at the comforting blankness of the ceiling.

They agreed to meet down in the bar after they'd unpacked. It didn't take Peter long. There was no point in getting to the bar before Dad, so Peter fired his laptop up to check Facebook. But although there was a wi-fi connection, he needed a password.

So he checked on his phone instead, which took for ever as the signal was almost non-existent, and because it always took an age. "God, this place is a dump," he muttered. He reckoned he'd probably be heading home in a couple of days.

His phone finally got its act together and Peter updated his status: "Peter Crichton is bored in the Cotswolds." The signal disappeared completely before he could send it.

Their rooms were on the same floor but off different sides of the main staircase. Peter hadn't really been paying attention, but reckoned finding the way back down to the bar should be easy enough.

Except, when he stepped outside his room, Peter couldn't even remember which way to turn. He set off to the right, and followed the corridor round and past several other rooms. But it didn't look familiar.

A side passage took him through to another corridor, which soon ended in a wall. Peter sighed with frustration and turned back.

Someone was watching him. He felt their eyes on him before he saw the figure standing in a doorway.

"Hello?" he said. Now he was going to have to admit he'd got lost. How embarrassing was that? "Sorry, can I ask...?"

It was a girl, about Peter's age or maybe a bit older. She was slim with angular features framed by dark hair that was cut off the collar and into a spiky fringe, like a rebellious public schoolboy. Her green eyes caught the light, like a cat's. Well, maybe staying here might not be so bad after all, Peter thought. He smiled.

But the girl's expression didn't change from a sort of grudging half-smile which might have been sympathetic or mocking. She pointed at a door in the opposite wall. She said nothing, but when Peter hesitated, she nodded like she was encouraging a small child to behave itself.

Peter tried the door, and found it gave out on to the main staircase. He knew where he was now. He turned back, and found to his disappointment that the girl had gone, the door closed behind her.

"Thanks," he said to the empty corridor.

His dad was already in the bar, talking to another man. It wasn't Mike from the university, who was working with Dad and Abby on the survey.

This man was older – in his fifties, maybe. His hair was steel grey and he was wearing a plain, dark suit. He spoke with an air of quiet authority, though Peter couldn't hear what he was saying. Professor Crichton was listening, which was unusual. He didn't listen to anyone who wasn't worth listening to. And in the professor's estimation that was very few people.

"Are you Peter?"

"Yes?"

He hadn't seen the young man sitting in the corner. Though Peter soon saw that actually he was only about his own age. He looked older as he too was wearing a suit. He had unruly fair hair that toppled forward, but there was an obvious resemblance to the older man.

"Thought you must be. I'm David Forrest. You want a drink? They'll be ages yet."

"Thanks, but I'm fine."

Peter sat down on a stool opposite David Forrest. "That your dad?"

He recognised the name – Forrest. The older man must be Sebastian Forrest, who was sponsoring the survey. That explained why Dad was listening – this guy was in effect paying his wages.

"It's all right here," David was saying. "We've got rooms in the new wing, round the back. You in the old part?"

"It's certainly old. I got lost just finding the stairs."

David grinned. "Tell me about it. Whole place is a maze. But the people are okay. Mrs Seymour is a bit..." He stopped to finish his drink. "I can't think of her as Faye. People that age shouldn't have first names."

Peter laughed, nodding. "I know what you mean."

David leaned forward, lowering his voice. "Especially as she calls him *Mr* Seymour."

Peter turned to look. A man had arrived behind the bar and was moving bottles and glasses round. He had a thick mane of grey hair, and walked with a slight stoop.

"Mr Seymour?" he said, turning back.

"That's all she ever calls him."

Peter gave a half-smile. "You here for long?"

David shrugged. "A few days. Dad's overseeing some of the building work, though it's pretty much ground to a halt for now. Recession, you know. Cash flow challenges. There's not a lot to do round here," he went on, "but I'll show you what there is if you like."

"Thanks."

"Not now, though. Looks like you're off." David got to his feet as his father came over.

Sebastian Forrest's eyes were as grey as his hair. He nodded at Peter and shook hands like David had done. It seemed a bit formal and old-fashioned.

"I was telling your father, you should see the stones at sunset. Quite a sight."

Dad was close behind. "Sounds like a plan," he said. "And I need to check what Mike and Abby have been getting up to. You ready for a field trip?"

"I guess so," Peter agreed. He'd have liked to stay and talk to David for longer. "Catch you later," he said.

"Are the stones close to the village?" Peter asked.

The professor pulled out of the car park. "As the crow flies. But we're not crows. The road doesn't take a very direct route."

As they left the last small houses behind, everything changed. A new roundabout had a wide road off it that seemed to go nowhere. In the distance, Peter could see several massive diggers. They stood idle and silent, stark against the white, cloudy sky. Beside them was a cluster of temporary buildings – workmen's huts, skips, a bright blue portaloo... Even the new stuff here looked neglected and *dead*.

A huge advertising hoarding at the edge of the roundabout announced:

WOLFSTONE MANOR ESTATE

A Forrest Domestic Estates Development

Three, four and five-bedroom homes of distinction

(Part Exchange Available)

Show Home Opening Soon

There was no sign of a show home, whether it was opening soon or not.

"Forrest is losing millions, apparently," Crichton said.

"The man you were talking to?"

The professor nodded, continuing on round the roundabout and down the lane. "His investors are getting jumpy, and they're waiting for the market to pick up. But all the time Forrest has interest payments on his loans, plus planning fees and God knows what else."

"You'd think he'd want to get on with it."

"Cash flow problems, I expect," the professor said, in a tone that Peter guessed meant he hadn't a clue what he was talking about. "But it's lucky for us," he went on,"because it means we've got more time to do a proper survey of the circle."

"But isn't the circle itself protected?" Peter asked. "He can't build on *that*."

"He could still build right up to it. Context is key, remember that. If we want to understand the Wolfstone Circle, then we need to know what was going on around it. Actually, that's all we'll ever know."

"What do you mean?"

Crichton took a sharp turn, and they bumped along a narrow track that seemed to lead nowhere.

"We're not allowed to dig inside the circle itself. We've tried non-invasive techniques like ground-penetrating radar, but we just get back a solid disc of rock. Could be natural, or it might be part of the construction. I'm hoping we'll learn more from peripheral evidence. And from looking back over the results of previous surveys."

"There have been some, then?"

"Years ago. Mainly amateur affairs. But yes, there's some stuff that might be useful."

The track petered out. Ahead of them was a young man, his long hair blowing round his face. Peter recognised Mike, one of his dad's post-graduate students from Hinton University archaeology department.

Mike and Abby had walked from the Red Fleece. Abby was actually Dr Abigail Messenger, who worked in Professor Crichton's department as a lecturer. She was already at work with tape measure, camera and theodolite.

"To be honest," she told Peter as she adjusted the theodolite's tripod, "the app on my phone's almost as good as this old thing. But your dad's brought a newer one with a built-in digital camera and GPS. At least, I hope he has."

Strands of her long brown hair had escaped from the elastic band that held it in a tight ponytail, and she paused to sort it out. The wind across the exposed fields blew her hair into a frenzy round her face as she untangled the band.

The Wolfstone Circle wasn't actually a circle. For one thing, it was incomplete. For another, if it had been complete it would have been a flattened circle – an ellipse.

Peter had seen stone circles before, but even so he

was impressed. Out here, in the middle of nowhere with the breeze tugging at his jacket, the atmosphere was palpable. These stones had stood for thousands of years, impassive and permanent. Peter counted nineteen of them in all.

The sun was low in the sky, silhouetting the stones. He could see why Forrest had said that the sunset would be impressive. As Peter ran his hand over the rough surface of one of the stones, it seemed to glitter.

"Quartz, or some similar crystal – do you see it?" Mike was standing beside him.

"Yes, I do."

"An unusually high level for granite like this. They chipped a bit off one of the stones for analysis back in the 1950s or "60s." Mike pointed across the empty field. "There's a track over there that leads back to the pub. Quicker than driving. And that way…" He turned to point in the opposite direction. "That way is Wolfstone Manor. Or what's left of it. Forrest Estates owns all this land now, so feel free to explore, if it gets boring."

They both turned to watch Peter's dad and Abby talking enthusiastically beside one of the larger stones.

"I'll give it ten minutes," Peter said.

Mike laughed. "Brave man."

Actually, he gave it fifteen. It looked like the professor and the others were set for the evening, so Peter said he'd see them back at the pub for a meal later. Once the professor got involved in a dig, he lost all concept of time. So Peter decided he might as well go for a wander.

The sun had become a deep red, touching the horizon and defying the remaining skittish wisps of cloud. Peter headed for a small area of woodland. Just as far as the wood, he thought, then he'd head back to the pub. Maybe he'd see the girl again.

Through the trees Peter noticed what looked like the remains of a stone wall. He skirted the wood. Dusk was gathering, and the area between the trees was receding into darkness.

He was about to turn and retrace his steps when he saw the gateposts. Two large stone pillars stood in the middle of the field, and from one of them hung an iron gate. It was tilting at a precarious angle, as if it might tear free of the hinge and fall at any moment. Originally there must have been a pair of gates. In the middle of nowhere.

Peter guessed the ruined wall he'd glimpsed had once reached these gateposts. On one of the posts – the one now without its gate – a stone plaque announced in weathered, crumbling letters:

WOLFSTONE MANOR

The wind was getting up, gusting through the trees so it sounded almost like a distant voice calling for help. Peter shook his head. Just his imagination.

The pillars were stark shadows against the setting sun. They were so old, yet so much newer than the stones in the circle. He reached out for the nearest pillar and felt the stone crumble and flake under his hand. Dry and rough. Only then did he glance up.

To see the wolf snarling down at him from the top of the pillar.

CHAPTER 2

"It scared the life out of me," Peter admitted.

"You *never* thought it was real?" David Forrest leaned back and laughed. Peter had found him in the bar again, absorbed in his iPad. Obviously David knew the wi-fi password.

"The sun was in my eyes," Peter said. "I didn't see the wolf statue until I was in the shadow of the pillar. Is the manor still there?" Peter asked, anxious to change the subject.

"Oh yes," David said. "It's just a shell now. About ready to fall down, I think. Best avoided, Dad says."

"Pity." It might have been interesting. If anything round here could be interesting.

"There's probably something about it in one of the books if you want to know more."

"What books?"

One whole wall of the restaurant was a single massive bookcase, with sections closed off behind glass-fronted doors. The contents ranged from old, dusty leather-bound volumes to modern paperbacks, from large-format illustrated guides to pamphlets.

"It's all local history," David said, opening one of the bookcase doors.

"And folklore, and a bit of magic," another voice added.

The girl that Peter had met earlier was standing in the doorway. She was leaning against the doorframe, her arms folded. She pushed herself upright without unfolding her arms and walked across to join them.

"What are you looking for?" she asked David, ignoring Peter.

"Just looking. Peter didn't know these were here."

"It's an impressive collection," Peter said.

The girl still ignored him, and he felt embarrassed and stupid. He wished he hadn't said anything at all.

She unfolded her arms for long enough to take a large hardback from one of the shelves. She handed it to David.

"There's something about the manor in here. Page 64, I think."

"Thanks," Peter said. He spoke to her back as she left. Only after she had gone did he realise she must have overheard them talking in the bar to know he was interested in Wolfstone Manor.

"Don't mind Carys," David said. "She's always like that. Ah, here we go."

Wolfstone Manor

Now sadly neglected and in disrepair, Wolfstone Manor was the ancestral home of the du Bois family, who lived there from the Norman Conquest up until the Second World War. After the war, following Lionel du Bois's ill-advised liaison with Himmler, the house was left empty.

Wolfstone Manor, as it was in 1952.

Grade-two listed, and described by Pevsner as "one of England's best examples of late Tudor architecture", the manor is sadly not open to visitors. Despite its robust appearance it is thought to be in imminent danger of collapse and is listed as 'At Risk' by English Heritage. Today it remains little more than a shell; its legendary wild parties long since over.

For those who are interested, the Gloucestershire County Archives include a copy of Doctor Ibbotson's 1952 survey of the property, complete with photographs and drawings of the du Bois coat of arms – the central wolf motif echoes through the general architecture of the property.

"I see you've found the library," Professor Crichton said a few minutes later when he, Mike and Abby arrived back from the circle. "Your father joining us?" he asked David before Peter could reply.

"He should be back soon." David took out his phone. "I'll give him a call, but don't wait for us." He went outside in search of a decent signal.

"Plenty to read while we wait for dinner," Abby said.

"Anything useful?" Crichton asked.

"Who knows?" Mike answered. "Well, Faye Seymour does, I expect. But she's not telling."

"Why not?" Peter asked.

Mike held his hands up and wiggled his fingers spookily. "Because no good ever came of anyone who dared to investigate the mysterious Wolfstone Circle," he said in an exaggerated rural accent. "Ooh-ah!"

Peter laughed. But no one else did. Mike went pink, and Peter realised that the room had suddenly gone quiet.

He felt himself colour up as well. Guilt by association.

"They say it because it's true," Mrs Seymour said quietly. "And you'd do well to remember that." She was carrying a pile of menus. "I assume you're eating?"

"Sorry," Mike muttered. "I was just…"

"I know." She handed him a menu. "I have no problem with you doing your survey, or taking the mickey. But you should seriously consider what's happened in the past."

"It's all just myth and legend," Abby said. "Folklore. Superstition." She held her hands up as if in surrender. "I don't mean to belittle it. But we're doing a proper scientific survey using the most modern techniques and equipment."

"Well, to be fair," Professor Crichton said, studying the new menu, "that's what they would have claimed in 1922." He closed the menu and smiled at Mrs Seymour. "Is the Huntsman's Pie as good as they say?" He could be charming when he bothered.

"Better," she told him. "You know what happened in 1922?"

Crichton nodded. "And I agree with you. We should understand and take seriously what's happened in the past."

Mike said nothing until Mrs Seymour had gone. "She's mad as a hatter," he told them all. "You shouldn't encourage her. I was actually making a serious point."

"So was I," Peter's father told him. "I don't agree with their ideas about why things happened, but happen they did. We all know that."

"I don't," Peter said. "I have no idea what you're all on about."

Carys came in to take drinks orders while Mike was explaining. "No one *knows* what happened. There was a survey, and it never got completed. Some trouble with the superstitious locals probably. People like..." He broke off as he realised Carys was watching him. "Well, you know. Er – I'll have a pint of Claw-Toe."

Carys nodded without comment and looked at Peter. It was the first time she'd looked at him properly and he felt his stomach lurch. How stupid was that? She obviously didn't like him.

The others were already talking about what they wanted to do the next day. At the mention of geophysics and satellite data, Peter tuned out and examined the menu.

"Hand."

"Sorry?" He looked up and found Carys staring down at him.

She sighed, and took hold of his right hand, lifting it up.

"You going to read my palm?" Peter wondered.

"Mum might. Not me." She slapped a book into his hand. "Homework. There's a whole chapter."

"What?"

She was already turning away. "You said you didn't know what they were talking about. You want to find out?"

The book was called *Neolithic Sites in the West of England*. There was a photograph of a standing stone on the cover, half of it faded from sunlight. The other half – perhaps protected by another book – was bright and vivid.

Sure enough, there was a short chapter on Wolfstone.

The Wolfstone Circle

The Wolfstone Circle – or the Dancing Wolves, as it is sometimes called in medieval literature – is not in fact a circle but an ellipse. Recent research suggests that the circle was never actually complete and one side has always been missing.

Local myths and legends about the circle are of course plentiful. According to one story, it is a broken bracelet dropped by a giant who quarrelled with his wife. The most colourful of these stories tells how the stones are actually the soldiers of Henry du Bois.

The legend says that Henry was given to drunken debauchery and excess. During a particularly wild evening some time in the late eighteenth century, he made advances to a servant girl, who fled in fear of her honour from Wolfstone Manor. Enraged at the rejection,

Henry rounded up his private troops and hunted the poor girl across Wolfstone Moor (now mainly farmland).

But unluckily for them, the girl's mother was a local witch. She confronted Henry and his men and invoked a curse that would only affect them if they did not stop their revelry. But as Henry and his men continued their taunts, she turned them to wolves. And when the wolves continued to dance round the witch and her daughter, she turned them to stone. Henry, however, is said to have escaped and fled for his life. Haunted by the events, he became a recluse and made generous donations to the village church – where his effigy remains to this day. He adopted the wolf as his family emblem…

The truth, of course, is far more mundane. The circle dates back to Neolithic times – long before Henry du Bois and his fabled excesses. As with all such monuments, the original purpose, if it had one, is unknown. Some stone circles are aligned with the movement of the sun, though there is a theory that the Wolfstone Circle is actually aligned with the lunar cycle.

The stones themselves are also unusual and distinctive, their high quartz content meaning that they glisten in the light of the sun (and moon). A composition analysis performed by Sir Gerald Swift in the 1950s also revealed an unusual level of silver compounds.

Photograph taken by Professor Matthias's ill-fated survey team, 1922.

The circle has been surveyed and studied several times – with mixed results. The noted seventeenth-century artist Tobias Fanshawe sketched the circle. A more accurate scale drawing was made by Lord Beckenhyme in 1876 as part of his *Survey of the Ancient Sites of Britain*.

Indeed this was the last site he surveyed, and his death from a suspected heart attack in the centre of the Wolfstone Circle, just after he completed his work, has given rise to more legend and speculation. There is no factual basis for the subsequent claims that two of his surveyors were found torn apart "as if by wild beasts" while a third was committed to an asylum for the rest of his life.

But even so, it was perhaps these stories and reports

that led to the famous Oxford University fiasco of 1922. Professor Matthias and his three students are said to have fled screaming from the circle after attempting to chart the shadows cast by the stones in the light of the full moon. What really happened that night, if anything – for Matthias was a notorious prankster – will never be known. Professor Matthias lived until 1963, but for the rest of his life he never spoke of Wolfstone again…

Peter passed the book round as they waited for the food to arrive. Everyone was keen to try the Huntsman's Pie, which turned out to be venison and mushroom.

"Bit sensationalist," Crichton decided, passing the book on to Mike. "Can't decide if it wants to stick to the facts or recount the legends."

"And what about 1876?" Peter asked. "Did that man really go crazy like it says?"

No one seemed to know. Abby asked Mrs Seymour about the 1922 'fiasco' when she and Carys came to clear the plates.

"There's a copy of the local newspaper report from November 1922 somewhere," she told them. "They took it seriously at the time, though there's a more recent theory that it was some sort of publicity stunt or hoax. Have a look for anything by Thomas Arterton."

"Is he an expert?" Mike asked.

"Local amateur historian. But he was living here in the 1920s. He was usually pretty meticulous."

"And what's he say about the 1922 survey?" Crichton asked.

"He hedges his bets, from what I remember. But he does mention an earlier dig."

"The one in 1876?" Peter asked.

Mrs Seymour turned to look at him. He was surprised how clear and sharp her eyes were. And as green as Carys's – you could tell she was the girl's mother from the eyes more than anything.

"That's right," she said. "Two of the men went missing. Their bodies turned up a few days later. Arterton suggests an attack by some wild animal. Probably just rumour and gossip. Local exaggeration."

"Probably," Mike agreed. "It happens."

"There are documented accounts of mutilated cattle, though," Professor Crichton said. "There was an incident with sheep quite recently, I seem to remember."

"Not since the 1970s," Mrs Seymour said. "If you call that recent."

He smiled. "I'm an archaeologist. That's *very* recent."

"The sheep probably died of something else, and the bodies were mutilated afterwards," Mrs Seymour told them. "Foxes most likely. Couldn't have been wolves anyway. Now, does anyone want pudding? Coffee?"

The talk turned to the dessert menu as Carys finished clearing away. She smiled at Peter when she took his plate. Not much of a smile, but a proper smile nonetheless. Peter hardly noticed. He was thinking about what the girl's mother had said.

Why had she said that? No one else had even mentioned wolves.

CHAPTER 3

Peter slept fitfully, waking to the sound of the wind, which sighed and growled round the windows like an animal out in the cold of the night.

He skipped breakfast, meeting Dad in the car park. Abby and Mike were already in the Range Rover and Professor Crichton was loading a rucksack full of equipment into the back.

"Sure you don't want anything?"

"Sure," Peter told him, grateful that Dad wouldn't make a thing of it. Unlike Mum – for her, skipping breakfast was tantamount to high treason.

"Carys asked where you were."

"Course she did." He didn't believe it for a moment.

A low mist hugged the ground. The stones of the circle poked up through it like a giant's broken teeth. The granite glistened where the mist had coalesced.

It always amazed Peter how boring so much of archaeology was. Painstaking, or meticulous, was how his father would describe it. But after a couple of hours Peter had had enough of measuring every possible aspect of the circle and each stone within it.

"Aren't you going to do any *real* archaeology?" he asked Mike, taking care the others didn't overhear.

Mike laughed. "If you mean digging holes and stuff, then yes. But not yet. We need to map out the site first, and do some geophysics – examine satellite images, read up on the previous expeditions – anything that will clue us in to where's best to dig. When we do start it will take a while with just the four of us."

"It'll take too long and it'll be just the three of you," Peter warned him. "Though maybe Sebastian Forrest will let you borrow a digger from the building site. Save a bit of time."

"Good idea," Mike agreed. "Tell your dad – he'll like that." He cupped his hand round a cigarette, swearing as the wind blew out the flame from his lighter.

After a sandwich lunch, Peter left them to it. Things didn't look like they were about to get any more exciting at the non-digging "dig", so he set off to find the remains of Wolfstone Manor.

Peter headed back to the gates he had seen the day before. The ancient driveway was overgrown but its path was still visible as a shadow across the fields. He followed it round the edge of the wood, and as he made his way up a slight incline, the house was revealed in front of him.

From a distance it was impressive – a large country house set in its own grounds. Square and imposing, it dominated the landscape.

But the gardens were overgrown and unruly. As he got closer Peter saw that the house too was neglected and in disrepair. Grass grew through the forecourt and moss clung to the walls. The heavy wooden front door was rotted and cracked. The stone walls and boarded windows were pitted and flaking, leprous with age.

A matted tunnel of vegetation clung to one side of the house. Looking up, Peter shielded his eyes from the sun and saw that the tunnel had once been an avenue of laburnum running alongside a paved terrace that was now broken and uneven. The vestiges of yesterday's rain dripped onto the blistered paving, dribbled out by a weathered gargoyle. Even from three storeys below, Peter could see the gargoyle's head was the face of a wolf.

A similar wolf's head stared out from above the shield over the front door – just as weathered and scarred. Wolves" heads were worked into the stone tracery round the windows and door frame, but they were indistinct and had lost their detail.

The ground floor was almost entirely boarded up. Peter peered through a crack in the wood, but could see very little – an imposing stairway rising from a large hall;

pictures hanging on the walls behind the bannisters… A new lock gleamed incongruously on the front door, probably put there by Forrest's workmen.

Not that Peter was intending to go inside. The exterior looked decrepit enough. Chimney stacks leaned at dangerous angles. In several places shattered stones lay where they had fallen at the foot of the walls, surrounded by starbursts of dust and chippings thrown out by the impact. A huff and a puff from the big bad wolf and the walls would come tumbling down.

There was a high tower at the back of the house. Making his way towards it, Peter was distracted by the landscape. Down from another terrace was what looked like the remains of a maze. From his raised vantage point, Peter could see how the straggly hedges met and intersected. If he screwed up his eyes and squinted, he could make out the shape of the green avenues, though most were now overgrown.

The entrance was still obvious – an arch of box over a rusted metal framework. Peter pushed his way through a mass of ivy that had woven through the box hedge. Inside was a claustrophobic green. But he could see that someone else had been here. Ivy and bindweed were pulled away where they had passed. Several branches were recently broken, exposing pale, new wood.

In places the walls of the maze were so overgrown they blocked the path. In others, they had become so thin that new openings gave into the next section.

The centre of the maze was obvious. It was overgrown, but still a recognisable square. In the middle stood a statue on a stone plinth. The features of the upright figure were washed away along with any inscription. But there was enough detail remaining for Peter to be sure of one thing.

It was a wolf.

Upright, snarling, and holding the stub of what might have been a sword or a cudgel in one paw. The other was curled into a fist.

"Bizarre," Peter said out loud. In fact it was creepy. The wind gusting through the tight-knit hedges sounded almost like an answering voice.

Tiny flowers were growing up through the cracks between the paving slabs at the base of the plinth. Peter smiled at the contrast between the muted savagery of the weathered statue, and the delicate beauty of the perfectly defined flowers as they shivered in the breeze and the bright sunlight. They were closed up, like snowdrops before they open, though Peter could see that the petals inside the hanging buds were a bright purple. They were supported by impossibly thin, pale green stems surrounded by equally slender green leaves.

The breeze rippled through the hedges again. This time Peter could hear clearly the voice that it carried.

"Help me – please..."

Yet it was so faint he felt he must have imagined it. Unless there was someone here in the maze with him? Peter whirled round, staring into the foliage. Nothing. He took a deep breath, suddenly desperate to get as far away from the place as possible.

The voice came again, fragmented by the wind.

Peter pushed through the hedges as fast as he could. The tiny leaves were still damp with yesterday's rain. Branches clawed at his clothes and his hands and face.

He tumbled out of the maze dishevelled, scratched and wet, and found himself at the foot of the terrace outside the house. He didn't know if he was running towards the voice or trying to get away from it. His heart pounded as the cry came again.

"Can you hear me? Please, help!"

Clearer now. Was it a child? The voice was coming from the end of the house – from the tower. Peter ran towards it. He slipped on a patch of moss, tripped on a broken flagstone, but kept running towards the voice.

It was a girl. He could hear her clearly now. But where was she? Was it Carys teasing him maybe?

Peter looked up as the voice called out again – and

skidded to a halt as he saw the girl.

She was leaning out of a window near the top of the tower. Too far away to see her clearly, but it certainly wasn't Carys. He had to shield his eyes from the sun, but Peter guessed she was just a little younger than he was – seventeen maybe. Her long, fair hair hung down below the windowsill as she leaned out towards him. One hand stretched down.

"Please help me. Get me out of here."

He couldn't see her clearly, but Peter could tell that she wasn't mucking about. She was desperate. Crying. Beautiful.

"Hang on," he shouted. "I'll find a way in."

His mind was churning as much as his stomach. Who was she? What was she doing in the house? How had she got trapped in there? He ran back towards the front door, imagining the girl exploring the decaying ruin. In his mind's eye he saw her walking through empty, dusty rooms. A trickle of plaster dust in her long hair. Then the roof collapsing and a beam crushing down on her legs, trapping her. He caught his breath at the thought. No, she's probably just got locked in. She didn't seem in pain. He hadn't seen any blood…

He rounded the corner, sprinting for the front of the house, checking his phone – no signal. Typical.

A sound came from inside the house. The crash of something heavy falling. The girl? Peter stopped, but his breath was the loudest thing he could hear for a moment. He stood by one of the boarded-up windows, straining to hear. Were those footsteps on the inside? Had she managed to get out of the tower? He leaned closer.

The board shuddered, then suddenly cracked as something heavy slammed into the other side. The wood splintered, a split appearing down the middle of the board. Peter leaped back, crying out in surprise and fear. His heart lurched and he felt suddenly sick.

"Are you all right?" he called, his voice tight with nerves. "What's happening in there? Just... hang on!"

The front door looked old and rotten. But it resisted Peter's attempts to shoulder it open.

He should just run and get help. But with no phone signal, it could take a while. Peter checked, just in case – one bar, thank God. But it was gone again before he could even think who to call.

He hurried back to the tower to tell the girl he was going for help. She'd have to wait. He tried to blot out the memory of the sounds from the house. They were inside and he was outside. Whatever it was, it couldn't hurt him.

Only this time, the noise came from right behind him. A pattering like a dog's paws scrabbling on the paving. He spun round – nothing. Imagination. Even so, his throat felt tight. He ran, fast as he could, glancing over his shoulder every few paces. He turned the corner of the house.

And slammed straight into something. Peter yelled in fright as hands grabbed his shoulders. A dark silhouetted figure held him tight.

CHAPTER 4

"Hey, hey, hey!"

Peter pulled away. It took him a few seconds to recognise David Forrest.

"Bloody hell! You scared the life out of me."

"I could tell. You look well spooked."

His heart was still racing and he felt cold with fear. "Spooked is right. Did you..." Peter hardly dared ask. "Did you hear something behind me? Or in the house?"

David shook his head. "It's old. Always creaking and making noises."

"And there's a girl."

David frowned. "What?"

"Come on – we have to help her. I think she's trapped inside."

"Inside?" David ran after him. "There's no one inside. They'd be mad – the place is ready to fall down."

"That's why we have to help her. Come on!"

"Who?"

They were back where Peter had first seen the girl. The sun was in his eyes again, and the tower was a dark shadow against the sky, devoid of any detail. He shielded his eyes as he pointed.

"Up there."

"Can't see anyone."

"At the window."

David laughed. "Probably a ghost. I bet this place is haunted big time."

"But I saw her," Peter repeated. Even as he said it he was less certain. The sun had been in his eyes. What had he really seen – shadows? What had he really heard – the wind? As if to make the point, a breeze whipped though his hair and sighed in the nearby trees.

"This place would give anyone the creeps," David said. "What are you doing here anyway?" He walked slowly back along the terrace.

Reluctantly, Peter followed. "Just looking. Then I heard… thought I heard a voice."

"Probably the wind. You thought it sounded like a voice, and your imagination filled in the blanks."

"I guess." Could it have been? But he was *sure* he'd seen the girl. He gave David a puzzled look. "Why are you here?"

David turned. "I came looking for you. Went up to the circle, guessed you'd be bored silly by now. Thought I'dshow you the local sights. Well," he added apologetically, "there's the church and some half-built houses. That's about it."

"And this place."

"Yeah, well, I'dkeep away from Haunted Manor. Even Scooby Doo wouldn't be seen dead here."

They retraced the route down the drive towards the ruined gates. "I was so sure," Peter said. But now it all just seemed silly. "Sorry."

"No problem," David assured him. "So what was she like, your spooky woman? Grey lady or screaming banshee?"

"Nothing like either of those. She was just a girl. Really pretty." He didn't like to say beautiful. "With long, fair hair. I just wanted to help her… What?"

David had stopped dead. He was staring open-mouthed at Peter.

"What is it?" Peter asked again.

"Nothing. It's nothing." David shook his head and smiled. "Really. I just thought I felt a splash of rain. Hey – let's see if they"ve found any buried treasure yet."

Most people wouldn't think of it as treasure, but Peter knew that to an archaeologist, finding a body was the next best thing. Maybe better.

Professor Crichton, Mike and Abby were hunched over an iPad sheltered in the open back of the Range Rover.

"The value of proper research," Crichton explained gleefully.

"Exactly where the 1920s expedition recorded it," Abby agreed.

Peter and David exchanged 'what are they on about' looks.

"A shallow grave," Mike explained.

He angled the iPad so they could see. To Peter this was just a jumble of different-coloured splodges and lines. He could see that David was just as nonplussed.

"Here, let me." Mike took the iPad and adjusted the settings. The colours and lines resolved themselves into a shape. The outline of a figure, hunched over. Broken and distorted, but obviously human.

"See that?" Abby pointed to a stab of orange at the back of the figure. The image enlarged in response to her touch. The orange blob was a discernable triangular shape.

"Arrow head," she explained. "Metal, but we're getting some strange feedback from it."

"Could be silver," Crichton said.

"Silver?" David echoed in surprise.

"Unusual, but not unheard of."

"So this guy was murdered?" Peter asked.

"You see it all in this job. Medieval murder victim," Mike said. "Shot in the back with a silver arrow while running away from a Bronze-Age stone circle."

"I doubt if they just buried him where he fell," Crichton said. "The body's been arranged. Positioned. Possibly ceremonially, so close to a site like this."

"And you're going to dig him up?" David asked.

"I wouldn't normally describe the delicate and sensitive operation of exhuming a burial site quite like that," Crichton said. "But yes, if you want to put it like that, we're going to dig him up."

David grinned. "Cool."

Professor Crichton and the others looked set to talk archaeology all evening, so Peter and David took themselves off to the far end of the bar. Carys brought them drinks and food, and seemed slightly less standoffish than she had the night before. She even smiled at Peter a couple of times, though most of her attention seemed to be reserved for David.

Peter didn't mind. Well, actually he did mind, but that was her choice of course. David was obviously better looking – and richer – than he was.

David told Peter that he was working in his father's business, but hoping to take time out next year to start a degree in business studies.

"You got any other family?" Peter asked.

"No," David said at once, a little sharply. He shrugged. "Sorry. There's just me and Dad now. What about you?"

"Mum's off lecturing round America. History of art.

Boston this week, I think." He should probably call her while David waited for his father to return and Peter's own dad was deep 'in conference' with Mike and Abby. Or text her maybe, in case she was busy.

"You leaving us?" Carys asked as he headed out.

"Just trying to find a decent phone signal," he told her.

"It's crazy in here, the building's so old the walls are really thick. Try across the car park. There's some maiden's tears..."

"Some what?"

"Little purple flowers. They're also called wolf's blight."

"Like snowdrops?" He remembered the flowers he'd seen in the maze.

"A bit. Stand close to them and you should get a signal."

"Thanks."

"That's all right. See you later."

She obviously didn't mean that. But he could hope. And this was the longest conversation he'd had with her so far.

Peter found the flowers growing in a clump against the hedge. These were fully open, not like the tight buds he'd seen before. They looked just as delicate, swaying in the moonlight. He sent Mum a text asking how she was and telling her archaeology was really boring. Though she knew that already. After that he texted a couple of friends, then he walked slowly along the road that turned off the main street by the pub.

"See you later," probably just meant she'd see him around the pub. It didn't mean she'd be looking for him. Of course it didn't. Maybe he'd tell Carys about the "ghost" girl he'd seen at Wolfstone Manor. Ghost or imagination? But he'd been so sure. Maybe he wouldn't mention it.

But in the still of the night, Peter thought he could hear the girl's cries again – breathing faintly on the breeze. Something else too – a dog maybe? More of a growl than a bark. Distant and distorted. It could be anything – a train, or a lorry, or…

Or it could be a wolf.

And voices.

He could hear voices.

There was a stone wall beside the road. With no streetlights in the village, everything was reduced to shadows and patches of moonlight. Above the wall loomed the dark shape of the church. It looked like there might be a gate in the wall further along, steps leading up to the churchyard.

The voices came from the other side of the wall. Peter wondered if he should call out a greeting. Instead he decided to head back to the pub.

A figure appeared above the wall – head and shoulders against the moonlight. Instinctively Peter stepped into the shadow of the wall. Immediately he cursed himself for being daft. But if someone saw him now it would look like he was hiding and eavesdropping.

"It has to be tomorrow," a voice said – not the figure by the wall, but another man. "If we wait any longer..."

Peter caught a glimpse of straggly hair over the man's collar as he turned. A beaky nose and thin-lipped mouth. One ear was a ragged mess, like a toy mauled by a dog. Peter grimaced, and held his breath.

"Tomorrow then," the man with the ragged ear said. "After what happened today that'd probably be as well. So long as it's before the Old One gets here. You know he doesn't approve."

"You think I care what *he* thinks?"

The voices were moving away, fading. With a sigh of relief, Peter stepped away from the wall. Who meets in a churchyard at the dead of night, he wondered. As he moved, his foot connected with a stone and sent it skittering into the road.

He froze, holding his breath. He was being stupid, he told himself – it was probably the vicar and a churchwarden. And he wasn't doing anything wrong. He was just out for a walk. He wasn't at school any more, caught where he shouldn't be. He wasn't a *kid*.

Heart thumping, Peter stepped out from the shadows

and turned towards the pub. At the same moment, a dark shape jumped out from the top of the wall, landing on the road, its hindquarters right in front of him. It was a dog. But huge – like a massive Alsatian. Peter pressed back against the rough stone of the wall, stifling a cry as he jarred his shoulder. Then, just as he thought the dog was about to turn and see him, it bounded off down the road.

CHAPTER 5

There was a man standing exactly where Peter had been, beside the flowers. Absolutely still, one hand raised to his head. Even from across the car park, even though he was barely more than a silhouette, Peter was sure the man was watching him.

In a sudden movement, the man stepped forward. He lowered his hand, snapping closed his phone. "Peter!"

Sebastian Forrest strode across the car park.

"Only place you can get a decent signal round here. Are you okay? You look pale. Maybe it's the moonlight."

They walked slowly back to the pub.

"I was just out for a walk," Peter explained. He felt he ought to say something. "Down to the church and back."

Forrest nodded. "Bits of it are thirteenth century, but it's not terribly remarkable. Some of the stained glass is interesting, I believe. Not that I'dknow."

"Nor me," Peter said. "But I did see..." He broke off and laughed.

"What?" Forrest pushed open the door and motioned for Peter to go in ahead of him. He smiled. "What did you see?"

"Oh, just a dog. Big though."

"A lot of the farmers have dogs. They're not uncommon."

"This one was," Peter said. "It was huge. Looked more like a wolf."

"A wolf?" Forrest seemed startled for a moment. Then he laughed. "Oh right, very funny."

"Sorry?"

Forrest's smile became a slight frown. "You don't know? About the wolves?"

"I know they're on the du Bois crest and this place is called *Wolf*stone."

Forrest checked his watch. "Look, I'dbetter find David and let him know I'm back. You free tomorrow morning?"

"I guess so... I can be."

"Good. Then let's meet down here – at, what, ten o"clock? – and I'll take you to see the wolves."

Forrest clapped Peter on the shoulder, amused, and headed off to the bar. Peter watched him go, wondering what the man meant. He turned, and almost bumped into Carys.

"Sorry. I didn't see you there."

She smiled. "That's all right. So, you're off to see the wolves tomorrow?"

She must have overheard. "Apparently. What did he mean?"

"You'll find out." She tilted her head slightly, watching

his reaction. "Mind if I come along?"

His father didn't seem at all fazed the next morning, when Peter told him where he was going. But maybe that was just Dad. You could tell him you were off to the moon, and he'd probably have the same reaction – a nod, a smile and, "Okay, see you later then. I'll be up at the circle most of the day."

Peter half expected that Carys wouldn't appear. But she was already waiting when Peter met Forrest in the bar.

"Got your phone?" she asked.

He pulled it out of his pocket. "Will it get a signal there?" Not that he knew where "there" was.

She took it from him, thumbing buttons. "Might do. But I meant for the camera. You'll get pictures."

Peter nodded. *But what of?* he wondered silently.

She gave him back the phone. "I've put my number in it."

He wasn't sure what to say to that.

"Isn't David coming?" Carys asked as they left the pub.

Forrest shook his head. "He's got work to do." He didn't explain what.

"We've all got work to do," she said.

Peter's heart skipped a beat – would Carys back out?

"But so long as I'm back to help Mum with lunch… If the weather holds we should get a few tourists passing through. What are you grinning at?"

"Sorry." Peter hadn't realised he was grinning. What an idiot! He turned away, catching sight of the clump of little flowers close by as they walked to Forrest's car. The flowers were closed up in tight buds again.

"They were open last night," he murmured.

Whether Carys heard him or guessed what he was thinking, he didn't know. "They open at night."

"That's unusual."

"Unique," Forrest agreed. "That's why they're called maiden's tears. Secret and closed up during the day, they only appear at night. Private and alone."

"Why?" Peter asked as they got into the car. He let Carys take the front seat.

"Best time to cry is at night," Carys said quietly.

"No, I mean… can they photosynthesise?"

"Yes, the leaves can. And there's the moonlight," she told him.

"Weird. I've never heard of them before."

"They only grow round here."

They returned to the main Gloucester road, then turned off again down a narrow lane. Peter reckoned they were curling round the back of Wolfstone Manor.

Finally, Forrest turned the car into a small gateway.

Ahead of them, Peter could see a modern building – low, red brick, like an office. Beside it were high metal fences, and behind was the edge of the wood that joined the grounds of Wolfstone Manor. There was a small parking area to the front, and Forrest drew up next to an old battered Land Rover.

"What is this place?" Peter asked as they got out of the car.

"Welcome to Wolfstone Lupine Sanctuary," Forrest said proudly.

"Is it yours?"

"It's a charity, but I sponsor some of their work."

"With wolves?"

"You'll see," Carys said.

A woman emerged from the office building. Her dark hair was streaked with grey and she had the slightly weathered features of someone who works outdoors. She greeted Forrest enthusiastically, shaking his hand.

"We're not interrupting?" he asked.

"Never. It's always a pleasure." The woman nodded at Carys, then turned to Peter. She extended her hand again. "Janey Donovan."

"Peter Crichton."

"It's just me today, I'm afraid."

She led them into the building. There was a plaque

beside the door with a logo on it. No words of explanation, just a symbol of two squares on top of each other, like a blocky number 8.

"Josh is down in London lobbying another MP or something," Janey Donovan was saying. "I haven't seen Eddie. I think one of the farmers called him out. He's our vet," she explained to Peter.

"Josh said there was some paperwork," Forrest said. "Why don't I sort that out while you show Peter and Carys around?"

"I think Carys knows her way around," Janey said.

The wolves were penned in by the metal fences Peter had seen. From a distance, they looked like large dogs – a sort of cross between Alsatian and Husky. Several of the animals paced along the side of the fences. There was a pent-up energy, a raw power in every step. Their grey pelts glistened in the morning light.

"Is it some kind of zoo?" Peter asked.

"Heavens, no," Janey said.

"And these are wolves?"

"*Lupus Ferus,*" Carys said. "Isn't that right?"

She was standing closer to the fence than Peter – closer than he was happy to go. One of the wolves was watching her through yellow-tinged eyes. Maybe it recognised her.

"*Canis Lupus Ferus*, yes," Janey said. "They're a Siberian

hunting wolf. Similar to the grey wolf, but rather larger. They're quite rare in fact. But they seem better suited to the environment here than some other breeds."

Peter watched the two women as, in turn, they watched the wolf staring back at them.

"Are you studying them?"

"We're taking the opportunity to observe the wolves" behaviour and how they cope with the change of physical and social environment. These animals have been specially imported from Russia, though they come via Poland."

"Why Poland?" Carys asked.

"They don't stop there long. Helps them adjust to the change in temperature, but it's really so they can get a proper medical check before being admitted to the UK. They have to be screened to make sure they're free of any infection or disease. The Home Office rather insists."

"The Home Office?" Peter echoed.

"They're following our progress carefully. After all, any reintroduction will need government backing. Possibly a change in the law."

"Reintroduction – of *wolves*? To *England*?"

Janey laughed. "Sorry, I'm not really selling us very well am I? To Scotland actually. But that's the ultimate goal, yes."

Peter was astonished. "But – they're *wolves*."

"Wolves aren't really dangerous," Carys told him. "Not usually."

"Which is why they're caged up, of course." It sounded more sarky than he'd intended.

"It's a controlled experiment," Janey said. "We can't let them just run free. They're all chipped so we can track them – this run links into others so they actually have several acres of space."

"You're sure they aren't dangerous?"

The wolf nearest them raised its head. It stared back at Peter, as if it was listening. Then it leaned back further, jaw upwards, and howled. It was a mournful, haunting sound. Like the wind. Peter was sure he'd heard it before, faint and distant.

"The wolf isn't a vicious or aggressive animal," Janey said.

"Just a large dog?" Peter asked. He'd heard that somewhere before.

"Like a hunting dog," Carys agreed. "Real wolves only harm humans when they believe they're in danger."

"What do you mean, 'real'?"

Carys blinked. "Sorry?"

"You said 'real wolves' aren't dangerous to humans."

"Well, you know – *real* wolves. Not wolves like in *Red Riding Hood* or the *Three Little Pigs*, or films or whatever."

Carys smiled. "Surely boys like Peter aren't afraid of wolves?"

Peter obviously looked confused, because Janey explained. "It's a quote. From Prokofiev's *Peter and the Wolf.*"

They moved on, walking alongside the fence. The closest wolf paced with them for a while, then got bored and loped off to join a few others a distance away.

"They're pack animals, but loners too if that isn't too much of a contradiction," Janey said. "It's good to see them back."

"There were wolves here before then?" Peter asked.

"How do you think Wolfstone got its name?" Carys asked. "There were wolves in the woods round here right up till the eighteenth century. Maybe later."

"And now you're bringing them back," Peter said. There was another group of wolves gathered round a clump of trees ahead of them. It was easy to believe they were no more dangerous than large dogs. Until one turned and looked at you. There was something about that look – a depth, an intelligence behind the eyes… a hunger.

"Not to here, not to Wolfstone," Janey said. "Not yet, anyway."

"Just Scotland, then?"

"The Highlands of Scotland," Carys said, "is where the

last wolf was killed in Britain in 1769."

"You know a lot about it."

She shrugged and moved closer to the fence, watching the animals. One hand against the wire, long-nailed fingers curled through the mesh.

"But why do it at all?" Peter wondered.

"All sorts of reasons," Janey said. "Tourism is an obvious one, and that would boost the local economy and provide jobs in areas where agriculture's in decline. But bringing back wolves, in controlled numbers of course, could also stop the red deer from becoming too prevalent."

"Is that important?"

"Reduces the cost and problem of culling them, and it'dincrease biodiversity. Control the deer and you'll get a greater variety of plants and birds. Helps reforestation too."

"Sounds like a no-brainer then."

"Except for the emotive issues. Most people, like you, think wolves are a danger."

Peter didn't reply. The wolves still looked pretty dangerous to him. Janey left the two of them to wander round while she went back to see how Forrest was doing with the paperwork.

"Probably gift-aiding another million," Carys said. They walked slowly back by the fence. "We're lucky to see so many of them. The fenced area includes part of the wood – they're usually off there. Josh says there's a whole pack arriving soon," she went on. "Josh is usually in charge here, but Janey's the one who's good with animals."

Peter watched Carys as she followed one of the wolves with her eyes. It bounded past them and off into the distance.

"You really like them, don't you?" he said.

Her expression of awe and wonder became a frown. "They're dreadful creatures," she told him coldly. "Terrifying."

"I'm sorry." He wasn't sure what he'd said, but her tone told him he should apologise. "I just thought you were… fascinated."

"You don't have to like something to find it fascinating," she said. "You fancy walking back?"

The change of subject threw him for a moment. "On my own?"

"With me, stupid." Her frown was gone and the half-smile was back.

One of the wolves paced with them along the wire. The fence led into the trees, but Carys followed a path that bent away from the pen and turned back towards the manor. Behind them one wolf gave out a mournful howl.

"If the wind's in the right direction, you can hear them at night back at the Fleece," Carys said.

"Especially when it's a full moon?" Peter joked.

But she wasn't amused. "That's not even a bit funny, you know."

"Sorry."

They walked on in silence. Peter was desperate to talk to her, but everything he thought of saying sounded completely daft or obvious when he practised it in his head.

Eventually Carys said, "So how long are you here for?"

"Don't know really. Till Dad finishes his survey, or Mum gets back from the States. Or until I get bored."

She gave a snort of laughter. "Surprised you haven't left already."

"*You're* still here," he pointed out. "Still in Wolfstone."

"Mum needs the help. But next year I might do a course. The college in Cheltenham does some catering and tourism and business management stuff."

"That what you're interested in?"

"No," she said simply.

"Then – why...?"

"It's what I know. It's what I do. Me and Mum."

"And Mr Seymour."

The path was getting narrower. Her hand brushed against his as they walked. For a fleeting, mad moment he thought about taking hold of it. Carys stopped and looked at him. Had she guessed what he was thinking?

"Sorry," he said.

"What is it with you apologising all the time?"

"I'm not falling for that," he said. "I'm not saying sorry about apologising. But you just stopped. I thought I'd done something wrong."

"Like what?"

"Er... not sure actually."

Her eyes narrowed slightly. "That way will take you back to the circle, across the fields." She pointed at another narrow path that intersected the one they were following. "This way is back to the Fleece."

"Right." He tried not to sound disappointed. "Time to part company, then?"

She nodded slowly. The light shining down through the canopy of trees dappled her face. "Or if you stay with me, there's a way back to the circle through the old manor grounds once we leave the wood. But that's a bit further."

He didn't hesitate. "That sounds good."

"Your choice." She walked on.

Peter hurried to catch up. "Sorry – did I do something wrong again?"

She gave him a sympathetic look. "No. Something right."

Before long, the trees thinned out and the bare ground

tufted with grass. Daylight broke through and they emerged into sudden sunshine.

Carys pointed the way across the field to where Peter could see Wolfstone Manor in the distance. He could use that as a landmark to find the circle easily enough.

"Thanks for walking with me," Carys said.

"Thanks for showing me the wolves."

"No problem."

"I'll see you later, then."

She nodded. "Yeah. Yeah, you will." Then she set off along the path that ran beside the hedgerow.

"Weird," Peter muttered. But good weird. Definitely good weird.

So close to the manor, Peter couldn't resist the urge to check the tower. He didn't really believe he would see the girl again. He didn't really believe he'd ever actually seen her in the first place. Maybe what he had heard was a howl from one of the wolves at the Lupine Sanctuary on the other side of the woods. But at the time he had been so *sure*…

The windows of the tower were empty blanks. "Hello!" he called. He wasn't really sure why, and his nervous, tentative voice was whipped away by the breeze. "Hello!" he called again, louder.

There was a sound. Like someone knocking on a door

to be let in… or to be let out.

It was the wind – it had to be. Catching at one of the boards. Knocking it against a window frame.

More knocks.

Had to be the wind.

Then silence.

He jumped down from the raised terrace and made his way through the remains of a rose garden. The house loomed above him, casting its shadow over the stunted plants and overgrown paths. Peter emerged from the shade, crossing the angular shadow of the roofline.

Once part of the shadow reminded him of the wolf that had stared back through the fence. The hint of a jawline, the shape of the head. One ear was standing upright, but where the other ear should be was a ragged stump.

He looked back at the terrace. Up at the roof. But he couldn't see what was making the shape.

When he looked down at the ground again, the sun had dipped behind a cloud and the shadow was gone.

CHAPTER 6

"Do you think there could be someone trapped inside Wolfstone Manor?"

Peter's father looked at him. "What, you mean like a tramp or squatters?"

Peter didn't know what he meant. "I thought I heard noises from inside." He wasn't about to mention seeing a ghost-girl.

"Probably something falling down. That whole place is about ready to collapse. You should keep well clear. Now come and look at this!"

He led Peter over to where Mike was digging, on the far side of the circle. The stones glittered in the sunlight.

"If the circle was complete, we'd be digging inside it," Abby said.

"One of us would," Mike said. He was leaning heavily on a spade, his face streaked with mud.

"Come on. You got to drive the digger."

"Forrest let us use one of the diggers from the construction site to scrape off the top layers," Crichton explained. He jangled a large bunch of keys. "Must remember to give him these back, though I guess his construction manager will have spares."

"I doubt he'll be needing them any time soon. And anyway, those probably are the spares," Mike said. "Except – a bit like me – they're only spare until some digging's needed."

"Have you got down to the skeleton yet?" Professor Crichton asked, ignoring the sarcasm.

"Just hit bone. Well, not hit – carefully uncovered." He took out a packet of cigarettes, looked at them, then put them away again without taking one.

"It's all brush and trowel from now on," Abby added. "Have you shown Peter the model?"

Crichton's iPad showed a three-dimensional model of the Wolfstone Circle built from digital photographs. Sitting in the Range Rover, he showed Peter how you could move around it, changing the perspective and viewpoint.

"It's just like being here," Peter said. "But we are here, so what's the point?"

"We won't always be here. This saves us trekking back from the university just to check a measurement or see how something looks." Crichton adjusted some settings, and the view of the stones changed to night-time. A full moon shone across the circle.

"That's cool," Peter admitted. "So you can check out the alignment of the sun and moon."

More adjustment filled the stones with bright colours – mainly blue, but with flecks of red and orange.

"Composition. The orange is quartz, for example. The red is silver compounds. That's mainly an extrapolation of Sir Gerald Swift's analysis from the 1950s, so it'll need refining. There's a copy of his report on the department server."

"Fascinating."

Crichton smiled. "Liar. But you'll like this… look."

The image changed again, this time showing a view of the stones from above.

"You can see it's half of an ellipse. It's parabolic. There's Wolfstone Manor, directly in line with the open end of the ellipse. Now, watch."

More stone faded into view, completing the flattened circle.

Crichton switched back to a view inside the circle at ground level, with the missing stones there as well. "Now we can see how the circle looked when it was first built. We know where the missing stones were, though we haven't found any geophysical evidence yet."

"Where did they go?" Peter wondered.

Crichton switched off the iPad. "Probably taken for building, centuries ago. Maybe some of the oldest parts of the manor are built from them. There are reports of other standing stones that have gone too. Like the so-called

Rogue Stone."

"Which was?"

"Like its name suggests, it was just a single large stone, outside the circle. A long way outside, so possibly unconnected. Though one version of the legend suggests it was the remains of the poor enchanted Henry du Bois himself."

"And where was it?"

"Over near the manor somewhere," the professor said vaguely, pointing past where Mike and Abby were busy in the shallow pit.

The outline of the skeleton was revealed, pale bone sticking out of the receding soil. Abby and Mike were cleaning it gently with paintbrushes. Peter knew from boring experience that the process would take for ever.

"If it's all right with you, I'll head back to the pub," Peter told them. "I want to check my email and Facebook. See you later."

There was a coach in the car park, and the bar was full of elderly tourists. From overheard snippets of conversation, they were fresh from a morning in Bath and heading for an afternoon and the theatre in Stratford-upon-Avon.

So Peter decided to take refuge in his room. As he reached the stairs, he passed Mr Seymour.

The man looked up, startled as Peter greeted him.

"Sorry," Peter said, and immediately cursed himself and wondered what Carys would say. "I just wondered if you could tell me the password for the wi-fi?"

The grey-haired man stared at Peter without moving. His forehead was wrinkled into a frown. His pale eyes showed no sign of understanding.

"So I can connect my laptop?" Peter offered. "Computer?"

"Computer password," the man said. His eyes flicked sideways, to the wall under the stairs. He stepped away from it. "I don't know."

"Do I need to ask Mrs Seymour? Or Carys?"

"I'll tell them you need it."

Peter thanked him, but the man didn't seem to hear. He was staring at the wall, and backing away. Abruptly, he turned and hurried back along the corridor.

Peter hesitated at the foot of the stairs. Was the man ill? Old age taking its toll? Or maybe he was just awkward round strangers?

He seemed frightened as well. Not by Peter, but by whatever was on the wall under the stairs. But there was nothing there. Just a plain wood-panelled wall.

Carys saw Peter look into the bar, hesitate, then leave again. She didn't blame him. The place was busy and noisy today, and given the choice she'd rather not be in a room full of pensioners either. But then, she didn't have a choice. She forced a smile and took another order for a cup of tea and a glass of sherry.

Eventually the tour leader and the driver managed to herd all their charges out of the Red Fleece and back onto the coach. Relieved, Carys set about clearing the tables.

"Password," Mr Seymour growled in her ear as he helped.

"I don't think I need one just to get into the kitchen," she told him.

"Your boyfriend – he wants the computer password."

"He's not..." There wasn't any point in trying to tell him Peter wasn't her boyfriend. So instead, she said, "Okay. I'll go and tell him. Can you finish here?" They were almost done.

Mr Seymour nodded and moved to the next table.

She knew he hadn't eaten, so Carys took Peter a ham roll. He called for her to come in as soon as she knocked. He was probably as bored here as she was, Carys thought.

"And Grandad said you wanted the wi-fi password."

She took Peter's laptop and typed in the network password.

"What do you want to do on the internet?" she asked.

"Just Facebook. Are you on? I'll be your friend."

Was he mocking her? She didn't really understand the

boy – but maybe he was as straightforward as he seemed. "Thanks."

"I was going to Google those flowers too," Peter went on. "Maiden's tears or whatever they were called."

"That's right. But actually, you could try looking under "wolf's blight". I doubt you'll find much information on them though. Want some help?"

She was surprised that he did. She kept her expression as neutral as possible. No way did she want him to know that the most exciting prospect on her social agenda was sitting in here with him, browsing the web. He must think she was so weird already.

They sat together on the side of the bed, Peter holding the laptop. He finally found a short mention.

> The Vale of Wolfstone is an area of outstanding natural beauty. It is, for example, the natural habitat of that rarest of plants, *maiden's tears* (also known locally as *wolf's blight*) – which is noted for its healing and restorative properties as well being unique in that it flowers only in moonlight.

There were other references too, but none of them said much more than this one.

"You could make it a tourist attraction," Peter suggested.

"You know, advertise it. Moonlit tours of the car park."

"More coaches of OAPs dribbling their soup on the table," Carys said. Her idea of hell. Best to move on… So she asked how the archaeology was going.

"Slow and boring."

"Bit like here then," she said before she could stop herself.

But he smiled. The uppity David Forrest would have laughed at her, not with her. Pitying, not amused.

"Dad's got this computer model which is pretty clever though," Peter said. "It can show the stones as they used to be, and you can even model the angle of the sun and phases of the moon."

"It's full moon in a few days, anyway," Carys said. "We're on the cusp."

"Cusp of what?"

Something else she didn't want to get into. Why was she saying this stuff? She was usually so careful. But there was something about Peter that made her trust him – made her want to tell him about… "So, you going to be an archaeologist?" she asked. "Is that what you're off to uni to study?"

"I'm doing history. So I could be, but I doubt it."

"Aren't historians just archaeologists who don't like getting dirty?"

He actually laughed at that. Carys laughed too. She felt more relaxed than she had for ages.

And immediately she felt guilty. She should be helping Mum finish sorting the kitchen, and setting up for the evening. She checked her watch, hoping he wouldn't think she was just bored.

"Hey, I need to get back. The oldies have gone, but Mum"ll want help clearing up. And there's a barrel that needs changing in the cellar. You okay?"

"Dad mentioned some study of the composition of the stones. I might try and find that."

Carys stood up. "I'll see you later, then."

"I'll tell you if I find anything interesting."

"Yeah, because that's so likely."

She grimaced as soon as she was out of the door. Why did she have to be so sarky? Peter was doing his best to be friendly. She must irritate the hell out of him.

Peter was sorry that Carys had gone, but to be honest, he was surprised she'd stayed at all. He probably bored her out of her skull. Why couldn't he talk about normal stuff? Trouble was, he didn't know what to say or how to interest her.

To take his mind off things, he went to the university website and found the archaeology department pages.

Sure enough, the entry he was looking for was in the archived research section.

The web page was headed Wolfstone Circle – Analysis of Composition. There was a short explanation, then a scanned page of typewritten material.

> The following is the page of summary results from Sir Gerald Swift's Analysis of Composition study of a fragment of one of the stones in the Wolfstone Circle, October 1954.
>
> The fragment analysed was found to be granite, probably originating in North Cornwall. It has therefore been brought some significant distance to its current location in the Cotswolds. The composition of the stone is broadly as one would expect, although the stone fragment has an unusually high quartz content. It has been suggested that it is the quartz crystals that make the stones at Wolfstone appear to gleam or shimmer, particularly in moonlight.
>
> That is not the case.
>
> Small quartz crystals do indeed catch

the light (from the sun or the moon, or any other light-source) and gleam. This phenomenon can be observed in most samples of granite.

However, the peculiarly strong nature of the phenomenon in the Wolfstone sample is due to the presence of silver. While metallic silver does occur naturally as crystals, the silver in the sample examined is especially pure. In its crystalline state it seems to resonate, not unlike the quartz, possibly due to some symbiotic bonding between the crystals. The effect is to make the crystals shimmer, and thus appear to shine even more brightly.

From observation at different times of the lunar cycle, this resonance is especially marked when the sample is subjected to high gravity waves. These are the waves that produce the tides, and which have in the past been supposed to affect the brain by resonating its fluid content. In short, the gravity waves produced by the moon. These waves wax and

wane as the moon moves around the earth, and are particularly strong at the full moon - which is when the silver crystals will resonate, and therefore shine, the most.

Peter skimmed through it, deciding that Carys would probably have been bored to tears if she'd stayed. At the bottom of the page there was a handwritten note. He had to zoom the image quite large to make it out. There was no way of knowing who had written it, and it could have been added at any time.

Worth noting that silver was seen as a magical defence. This may be because of its very real medicinal properties. Silver is a powerful antimicrobial agent, only recently superseded by modern antibiotics. (Silver was used as late as WW1 to combat infection in wounded soldiers.) Silver has a toxic effect on some fungi and algae, as well as viruses and bacteria. Silver nitrate has now been replaced by silver sulphadiazine in prepared dressings, bandages and gels.

Another search on "silver sulphadiazine" suggested that the handwritten note must have been written in the last twenty years. Peter also found an explanation of how silver fights infections.

It is probably effective because in ionised form (Ag^{+}), silver forms strong molecular bonds with those elements the bacteria need to support their life. For example: sulphur, nitrogen, oxygen. Denied these, bacteria, for want of a better term, suffocate.

Again, he thought Carys would find that boring as hell. But what *would* interest her?

Without really thinking, he searched for "Sebastian Forrest". He got back a load of hits. Most of them corporate news or links to websites of Forrest's various companies. But halfway down the second page, a headline jumped out. Short, shocking and to the point.

Millionaire's Wife Brutally Killed

He hardly dared click on the link. When he did, Peter could only read the first paragraph. No wonder David had reacted when Peter asked about his family. He felt sick.

> Katherine Forrest, wife of millionaire businessman Sebastian Forrest, was found dead in their Kensington flat yesterday morning. There has been no official statement on the cause of death, but it is understood that she suffered multiple lacerations and stab wounds in what unofficial sources are describing as "a frenzied attack". Mr Forrest is currently out of the country and the couple's two children are away at boarding school.

The article was over five years old. Numbed, Peter closed the lid of the laptop. Then he opened it again – *two* children? David had said, "There's just me and Dad now."

It didn't take long to find a recent picture of the Forrester family. It showed the *three* of them arriving for the premiere of a film that Forrester had helped finance.

Sebastian Forrest was instantly recognisable. Over his shoulder, David was grinning at the photographers. Beside him, looking less comfortable, was his sister – Annabelle, according to the caption. The photographer had got a good shot of her, even though she was furthest away. Peter guessed she was about sixteen, with long, fair hair tumbling down her back. Even in the small photo she was beautiful. Distinctive. Unforgettable.

She was the girl he'd seen at the tower window of Wolfstone Manor.

Peter walked down the stairs in a daze. How could he have imagined the exact likeness of a girl he had never met? Of course, he couldn't. But that meant...

He wasn't sure what it meant. Was Annabelle Forrest really living – or trapped – in Wolfstone Manor? But why? Could he have imagined the similarity between the girl in the picture and the 'ghost' he'd seen?

How had David reacted when he described the girl? Peter couldn't remember. But he hadn't rushed to investigate, like Peter would have done if it had been his sister...

He reached the bottom of the stairs in time to see Carys hurrying away down the corridor. Where had she come from? She seemed to have appeared from nowhere.

There was a door under the stairs. He hadn't seen it before because it just looked like part of the wood panelling. There was no handle, but the door was not quite shut and a key stuck out of a small lock. Curious, Peter gave it a tug. The door was thick, and very heavy, but it opened easily on well-oiled hinges.

On the other side, stone steps led down. A cellar. Carys had said she had to change a beer barrel.

The cellar smelled damp. Whitewash was flaking from the walls. He shouldn't be down there, Peter thought. Not without asking.

But there was nothing much to see. Half a dozen metal barrels stood along a wall. Several others were attached to plastic tubes that must lead up to the bar. Boxes of bottles, spirits and mixers, were stacked on the floor. One whole wall was taken up with a wine rack.

A narrow opening led into another room beyond, but that was in darkness. Peter leaned through, and his hand found a light switch.

The room was small and empty. There were no windows. The door opened flat against the wall. It was made of thick wood, braced with metal. It had three heavy bolts, at the top, bottom and middle.

But Peter's attention was focused on the back wall. The stone was deeply scored and scratched. Dark stains ran down the damaged whitewash and pooled on the floor. A thick chain was attached to the wall by several large iron staples. Each end of the chain ended in a clasp – a manacle. In the bright light, the chain and manacles gleamed like silver.

What was this place? Why had Carys been down here? There was good weird and bad weird – and this was definitely bad weird.

He flicked off the light and stepped back into the main cellar. His foot caught on a bottle, knocking it over. It rolled into a corner. He froze, holding his breath. Carys had left the door open – so she'd be back soon. Was that her now? Could he hear footsteps on the stairs? Or was it his heart thumping?

He hurried back up the stone stairs. Was he being stupid? So was this the remains of some medieval dungeon in the cellars of the old pub? Or was it maybe some way of holding beer barrels in place? Or...

The stains on the walls and the floor. They didn't look medieval. They looked recent.

They looked like blood.

CHAPTER 7

Peter wasn't sure how he felt about Carys after that. He certainly didn't want to tell her he thought he'd seen Annabelle Forrest trapped in Wolfstone Manor.

David Forrest was sitting in the bar when Peter ventured down in the early evening to see if there was any sign of Dad. He felt his stomach lurch, but David had seen him so he had to go over. But what could he say – what *should* he say? Maybe he'd ask again about his family – if he could do it in a subtle way.

Talking to David, Peter could almost forget what he'd found out. Could almost pretend the last couple of days had been normal. Almost.

David's father soon joined them, and then Peter's own father, with Abby and Mike. They moved into the restaurant, returning the usual peace and quiet to the few locals camped in the bar. Mr Seymour stood silent and still, waiting for the drinks orders.

"So where did you go to school?" Peter asked David as the talk became more technical. He was hoping to be able to ask about David's sister. As it turned out he didn't have to.

"Cheltenham," David replied.

"Is that where you're from, then?"

"God no. It was a boarding school. We both went to school there. Well, Annabelle to the Ladies' College, obviously."

"Your sister?" Peter asked. He turned away as he spoke, like he wasn't at all interested.

"That's right."

"So… where is she now?"

"She's younger than me. She's still at school."

"Oh, right."

David laughed. "At least, she'll be in trouble if she's not."

Too right, Peter thought. But what sort of trouble *was* she in?

He didn't have time to wonder. There were other distractions. Carys came to take orders for food. Peter tried to act normal, putting all thoughts of dungeons and manacles and blood out of his mind. He wasn't sure if he managed it. But the next time she appeared, Carys was looking for Professor Crichton.

"There's someone on the phone for you. Said they"ve been trying all afternoon on your mobile but couldn't get through."

"No signal probably," Mike said.

"Battery's flat, actually," Crichton admitted.

"Typical," Abby muttered.

"Anyway," Carys went on, "it's some guy called Rutherford or something. From the university."

Dad sighed. "Funding committee, I'd better talk to him."

The food came while Dad was still on the phone.

"Sounds heavy," Carys said quietly to Peter. "We'll keep his warm."

She seemed just the same. Tomorrow, Peter decided, he'd ask her about the cellar. There had to be some straightforward explanation. He could imagine her laughing and saying, "Oh I don't know, they were here when we took the pub over." Maybe.

Then his dad was back – another distraction. "Apparently there's a funding meeting first thing tomorrow. I have to be there."

Abby and Mike both spoke at once. Crichton held his hand up. "Three-line whip – I can't escape. But the good news is there may be a couple of corporate sponsorship deals coming up. They want me to talk to the high-ups at the companies."

"So you'll be gone all day," Abby complained.

"Couple of days probably. They're still setting up the meetings. In London."

Great, Peter thought. The last thing he wanted was to be dragged off to the university or have to sit in some coffee shop in London waiting for Dad.

So he was relieved when Crichton said, "You'll be all right here, won't you, Peter?"

"Yeah, no problem."

"You can help Abby and Mike. Keep them in order."

"Yeah," Mike agreed, grinning. "Because we so need that."

"What time's the meeting?" Abby asked.

"Nine-thirty. Prompt."

"Early start," Mike pointed out. "And we're going to be without a car except for Abby's old banger."

Sebastian Forrest cleared his throat. "You could go tonight."

"I would," Dad agreed. "There're papers I need from home. But it's been a long day and I've already had a couple of glasses of wine."

"That's no problem. I can organise a car for you."

"That'dleave the Range Rover for us," Mike pointed out.

"I've still got to get to the meeting. And down to London."

"Mum's car's at home," Peter reminded him. "You can use that."

"That's agreed, then," Forrest said.

Crichton left straight after he'd eaten. He promised to text Peter as soon as he got home, and to let him know where he was and when he'd be back. But Peter had no expectation of hearing from his dad at all. Most likely he'd just reappear suddenly in a few days" time.

Peter left Abby and Mike talking with Sebastian Forrest and David. Now he was connected, he could catch up with what everyone was up to on Facebook. But he couldn't concentrate. He kept seeing Annabelle Forrest's face. Kept imagining her trapped in the tower of Wolfstone Manor. Had he really seen her? Or was he adding her image into his imaginings?

After an hour, he'd had enough. He closed the web browser – the last tab to close was the scanned report on the composition of the stones in the circle.

He caught a few words before they disappeared along with the window: *"... the full moon – which is when the silver crystals will resonate, and therefore shine, the most."*

Peter hadn't drawn his curtains, and he could see the moon in the clear sky. Just an edge of it was missing, like it had been folded back. There would be a full moon in a couple of days. Close enough, surely, to see if the stones really glittered in the moonlight.

Abby and Mike were laughing in the restaurant as he passed. Peter considered asking them if they wanted to join him, then changed his mind. He'd rather be on his own. There was no sign of Carys, but her mother passed him as he headed for the side door.

"Going out?"

"Thought I'd go and see the circle in the moonlight."

"Good idea. It's quite something. Hang on..."

Peter waited while she disappeared for a few moments. She returned with a key and a torch. Her bracelets jangled as she handed them to him.

"It's quiet tonight, so I might lock up early," she explained. "This opens the side door. I won't bolt it unless I know you're back."

"Thanks."

"Be careful."

Peter paused in the doorway. "Of what?"

"Nothing. Everything. Just – watch out for yourself."

The moon was bright enough that Peter didn't need the torch. Disappointingly, as he approached the stones they didn't seem to be glowing. He wasn't sure what he'd expected – a ghostly light emanating from the centre of the circle, maybe. But it was just a half-circle of standing stones bathed in the pale light of the moon.

Then, as he got closer Peter began to notice the effect of the light on the crystals of quartz and silver embedded in the stones. It wasn't a glow so much as a sheen. A faint sparkle. Like glitter make-up catching the dim light in a nightclub.

Somewhere in the distance he fancied he heard the baying of a wolf. If he listened carefully, would he also hear a teenage girl calling for help?

In his mind's eye, Peter replayed what he had seen. What he *thought* he had seen. The girl at the window. The boarded window cracking as something thumped into it. Standing with David looking up at the window where the girl might have been.

He realised in the same moment that he was walking away from the stones now, down towards Wolfstone Manor, and that he knew how to get inside. If the girl *was* there, he'd find her.

Moonlit shadows deepened as Peter reached the woods. He took the torch out of his coat pocket. But there was something about the stillness of the night that made him wary of turning it on – the back-of-the-neck feeling that he was being watched. Eventually, the stark silhouette of the house loomed against the sky in front of him and he slipped the torch back into his pocket.

Just as Peter had remembered, the plywood board across the window had a crack running through it. The bottom corner had torn free of the fixings. He pulled it as far from the stone mullion as he could – far enough to wedge it open with his arm and shoulder. Then he could lever the board further away.

The wood protested, creaking and straining. Finally it gave a loud crack, and snapped back along the line where it had already splintered. He squeezed through the window and dropped into the darkness beyond, holding his breath – listening for the slightest sound. The air was heavy with dust. It seemed to press in against him. He shouldn't be here – every instinct told him to get out now. But he had to know – did he imagine the girl in the tower, or was there really someone there?

The torch seemed weak compared to the moon outside. Its narrow beam picked out claustrophobic details. Cracked plaster, the bare lathe work where the ceiling had crumbled away. Wall lamps – rusty and hanging loose. Floorboards that were slick with dust…

Peter crossed the room and emerged into a corridor. The wood panelling was bowed and misshapen with damp, pitted with age, dull with dirt. Floorboards creaked ominously beneath his feet. He hardly dared breath. Every sound was amplified by his fear. Every shadow waited to leap out at him.

The corridor led to a large open hallway. The front door was ahead of Peter, a wide, imposing staircase leading up behind it. An enormous glass chandelier hung over the centre of the hall, the surfaces dulled by dust.

The walls above the panelling were discoloured, shadowy rectangles revealing where pictures had once hung. But he was sure he'd seen the paintings through the window last time. Or had he imagined that too? Another reason to get out now. He swallowed, mouth dry, and turned, trying to get his bearings. If this was the front door, then he'd come the wrong way…

He set off back down the corridor. His footsteps echoed through the empty shell of a house.

If it *was* empty.

The house groaned and creaked around him. It seemed to breathe as he breathed, to pound and thump as his own heart pounded and thumped. The building was like an extension of himself – he could almost believe he was dreaming, and hearing himself asleep.

Another staircase led both upwards and down into blackness. This must be the tower. The girl had been one level below the top – the third storey. He paused at the bottom of the stairs – he didn't want to do this. But he had to find out what was up there. He pressed on upwards.

There was a short corridor off the stairs on the floor where Peter reckoned he had seen the girl. Only one door was closed. It was badly splintered and looked like it had been forced back into the frame. There were bolts top and bottom, their sockets bent and twisted. Peter swung round, peering into the shadows, half expecting to see whoever had done this standing behind him, smiling from the shadows. But he was alone.

He'd come this far. He couldn't go back now, however much he wanted to. He had to put his shoulder to the door to force it open. It slammed back against the wall, making him flinch and look quickly over his shoulder. Then, summoning every last bit of his courage, Peter stepped into the room.

It was a bedroom. The first sweep of the torch picked out a small bed against one wall, duvet pulled half across. Then a table with books piled on it. A free-standing wardrobe. It wasn't tidy, but it was clean. There was none of the dirt and grime or the musty aged smell of the rest of the house. It smelled faintly of roses. Someone had lived here recently.

But they weren't here now.

A second door led into a tiny bathroom. Make-up and lipstick lined up under a cracked mirror. A towel lying on the floor between the toilet and a narrow shower cubicle. The smell of roses was stronger – coming from a bar of soap. Peter felt like he was intruding.

He also felt elated – the girl *had* been here. He had *seen* her. He really had. But then again, his vindication came at a price. It looked like she'd been locked in this place.

He looked round again, biting his lip, trying not to think about how she'd asked for his help. And now he was too late. He'd failed her. He knew who she was, but why was she being kept here? Did her father know? Did David?

Peter sat down at the table. What the hell should he do now? He must tell someone what he'd found. But who? Dad was gone. The police? But then he'd have to explain that he'd broken into the house. And possibly – just possibly – there was some reasonable, sensible, innocent explanation for all this.

"Yeah, right," he murmured, sweeping the torch beam over the desk in front of him.

There was a book. It had a plain cover. A notebook. Or rather, just the cover of a notebook. Most of the pages had been ripped out, leaving ragged marginal stumps of paper. He angled the torch, to see that one word was scrawled in red across the inside back cover:

AFRAID

Peter dropped the notebook, feeling suddenly sick. The torchlight picked out a piece of paper that had been under the book. The stub of a boarding card for a flight from LED to LHR.

As he stood up, the torch beam moved across the floor. Something was sticking out from under the bed. He hesitated, then moved the torch quickly on. It looked like dark fur. Cautiously, Peter backed away. Whatever it was didn't move. He risked shining the torch directly at it. A paw.

He almost laughed with relief as he realised what it was. The arm of a teddy bear. He pushed the duvet out of the way, revealing the toy. The light shone full on it for a second. But that was more than enough. With a yelp of fear, Peter dropped the torch. The light danced round the walls as it rolled away. But the image it had shown was stamped on Peter's memory.

Stuffing had exploded from the bear's stomach. One arm was missing, a leg torn almost off. A single glassy eye stared impassively at Peter.

The thing had been ripped to pieces.

Peter grabbed the torch. As he fumbled with it, the beam cut across the deep parallel scratches running down the back of the door, and the walls either side. They echoed the slashes across the toy.

He didn't care how much noise he made as he clattered down the stairs. The torch lurched erratically across the floor and walls.

He missed the ground floor, only realising as the steps changed from wood to stone. The air was suddenly damp and heavy. He turned quickly to retrace his steps.

He couldn't wait to get out of the house. Whatever had happened here, he was never coming back. Just, please God, let him get out again in one piece.

"Who's there?"

The voice caught him as he turned, and Peter almost leaped up the next few steps.

The voice was faint – weak and nervous. "Hello? Help me, please."

His every instinct was to run. But the voice was afraid. Begging for help. He'd run away last time, and been no use at all.

"Who is it?" he called back. His voice was so husky with nerves he doubted anyone would hear him.

The voice seemed to rise up from the bottom of the stairs. "Oh thank God. Thank God..." The voice dissolved into tears.

Peter stood for seconds that seemed like an age, torn between getting the hell out and going to help. The image of the blonde girl in the window vied with the slashes ripped into the door above. Finally, taking a deep breath, mustering his courage but ready to turn and run, he took a step downwards, towards the voice.

The steps seemed to go down for ever, arriving at last in a huge vaulted chamber that was more like a crypt than a cellar. There was light – flickering lamps stood on tall iron stands in the alcoves. Candles, fixed with their own wax to stone shelves, gave off a smoky light. Some were burned almost right down, others snuffed out.

Moonlight streamed in through small windows high on the outside walls – windows that were no more than narrow, curved holes cut into the stone roof. Crescents of moonlight, shining down on a line of carved tombs down the centre of the vault. Like crusader knights lying on stone caskets…

But Peter barely registered any of this.

His attention was on the girl.

She lay sprawled on the floor, her long, fair hair spilling round her hands as she wept into them. His fear was washed away by the sight of her. Peter wanted to run to her, to hold her, to tell her everything would be all right. He'd make sure everything was all right.

But he couldn't get close. Because she was lying inside a huge cage, its bars gleaming in the moonlight like polished silver.

CHAPTER 8

The cage was locked, like a prison cell. Peter shook the door, but there was no way it was going to open. The girl shuffled away, across the stone floor, pushing herself backwards on scratched, bare feet, watching him through red-rimmed eyes.

"Annabelle?"

She didn't react.

"You're Annabelle, aren't you?" Peter said gently. "Who put you in here?" The question made him suddenly aware of how much danger they must be in. He looked round, listening for the slightest sound. As far as he could tell, they were alone. But that didn't stop the cold prickle of sweat between his shoulder blades, or the lump of fear in his throat.

She didn't answer, but watched Peter warily. Her face was grimy and tear-stained. Her hair matted and her plain white dress torn and discoloured. Her eyes were wide with fear – and just possibly hope.

He reached through the bars. She didn't react, but she didn't back away again either. She was crying quietly, whimpering like a wounded animal.

"It's all right," Peter assured her. "I'll get you out of there, I promise. Is there a key somewhere? We have to hurry."

She had her face buried in her hands again. Was she even listening?

"Annabelle!"

She looked up, startled by the urgency in his voice.

"I said, I'll get you out of there, all right?" He took a deep breath, trying to stay calm. But his heart was racing and he was sweating, despite the cold. Angry as well as afraid. Who the hell had put her in here? "My name's Peter. I saw you in the tower, do you remember?"

He checked his phone. The signal bars had been replaced with 'Searching...'

Her hair had fallen forward but he could see her eyes watching him closely from between lank strands. She leaned forward, and crawled slowly towards him on hands and knees. Peter reached through the bars again, and this time she took his hand. Her body was trembling. Her long fingernails dug into Peter's hand as she held it tight.

He put his other hand through, and patted her shoulder. Stroked her hair. He didn't know what to do really. She flinched at his touch, but then seemed to accept it. It was like comforting a frightened cat.

"I'll find something to open this cage," he said. "Something I can use as a lever, maybe."

He made to withdraw his hand, but she gripped him even tighter, pulling him close. Her other arm thrust through the bars, and round his neck. He thought she wanted to whisper something, and let her pull his head close. Instead, she pressed her own face to the bars on the other side, and kissed him.

He was so shocked, he didn't move. All he could think of was that despite the dirt and the dust, the tears and the smoking candles, she smelled of rose petals.

He slowly withdrew his arms from the cage. She kept hold of his hand for as far as she could reach. She was holding on so tight it hurt. A ring on her finger dug into Peter's flesh – a large, silver ring. He gently eased her finger open with his other hand. The ring caught the flickering candlelight and he saw that it was engraved with the head of a wolf.

She pulled her arm back into the cage, and sat with her knees pulled up tight to her chest, watching Peter as he backed away.

"There has to be something," he said out loud. "A crowbar, maybe?"

The metal stand on which one of the oil lamps stood was too large and unwieldy to fit between the bars of the cage. The nearest tomb offered no help either, just the effigy of a knight lying impassive and useless, his features worn away by age. The sword he clasped to his chest was carved stone. The cracked and worn remains of an animal lay curled at the knight's feet. A hunting dog… or a wolf.

The edges of the chamber disappeared into darkness and shadow. Peter shone his torch into the gloom. He took a step backwards as the torchlight revealed another shape. It glittered as the torch picked it out, as if hungry for the light. A standing stone – just like the ones in the Wolfstone Circle. But this one was built into the wall of the chamber, so that it seemed to jut out from the stone like a rocky pustule about to burst.

"I'll have to go for help," Peter decided. He ran back to the cage, pressing his face to the bars. "Sorry – I'll be as quick as I can." He thought for a moment she was going to grab and kiss him again. His heart leaped at the thought. But she just stood on the other side of the bars, looking back at him. Afraid. Alone.

There was noise from above. The unmistakable sound of footsteps on the stone steps down to the chamber. Someone was coming.

Annabelle looked up, then back at Peter. Her eyes were wide open with terror. She knew who it was – and they weren't coming to help.

"I'm sorry," he whispered, hoping she would understand. "I'll be here. I'll do what I can." He switched off the torch and pressed back into the gloom, hiding behind the protruding stone.

She continued to stare across the chamber, even though Peter was sure she couldn't see him. He was desperate to help her, to do something – anything. Whoever it was, Peter would charge at them – knock them to the ground and find the keys to the cage. But any hope that he could free Annabelle was dispelled as soon as the figures emerged into the guttering light.

There were four of them. Their dark cloaks seemed to absorb the light. Hoods shadowed their faces. Two of the figures stood either side of the entrance – sinister sentinels framing the steps behind. The other two approached the silver cage.

Annabelle scuttled back, as far away from them as she could get, pressed against the bars at the back of the cage. One of the cloaked figures unlocked the door and swung it open.

Immediately, the girl hurled herself at him, snarling and scratching, punching and biting. Peter forced himself to stay still. The two men grabbed Annabelle. One held her wrists, the other caught her round the waist. Peter forced himself to stay still, his hands bunched into tight, frustrated fists. If there had just been the two of them he might have been able to help her escape. But the other two figures watched impassively as their fellows dragged Annabelle towards the stairway.

Peter had surprise on his side. They couldn't know he was here, watching. Maybe he'd get his chance. He had to follow, see where they took Annabelle. As she struggled, she twisted and turned, looking back over her shoulder, her expression pleading and terrified.

The fight seemed to go out of her. A sudden acceptance of the inevitable, or perhaps she was saving her strength for whatever was to come. For a moment, the chamber was silent. Then she yelled out, and kicked and struggled again.

One of the figures slapped Annabelle hard across the face. Her head snapped round under the force of the blow. Her screams and shouts became a wail of pain. Peter took a step forward. It was all he could do to stop himself rushing at them there and then – yelling and screaming. But it wouldn't help.

The man who had slapped Annabelle reached out for her again. He took hold of her chin, and turned her face gently back towards his. Her whimpering died away as she stared into the blackness under his hood.

"I'm sorry," he said. "But the sooner we get you to the circle, the sooner we can finish this."

Peter watched in surprise as the man stroked Annabelle's

cheek. She closed her eyes, did not resist as they led her away.

As soon as they were gone, Peter checked his phone. There was a signal. Here beside the standing stone, the phone had two bars. Should he call someone or follow the men who had taken Annabelle? If he moved, he might lose the signal. They were going to the circle – the man had said so. Call, then follow.

But call who? Dad was miles away. Whose number did he know? He scrolled down his list of stored numbers. He paused at Carys's name. But in his mind's eye, Peter could see the silver manacles and chain – it had to be connected somehow with the eerie silver cage across the chamber from him. He scrolled on...

A tired voice answered on the third ring.

"Peter? What time is it? I was asleep. What do you want?"

"Just listen, David," Peter hissed.

David Forrest sounded more awake now. He could probably hear the urgency in Peter's voice. "What is it? What's wrong?"

"I'm at Wolfstone Manor."

"Where?!"

"There's some sort of crypt or vault underneath that tower at the back."

"What the hell are you— "

"Just listen, will you?" Peter demanded. "I tried to help her, really I did. But I couldn't get the cage open. And now they"ve taken her away. They're taking her to the circle."

"What are you talking about?" David said. "Have you had a nightmare or something? Who couldn't you help? Who have they taken?"

"Annabelle!" Peter almost shouted into the phone. "Don't you understand? She was here. I saw her at the window, and now they"ve taken her away. They"ve got your sister!"

There was silence at the other end of the phone.

"David – are you still there? Did you hear what I said?"

But the signal had gone, and the phone was dead.

The journey through the manor grounds was a nightmare. Peter didn't dare use the torch. Although the sky was clear and the moon was almost full, he tripped and stumbled more times than he could remember. With every step, every stumble, he thought the men in cloaks would materialise out of the shadows to grab him.

Even before he reached the Wolfstone Circle, he saw that the whole area was lit by the headlights of vehicles parked close by.

His phone signal was still intermittent. Should he call the police? But what would he tell them – he had no idea what was going on. Hooded figures stood inside the circle – more of them now, maybe a dozen.

Right in the middle, two of the cloaked figures held Annabelle by the arms, stretched out between them. She stared defiantly into the night, the breeze tugging at her dress. The other figures stood at the edge of the circle, mirroring the stones.

Peter dropped to the ground, as close to the circle as he dared. Any closer and he'd be picked out by the headlights. But what now? If they saw him, if they caught him, that wouldn't help Annabelle.

The closest of the cloaked figures turned towards where Peter was lying on his stomach. Peter pressed himself down into the cold grass. He could feel the damp ground give under his weight. Tufts of grass pressed uncomfortably into him. After a moment he dared to raise his head, ready to leap to his feet and run for it.

Mercifully, the figure was moving back towards Annabelle and the circle. As he turned, moonlight filtered through the darkness beneath the hood. For a moment, Peter thought he saw a grotesque, misshapen face – an elongated snout, massive jaws, yellowed eyes…

Carys. If there was anyone Peter wanted with him now, it was Carys. He didn't care what he'd found in the cellar. He just wanted her there. He had to move to tease his phone out of his pocket. Every movement was a risk. Every breath an effort.

His phone had a weak signal. He didn't dare call – his voice might carry to the circle. He'd text her. But – would she come? Would she believe he needed her help?

He held the phone as steady as he could, making sure the flash was turned off. The click of the camera seemed incredibly loud. The image was blurred – distant and indistinct.

Peter texted the image and a short message to Carys. As soon as he sent it, he wished he hadn't. What if she and her mother were actually *here*, at the circle, right now? He strained to hear if anyone received a text. Stared at each of the cloaked figures to see if any of them checked their phone. The cold of the ground was seeping right through his body, chilling his blood.

Noise and confusion now. Just one of the robed figures remained at the edge of the circle, close to one of the stones, reaching down under its edge. The others closed in on Annabelle. Her screams split the night.

At the sound, Peter leaped to his feet, all thoughts of his own safety gone. She needed help, and she needed it *now.*

He charged forward, shouting at them to stop – to leave her alone. Annabelle's screams had changed to snarls of anger. He couldn't see her – the figures were so close round her. A blur of movement between them. Somewhere a dog barked.

Peter charged into Annabelle's captors. One staggered away. Another snatched at Peter's arm, pulling him almost off balance. As they turned towards Peter, a grey shape hurled itself at the cloaked figures from inside the circle, from behind them. Peter had no chance to see what it was. Hands grabbed at him. He struggled, fought, yelled, punched, kicked...

Then he was on the ground, his arm yanked up his back so far he thought it would be torn from the socket. A cloaked figure dropped to its knees beside Peter.

Hot, rancid breath reeked out from beneath the hood.

He was hauled to his feet. The figure in front of him threw off its hood and stared angrily at Peter.

He could only stare back in astonishment. "You?!"

CHAPTER 9

"What the hell do you think you're doing?" Sebastian Forrest demanded. "You almost ruined everything."

"Me?" Peter was aghast. "What about *you*? What are you doing? You keep your own daughter caged up then bring her here for this..." He didn't know what the word was.

Forrest was taken aback. For a second, Peter thought the man was going to hit him. He seemed to be struggling to keep control.

"You know nothing," Forrest snarled eventually. His head was swaying slowly, like a dog scenting the air. "Get him out of here."

"Where shall we take him?" one of the men holding Peter asked. His voice was a guttural bark.

"I don't care... Just away from here. Now! Then we'll try again."

As the two men holding Peter dragged him out of the circle, someone was running towards Forrest and the others – a silhouette in the headlights of the parked cars. As the figure grew closer, Peter recognised it. He didn't know whether he should be surprised or relieved to see David.

Forrest was clearly shaken by his son's arrival however, and though Peter was too far away now to hear what they said, the body language between them was tense and confrontational. David pointed angrily into the circle, past the cloaked and hooded figures that stood within it.

Sebastian Forrest jabbed his finger – as if emphasising a point he had made in previous arguments. He shook his head, turned away. But David grabbed his arm and pulled him back round.

Forrest shook off his son's hand and pushed him away.

This time Peter caught the words. "I've told you," Forrest shouted. "It's too late. Do you think I'd lie about it? About something like that?"

"But you kept Annabelle locked up and didn't think to even mention it?" David yelled back. "You'll try for her, but—"

The rest of his words were lost in the sudden noise. Searchlights raked down from above. Peter's hair was blown back. The whole place was a maelstrom of sound and wind and light.

The helicopter was coming down on the side of the circle where the men were holding Peter. They stared up in surprise at the dark shape hidden in the glare of its own searchlights, which now illuminated the scene. Peter wrenched himself free and sprinted for cover. The men who'd held him ran the other way, towards the circle.

"It's him!" one of them yelled. "It's the Old One!"

The figures in the circle all turned to watch the helicopter settle heavily on the ground, its searchlights angled towards the Wolfstone Circle. A dark shape charged through the ring of figures and bounded off into the darkness. Forrest started to run after it, but his son grabbed him and pulled him back.

The dark shape charged straight at Peter as he crouched in the long grass. It was a large dog – like the one he had seen at the churchyard, but sleeker. A streak of lighter fur ran from the top of the animal's head down its back. It grazed past Peter, knocking him sideways, then it was gone – bounding off towards the woods.

What the hell was going on? He dropped down so that he was lying in a slight hollow, concealed in the longer grass, and watched as the side door of the helicopter slid open.

Half a dozen uniformed figures jumped down from the helicopter and approached the circle. They carried guns, and moved together with the practised ease of soldiers. Or a pack of animals hunting their prey.

One of the soldiers paused, caught full in the beam of the searchlight. Instinctively, Peter shuffled backwards as the soldier glanced his way. Even so, he had a clear view. He saw the dark grey uniform with its high collar and double-breasted tunic. The black boots. The dark frame of what looked like a machine pistol, which the man held in black-gloved hands.

If it was a man.

There was something about him – the slight hunch when he walked; the shape of the face…

The soldiers formed a double line, like an honour guard. Peter held his breath. A root or branch was pressing painfully into his side, but he didn't dare move. What now?

Another figure stepped out of the helicopter. He was tall and thin. He stared up at the moon for a moment, the pale light illuminating his pinched, emaciated features.

The man wore a long, dark leather coat, like that of a German SS officer from the Second World War. His left arm hung loose, the shoulder dipped and hunched. As he walked, the man did not move this arm at all. In the glare of the searchlights, his face looked bluish-grey, like it was bruised. He paused to peer at the trench where Mike and Abby had been digging, now covered with a tarpaulin, then he continued towards the circle.

There was something about the SS officer that drew attention away from everyone else. Peter was transfixed. He couldn't look away. This must be the Old One, but who *was* he? Why was he here?

Sebastian Forrest stepped forward. He greeted the

man and they shook hands, like equals. But from the way the cloaked figures shuffled nervously while the soldiers stood to attention, it was clear who was really in charge.

Forrest shook his head, pointing off in the direction of the woods. The other man also gestured – always with his right hand. His left arm remained still throughout.

Peter peered into the circle, trying to see past the cloaked figures, desperate to know if Annabelle was all right.

Finally, the tall, lean man turned away from Forrest. His deep-set eyes scanned the area around the circle. Even at a distance, Peter was sure the dark eyes fixed on him, bored right into him. The man raised his right hand and snapped his fingers. Then he pointed right at Peter.

He *couldn't* have seen him. But in unison, the soldiers turned and started running – straight towards Peter. If he didn't move, they'd find him in seconds. If he did, they'd see him at once.

He crawled backwards, desperately, pulse racing. How far was it to the woods? He jumped to his feet, praying the darkness afforded some cover, and ran as fast as he could. The ground thumped at his feet and his heart thumped in his chest. He gulped in painfully cold night air – afraid to look back, but unable to stop himself. The soldiers were gaining on him. But not just soldiers.

They came out of the darkness. Bounding across

the stone circle, racing through the open countryside, overtaking the soldiers and racing towards Peter.

One of them passed him, ignoring Peter and charging on into the wood. Another massive dog, bigger than Peter, its tongue lolling hungrily from the side of its mouth as it ran.

Peter reached the woods, staggered onwards, deeper and deeper. Until, exhausted and terrified, he sank down in the undergrowth.

As soon as he'd stopped, another of the huge dogs barrelled through the trees. It stopped, front paws up on a fallen trunk, eyes glinting red in the reflected moonlight as if they were lit from within. One of the animal's ears was twisted and torn, a ragged stump of gnarled gristle. It snapped its jaws hungrily as it looked round – not a dog at all. A wolf.

It stood for a few moments, absolutely still except for the breeze riffling its fur. Its head was raised and Peter realised it was sniffing the air. The way he was sweating it would smell him in no time. But the wolf set off deeper into the wood, away from Peter. If it wasn't looking for him, who *was* it after?

He didn't have time to think about that. The soldiers were coming, crashing through the undergrowth – snarling and growling like the wolves. Peter burrowed into the middle of a clump of bushes as one of them charged past. Branches scraped at his face and he stifled a cry of pain. The soldier stopped, breathing heavily, looking round.

The moonlight was broken up and scattered by the trees. But the soldier would see Peter if he looked the right way.

And there was enough light for Peter to see the soldier. He struggled not to make another sound, forced himself to stay absolutely still.

Tufts of dark hair erupted from the soldier's collar, and more bristled where the gloves met the wrist. But the face was the worst – silhouetted against the almost-full moon as the creature in uniform turned. A long snout, vicious jaws, deep-set red eyes, and matted hair... It was the face of a savage wolf.

CHAPTER 10

The wolf-soldier stood for what seemed an age, as if sensing its prey was close. Peter pressed slowly, carefully, back into the shadows.

A fallen branch snapped under his foot. The wolf-soldier swung round towards the noise. Its face was a snarl of triumph. A thin dribble of saliva escaped from its hideous jaws as it started towards Peter.

He couldn't move – frozen with fear. Shivering. A cry of panic welling up in his throat.

Then one of the *real* wolves charged into the undergrowth behind him. It forced its way through the tight-knit branches, ignoring Peter. The soldier-wolf gave an angry bark as the creature ran past it.

Distracted, the soldier-wolf moved off through the trees, still snarling. Its gun was slung over its shoulder, hanging loosely as the creature swept aside the foliage with massive, gloved paws. Peter had never seen a gun like it – a narrow barrel and light stock.

As soon as the sound of the figure's angry progress through the wood had faded, Peter pushed out of his cover. He had to get back to the pub. He'd be safe there. He could crawl into bed and hide under the covers and hope that Dad would be back soon.

Staring after the soldier, Peter didn't see the blood-red eyes glinting in the shadows. The massive animal charged out of the gloom, leaping at Peter. Its front paws slammed into his chest, knocking him backwards.

Peter rolled out of the way instinctively as he landed, and the huge bulk of the animal crashed into the ground where he'd been. It would have crushed the life out of him. Immediately the wolf was up and heading straight for Peter as he lay winded, confused and terrified.

His hands scrabbled at the ground, found something – a broken branch he'd trodden on. He rolled again, bringing up the branch as the wolf leaped out of the darkness. The end of the branch was a broken, ragged point. The wolf saw it, but too late.

The point connected with one of the wolf's paws. Peter felt the animal's weight, like the recoil of a gun, knocking back into him. The speed and size of the wolf drove it on. The branch emerged from the back of the paw, accompanied by a shower of blood. The branch was torn from Peter's grip, snapped as the wolf landed on it.

The animal's high-pitched screeches of pain echoed in Peter's ears as he dragged himself to his feet. The wolf lay on its back, clawing at the stump of the branch with its good paws, trying to pull it out. Its red eyes locked onto Peter's, and for a moment there was something in them, something he thought he recognised.

Peter ran.

He didn't care how much noise he made, didn't know which way he was running, had no idea if the wolves or soldiers were after him. He ran until his lungs were about to burst and his throat was raw from breathing so hard. His face was scratched by branches and his ankle ached where he'd twisted it and not even noticed.

A soldier-wolf turned at the sound of Peter's approach. It brought its gun up.

Peter didn't see it until it was too late – his only chance was to keep running. He put his head down and charged, shoulder slamming into the creature's midriff. Unbalanced, but still on his feet, Peter ran.

The sound wasn't loud. He felt something whistle past his cheek. The shot missed, embedding itself in a tree ahead of him. Peter could see it, not a bullet but a metal dart with a tufted end, sticking out of the bark of the tree.

Another shot – and a sudden pain in Peter's arm. But he kept running. He clawed at the pain with his other hand, and felt the dart. It had stuck in his coat, but the tip of it must have penetrated the skin. He pulled the dart out and stuffed it into his pocket. He could feel blood running down his arm, inside the coat, slick and sticky.

He dived to one side, rolled under a bush and was up and running again. Peter felt light-headed, like he could run for ever. But the world around him seemed to be slowing down. Blurring. He emerged from the trees and the moon was a double-disc. His head was swimming.

At least he knew where he was. The distinctive, forbidding shape of Wolfstone Manor loomed in front of him. He struggled to keep it focused, realising now that he'd been drugged. The dart was a tranquiliser. He had to keep going, had to find somewhere to hide. To sleep it off. Inside the house? Too far. Too dangerous.

But where in the grounds could he hide? Where would they be unable to find him?

The answer was so obvious he'd have laughed out loud if he'd had the strength. But he could barely move his fingers over his phone, could hardly see what he was doing. He forced his way through a hedge. Pressed the dial button.

Signal – please let there be a signal.

He was falling. The whole world was getting darker. There was a throbbing in his ears – or was it the sound of a phone ringing somewhere in the distance?

"Hello?" a voice said. Even that seemed so far away.

Focus – he had to focus on what he was doing.

"Hello?" the voice said again, even fainter now. "Have you any idea what time it is, Peter? Hello?"

He struggled to speak – to explain. He must tell... must...

His head fell back, and he felt the cold, hard earth under it.

The last thing he saw was a vivid purple flower swaying gently close to his face. Maiden's tears.

The best time to cry is at night.

Wolf's blight.

Then even that was gone.

CHAPTER 11

The helicopter had woken Carys. She had heard it in the distance, cutting through the still of the night.

She got out of bed and went to the window to see what the noise was. Searchlights shone down from the dark shape that traversed the pale disc of the moon. It looked like it was somewhere between the circle and the manor. She watched, as the helicopter descended out of sight.

She got back into bed, and tried to get back to sleep. Her phone buzzed to tell her she had a message. She ignored it. She was just drifting off when her phone rang. Not a text, but a call. Who calls in the middle of the night? she wondered as she fumbled for it.

A few moments later, she was wondering if Peter was drunk. He'd sounded woozy, half asleep. He'd not made much sense, apart from telling her that he was in trouble. He'd said something about the circle, and he'd mentioned the helicopter.

She heard it again. The dark shape hovered like an insect above the trees before disappearing into the distance. Carys's phone buzzed in her hand, reminding her she had an unread text.

She stared at the blurred picture. She could make out the stones of the circle, the dark figures. A pale shape in the middle of them – another person. A girl?

The obvious, sensible thing to do was to get Mum. But she was looking after Mr Seymour. A glance at the sky out of the window was enough to remind Carys of that. She felt guilty enough about not being there to help, but she'd been so tired that Mum had packed her off to bed. No, Carys must handle this on her own.

Peter wasn't drunk, she decided. He wasn't that sort of boy. He was out there somewhere and he needed help. He'd called *her* for help, she thought as she pulled on her jeans. Not his dad (though, okay, he was on his way to London), not smarmy spoiled David Forrest, or one of the archaeologists, but *her*.

He'd said – she thought he'd said – he was in the maze. She called him back, but the phone just rang and then went to voicemail. Mum's bed was empty and hadn't been slept in, and Carys grabbed the keys from her bedside cabinet. Would Mum hear the battered four-by-four as it spluttered into life? Well, if she did she could call – Carys had her phone.

Ahead of her, a car turned out of the narrow track that led down to the circle. Its brake lights flashed briefly in her rear-view mirror, then it sped away.

There was another track further on, hardly more than a footpath, but it led to the Manor's old driveway. The four-by-four bounced along, lurching from side to side. Carys fought to keep going in a straight line. The steering wheel twisted in her grip as the wheels caught in ruts or bumped down rabbit holes.

After what seemed an age, Wolfstone Manor loomed in the distance. Its roof merged with the grey of the night sky. The going was easier for a bit, but it soon became slow and bumpy again. How close could she get?

A dark shape charged towards her out of the night, and Carys stamped on the brake. The four-by-four slewed and skidded to a halt. She breathed deeply, telling herself to stay calm. But she'd caught a glimpse of the animal as it crossed her path. It was an enormous wolf.

The engine had stalled. But she was about as close as she could get anyway. Carys clambered out, feeling weak and sick as she started towards the house. The sight of the wolf had made her stomach lurch. "Oh God, oh God," she muttered as she hurried forward. "Please let him be all right."

In her imagination, Carys saw Peter lying in a pool of thickening blood, his throat ripped out by the beast…

Across the terrace, the maze was a mass of shadows. She called out – hesitant and nervous at first; increasingly loud and frantic as she got no reply.

Along overgrown paths, through hedges that were more branches than leaves. She scraped and clawed her way onwards, painfully aware that there was no method in her search. Stop, she told herself, stop and think. Just think.

He wasn't answering, so either Peter wasn't here at all... or perhaps he couldn't answer. She had her phone out – but that was stupid. If he couldn't answer her shouts he wasn't going to answer his phone.

Then she realised. He didn't have to. She made the call – and somewhere in the distance a phone started to ring, a good old-fashioned bell sound. Thank God he didn't have some crazy, childish ringtone.

The ringing stopped as the phone went to voicemail. Carys ended the call and immediately rang again. She edged closer to the sound, shoving through the overgrown hedges and ducking round the larger branches. She was desperate to reach Peter; terrified of what she might find.

And suddenly, there he was – lying on his back, eyes closed. But his chest was moving – he was breathing. Carys ran to him, dropped to her knees, grabbed his hand.

It was covered in blood. She gasped in horror, and he stirred slightly. His forehead was glistening with sweat in the dappled moonlight that filtered through the hedges.

The blood was coming from higher up his arm, yet his coat wasn't torn – wasn't ripped and clawed to shreds. But he was feverish, shivering, unconscious...

She tried to lift him, to drag him. She managed a few metres, then gave up, breathless and frustrated. She'd never get him back to the four-by-four like this.

"I need to get the car closer," Carys told him. Could he hear her? Did he even know she was there? "Really – I won't be long... You'll be all right. I promise – you'll be all right."

As she gently lowered his head, she caught sight of the small purple flowers nestling under the hedge and almost cried out with relief.

Quick as she could, Carys plucked the flowers and crushed them in her fist. She felt the moisture welling up. With her other hand, she prised Peter's mouth open slightly. Then she let the juice from the flowers drip out of her fist and into his mouth. It might be enough.

"I won't be long," she said again. She hesitated for a moment, before leaning down to kiss his forehead. Then she was running back through the maze.

She didn't see the shape that stepped back into the shadows, all the time watching Peter as he lay shivering on the cold ground.

CHAPTER 12

He was running, running for his life. But it wasn't like before, when he'd been pursued through the woods. Peter was running, but he couldn't feel the ground under his feet. It was like he was floating just above it, never quite touching reality. And he was not alone.

The girl ran with him. It was Annabelle, and yet it wasn't Annabelle. She looked similar – long, fair hair blown round her determined, frightened face. She kept looking back. She stared right at Peter running alongside her, and didn't see him.

He didn't know who she was, but she was running for her life.

They ran through formal gardens, along a tree-lined path, and out onto a wide driveway. Distant gates set into a high wall stood impassive and impressive ahead of them. The statue of a wolf looked down hungrily from the top of each gatepost.

From behind came the thunder of the horses" hooves, the bark of the hounds. The shouts and laughter of the men chasing them. Chasing *her.* Because Peter wasn't really there at all.

"You're the girl from the legend, aren't you?" His voice was loud despite the sound of dogs and horses.

She didn't answer. She kept running. When she fell, sprawling headlong on the grass, Peter reached down to help her up. But he couldn't. Even though he was right there beside the girl, he couldn't reach her.

He looked round, confused, and found that they were suddenly in the middle of the Wolfstone Circle. Or rather, where the circle should have been, because there were no stones – just the view down to the woods one way and back towards the road the other.

The girl struggled to get up, but the dogs were on her before she could move. Snarling and snapping, they forced her back to the ground. The horses were close behind, the men riding them laughing as they watched.

She managed to drag herself out from under the hounds. Her dress was ripped, her face spattered with blood. Her eyes wide and pleading as she staggered towards the nearest horseman, hounds snapping at her ankles. He twisted in his saddle and pushed himself down from the horse, landing in front of the girl. He raised his whip.

And suddenly in place of the man there was a stone; a flattened semi-circle of stones replaced all the men and their horses. A faint echo on the breeze was the only memory of the laughter.

The echo of the barking dogs became the chant of the approaching robed figures. They pushed a man ahead of them. He was exhausted, his dark hair and beard matted with sweat. A medieval peasant – his rough clothes torn and muddy. His hands were bound together with a thin silver chain. If he'd had the strength, he'd have run – Peter could see that in his eyes. At the back of the group of robed men stood an archer, silver-tipped arrow already slotted to his bowstring.

One of them shoved the captive into the middle of the stones, where he stumbled and fell to his knees. His eyes were wide with fear.

The robed figures stopped at the edge of the circle, closing together, obscuring Peter's view of the peasant. One of the robed men stooped down beside a stone. The movement was familiar. It echoed in Peter's memory. The man reached beneath the edge of the stone, into the grass.

The cry was a mixture of surprise and fear and pain. It could only have come from the shackled man in the circle. But as the robed figures stepped back, Peter saw that the man was gone. The circle was empty...

Suddenly faint, Peter sat down heavily – not on the ground, but on a wooden chair. The world shimmered and blurred, and he was inside Wolfstone Manor again.

A long wooden table was loaded with food. Plates of

meat and bread, bowls of fruit. Flagons of wine and ale. A whole pig, crisp and hot, laid out on an enormous pewter dish.

The noise was sudden and confusing. So many people eating and talking and laughing. There must have been twenty guests sitting along the table. None of them looked at Peter.

A young man and woman sat at the head of the table. The man wore expensive, elaborate robes. The woman's dress was elegant simplicity. She had small purple flowers braided into her hair. They each wore a heavy silver ring, and Peter knew there would be a wolf engraved on them.

The man got to his feet. He gestured for the woman to do the same. Arms linked, they stared along the table. The man raised his goblet. Dark red liquid lipped over the top.

His voice cut through the noise of the guests. "It is time," he declared.

All other speech and laughter died away. One man banged his goblet on the table in appreciation. A woman beside Peter took a deep fulfilling breath, head back and eyes glistening in anticipation.

The young man and woman raised their goblets and drank. They gulped hungrily at the viscous dark red liquid that ran down their chins and splashed to the floor. Then they hurled the empty goblets away across the room.

The other guests were on their feet. Peter remained rooted to his chair as he watched them. They downed their drinks, hurled their goblets away, snarling with eager delight. Their features shimmered. Clothes ripped away to reveal the fur beneath. Claws raked down faces – the wolves within bursting out through their human skin.

One of the wolves tore into the pig with its massive jaws. Plates were knocked aside as others joined in. Red wine spilled across the table, ran along the grain of the wood, and dripped like blood to the stone floor.

Gradually, the animal feeding and the noise stopped. All the hideous creatures turned towards the two wolves standing upright at the head of the table. Their rheumy eyes swivelled slowly round until they were staring at Peter. Then suddenly both creatures leaped up onto the table, and charged towards him, scattering food and plates.

Peter fell backwards, the chair tipping away as he tried to escape. He landed painfully on his back, staring up at the sky. Knowing that, in a moment, the wolves would be on him.

Staring at the *sky*. Not the ceiling of the great hall of Wolfstone Manor, but the nearly full moon emerging from behind a cloud.

The ground was cold and damp under his head. He felt

incredibly hot, yet he was shivering. He tried to sit up, but it was too much of an effort. He must have been dreaming, he realised. But how much had he dreamed? The girl in the cage? The ceremony at the stones and the helicopter? The *wolves*?

Maybe he was still dreaming. As he slumped back down, he was sure he saw someone watching him from the shadows. Just a glimpse of a girl's face – young, pretty, sad, framed with long, straggly fair hair. He forced his body to move, twisting round to see her properly.

But there was no one there.

Instead movement came from the opposite direction. The sound of something forcing its way through the remains of the hedge; a dark shape, blotting out the moonlight, reaching down to him.

"You're awake," Carys said. "Thank God."

She got her arms under him, and hauled Peter up to standing. He slumped against her, legs like jelly. He said thank you, but no sound came out of his mouth.

Carys held him tight, both arms round his waist. She tentatively let go with one arm, bracing him against her with the other. She felt warm and reassuring. "It's not far now. Can you walk?"

"Yes," he managed to gasp. And collapsed to the ground.

CHAPTER 13

The room swam into clarity for a few moments before slipping away again into the haze. If he concentrated, Peter could focus, at least for a short while. He was lying in bed. Had it all been a dream?

He fell asleep again before he could decide.

Sunlight was streaming in round the edge of the curtains when he woke again. He felt less woozy. But his arm ached.

The third time he woke, Carys was sitting beside his bed.

"How are you feeling?"

Peter mumbled a response. He was acutely aware that he seemed to be wearing only his underpants beneath the covers.

"How's the arm?"

It was only when she asked that he noticed there was a bandage round the upper part of his forearm.

"It aches. But then, so does the rest of me." He summoned up the courage to ask, "Sorry – how did I get here?"

Carys smiled. "Don't worry, Mum put you to bed."

"Right." Was that less embarrassing? Not much.

"I just carried you back to the car and drove you here." She watched for his reaction, and seemed amused at his confusion. "Never mind. We can talk about last night later."

"Why – what happened last night?"

"You tell me."

Mrs Seymour checked on Peter after lunch. He told her he was feeling fine, and she suggested he come down and have some soup in the bar. Abby and Mike were up at the dig apparently. He asked whether Sebastian Forrest was still here.

She didn't seem surprised at the question. "He had to leave first thing this morning. David too." She laid her hand across his forehead. "Your temperature's down, which is good. A fever that high and you begin to hallucinate."

Was that it? Or was she trying to convince him he'd been imagining things?

"Let me check your arm while I'm here."

Peter sat up in the bed so Mrs Seymour could undo the bandage. "Did I cut myself?"

"Something like that. It's a small wound," she said quietly as she examined it. "Not like a bite at all."

"It was a dart," he remembered. "They shot me."

She nodded as if this made perfect sense.

"What is that stuff?" The bandage was lined with dark purple, the colour of an old bruise. It was cool and damp.

"Just an old traditional remedy. Your arm will be better in no time, though you're lucky Carys found you before..."

"Before?"

"Before the infection took hold." She bound the arm up again quickly and efficiently. "There."

"The remedy – it's the same colour as those little flowers."

"That's right. There are a few other ingredients, but mostly it's crushed wolf's blight. The only remedy there is."

Professor Crichton rang while Peter was having his soup. Mr Seymour watched curiously from behind the bar as Peter answered. He assumed someone had told Dad he was ill. But it was soon clear that that wasn't why his dad was calling.

"It's going to take a few days to sort out, I'm afraid," the professor said. "Bureaucracy, that's all it is. But I'd better hang on or the funding will vanish in a puff of paperwork. Will you be okay?"

"I'll be fine," Peter lied. "And anyway, Abby and Mike are both here."

"You could go and stay with Aunt Sarah," Dad offered.

"I'll be all right," Peter said quickly. He felt better for having something to eat.

"All right then. I'll let you know when I'll be back as soon as I know myself."

Mr Seymour came over as Peter ended the call. He assumed the man was coming to take away the empty soup bowl. But he didn't touch it. Instead he peered suspiciously at Peter from close range. His nose wrinkled slightly as he sniffed, like an animal scenting a predator.

"Are you okay?" Peter asked nervously.

The man sniffed again. Then he glared at Peter, and moved away. "Should be all right now," he muttered as he went.

Before Peter could comment, Abby and Mike walked into the bar. Both were soaking wet, and a glance out of the window told Peter it was raining heavily.

"Can't do much in this," Abby said, slumping down on the seat beside Peter.

"How are you doing?" Mike asked Peter. "Faye said you had a disturbed night. Caught a chill or something."

"I'm fine," Peter assured them, and asked how the dig was going.

"Found another body," Abby said proudly. "Same sort of period, again facing away from the circle."

"And shot in the back with a silver-tipped arrow," Mike added. "Bizarre, but there you go."

"Doesn't really fit with the current thinking that some stone circles were places of healing, does it?" Abby said. "But maybe Wolfstone is the exception."

"Kill or cure," Mike joked.

"His hands were tied with a silver chain. Probably part of some ritual," Abby told Peter.

"They did find something similar at Stonehenge," Mike said. "A grave facing away from the stones."

But Peter wasn't listening. In his mind's eye he could see a man walking slowly towards the Wolfstone Circle, his hands tied with thin silver chain. He could see the cloaked and hooded archer following behind, silver-tipped arrow slotted to the bowstring. Waiting for the man to run...

"... somewhere near St Petersburg, I think," Abby was saying as Peter snapped out of his waking dream.

"What is, sorry?"

"This other circle that's not a circle."

"We were reading up on it last night," Mike said. "Bodies found there too, it seems. Anyway, the original number of stones and the shape of ellipse were virtually identical to Wolfstone. Quite a coincidence."

Peter spent the afternoon lying on his bed. He dozed

between texting friends and checking Facebook. He barely noticed the time, and it was already getting dark when there was a knock at his door. It was Carys with two mugs of tea.

"Mum says the fever should have gone by now." She sat on the upright chair while Peter perched on the edge of the bed. "There shouldn't be any lasting effects, but I just wanted to check."

"Check – how?"

She stood up and walked slowly round the room, pausing at the window. She opened the curtains slightly, just enough for Peter to see the full moon outside. She stared out into the night for a moment, then drew the curtains again.

"You seem all right. How do you feel?"

"Fine. A bit tired, but then I guess I was up half last night."

Carys tilted her head to one side, the way she did when it seemed she was thinking. "Let's get some air. Mum will need me later, but apart from Mike and Abby the bar's quiet tonight."

"Really?"

"You saw it – the full moon. No one goes out when there's a full moon."

She didn't wait for him to ask why not, but headed for the door. Maybe she thought it was obvious. Maybe it was.

"Tell me about last night," she said. "Tell me everything you remember."

They walked slowly down the lane towards the church. Peter expected her to interrupt, or tell him he was being stupid, or laugh. But she was silent until he finished. He told her about going to the manor, about the girl's room and finding Annabelle in the cage in the underground vault. He told her about the robed men who took her away, and the helicopter – the 'Old One' and the soldiers and his own escape into the woods. He told her about how he saw Wolfstone Manor and its gates as they used to be, intact and complete, about the pursuit of the young woman, the peasant taken to the circle, and the banquet...

"So," he asked when she still said nothing, "do you think I was hallucinating because of the fever?"

"You saw the manor as it was hundreds of years ago, a medieval peasant, and some bizarre banquet. Of course you were hallucinating."

They were standing in the churchyard, the tower looming over them. The gravestones were ragged dark slabs in the grey night.

"And wolves," Peter said. She was right, the whole thing was ridiculous. He must have imagined it all. Even Annabelle – he'd seen her face on the website and imagined meeting her, helping her... He forced a laugh.

"*Were*wolves, how daft is that?"

Carys's face was illuminated by a shaft of moonlight as she answered. "Oh no," she said. "The werewolves are real. It was only after you were bitten that you started hallucinating."

"Bitten?" He latched on to the word as though it was the only one he understood. "I wasn't bitten. Why do you think I was bitten?"

"You were *infected*. I saw. I was there – I found you."

"Infected? Maybe – but I wasn't *bitten*." He pushed his sleeve up, and pulled the bandage aside. In the moonlight he could see the slight swelling, like a blister with a small scab in the middle. "Does that look like a bite? I was shot."

"Shot? What do you mean shot?"

"With a gun. Shot. Bang,bang. I told you they had guns." He rolled his sleeve back down. "Some sort of dart. I pulled it out. Hang on…" He was remembering something from earlier. "Your mum said it didn't look like a bite. Does *she* know about the werewolves?"

Carys tilted her head and pursed her lips.

"Just me who doesn't then," Peter realised. His head was swimming. "But – that means… Annabelle. She was real."

"Yes."

"And they did something to her. In the circle." Suddenly

he was angry. He'd let a whole day go by. He'd promised to help her and now it was probably too late. "We have to do something."

"We don't even know where she is."

He ran back towards the churchyard gate. "Then let's find her."

"Get real," she called after him. "Annabelle could be anywhere. She could be..." She didn't finish the thought.

"I promised I'dhelp her. We can't just abandon the girl."

She caught Peter up in the lane. "It's a full moon," Carys said. "It's the worst possible night to help anyone. We don't even know where to start."

"Wolfstone Manor?"

"Possibly... All right," she conceded. "I suppose. But not tonight. In daylight."

"It wasn't a full moon last night," Peter said. "Not quite."

"So how come they were wolves, is that what you're wondering?"

"One of the things."

"Several nights either side of the full moon are what are called "cusp" nights. How many depends on the strength of the moon, the weather, the individual werewolf... But on those nights, they can *choose* whether or not they change. Though some have more control than others. Some of them..." She looked away, and didn't finish the thought.

Peter looked up at the perfect pale disc above them. "And tonight?"

"Tonight there's no choice."

They walked on in silence, until Peter got up the courage to ask, "And how do you know so much? Are you? I mean, I don't want to be rude, but are you?"

Carys stopped and stared at him, hands on her hips. "Am I what?"

"Are you a werewolf?"

She looked up at the sky. "Like I said – tonight there's no choice. The werewolves all change. Do I look like a wolf to you?" She shook her head. "No, don't answer that. Come on – there's something you have to see."

Peter could hear Abby and Mike laughing and joking in the bar as Carys led him through the door concealed beneath the stairs. He felt numb and light-headed. Like he had wandered into a dream.

Except that it wasn't a dream.

"Wait here," Carys told him. "I need to talk to Mum."

He waited while she disappeared through the door. The sound of her footsteps echoed back up. As the door closed, it cut them off. There was no sound at all from the cellar, the door was so thick and heavy.

When it opened again, a few minutes later, the sound of

raised voices was immediate and shocking. All the more so as Peter recognised the first angry voice as the usually calm and even-tempered Mrs Seymour.

"...can't see what good it will do!"

Her daughter's response was even more fiery. "He needs to know! He has to see this."

"But why?"

"Because!" Carys was shouting from just inside the door as she swung it open. "Because of what might happen. Because of what's *already* happened."

Peter wasn't sure he wanted to see whatever was in the cellar. He certainly didn't want to face Faye Seymour and it sounded like she didn't want him there either. But Carys gestured for him to follow her back down the steps.

"Come on," she urged.

Maybe facing an angry Carys was even worse. Peter followed nervously.

Mrs Seymour stood at the bottom of the stairs, arms folded and head to one side. There was no mistaking the similarity between mother and daughter, though Faye Seymour looked tired, her eyes sunken and her cheeks streaked with tears.

"I'm sorry," Peter told her. He didn't know what else to say.

She nodded. "I'm sorry too. I'd rather spare you this, but

Carys is right. It's too late now."

Mrs Seymour gestured for him to follow Carys through to the back room. The room with the chains.

The room was no longer empty. Inside, Peter could hear the sound of an animal growling, snarling, scrabbling at the stone floor.

Carys stood aside from the doorway so that Peter could see the creature chained up to the wall by the silver chains and manacles. A huge wolf, its grey-white fur matted and stained. Red eyes gleamed hungrily in the light filtering in from the main room. Massive jaws crunched together as the animal strained at its bonds. Claws raked the air as it tried desperately to reach its prey. To reach Peter.

He stepped back, throat dry and stomach dropping away with fear. Even though he knew, he breathed. "What the hell is it?"

"It's Mr Seymour," Carys said, looking back the creature. Fear, pity and anger all mixed together in her expression. "It's my grandfather."

CHAPTER 14

"The reaction's more extreme in direct moonlight," Carys told him.

"More extreme? It looks pretty extreme to me right now," Peter said.

He was sitting on the bottom step. The creature that was actually Mr Seymour growled and whimpered in the next room. Occasionally it let out a howl of rage. The heavy cellar door from the pub blocked the sound.

"I thought you should know. Since you've already seen, already experienced..." She didn't need to say what.

"Thanks."

Mrs Seymour came through from the room where the creature was chained up.

"He's calmer now. We do what we can for him," she told Peter.

"I'm sure. Has he always...?"

"My father-in-law has been like this for as long as I've known him," she said. "Though when I married Jeff, I didn't... Well, never mind. It's not hereditary, not in this form. Thank God."

"Just so long as we don't let him bite any of us,"

Carys said.

"There's no cure?" Peter asked. Immediately he felt daft. "Of course not," he answered his own question.

"The wolf's blight can counteract the effects of a bite," Mrs Seymour said, "but it has to be administered almost at once." She turned to Carys. "I can cope for now. If you two want to take a break."

Carys nodded. "I should get back to the bar. Just in case anyone comes in." She gave her mum a hug.

Abby and Mike had gone and the pub seemed deserted.

"Does everyone know about... you know?" Peter wondered.

Carys shook her head. "Not specifically. But the locals know not to go out when it's a full moon. That's just the way it is round here. Always has been."

They went into the restaurant, and sat at a table by the glass-fronted bookshelves.

"What do you know about werewolves?" Carys asked.

"Loads," Peter said. "And nothing... I mean I've seen films and stuff. So I know that if you get bitten you turn into one. Then you change into a wolf every full moon, and you can only be killed with a silver bullet. But is any of that actually true?"

"There's some truth in it. Though lots of it was made

up for the movies. Even more is rumour or gossip passed down through the centuries."

"But – I mean, werewolves – they're just a story, a myth. Well," Peter corrected himself, "they're obviously not, but even so..."

"There's a lot of legend and myth surrounding them, shrouding the truth," Carys agreed. "I already told you that most werewolves can choose whether or not they change in the days and nights close to a full moon – what we call the cusp. They only really lose control when the moon is actually full. Though Grandad's so old and weak now that he finds it hard not to change on any cusp night."

"But why do they change at all?" Peter wondered. "I mean it's not, well, *magic,* is it?"

"There are theories. Lunacy gets its name from the fact that some people who are mentally ill seem even more insane on a full moon. There are suggestions that it's maybe to do with the moon's gravity affecting the fluid content of people's brains."

"Like it affects the tides?"

"Exactly."

"But don't people know? Important people – like the government? Surely there would be scientists working on it."

Carys sighed. "It's always been ignored. People try to

forget about it or pretend it really *is* just a legend. And, to be fair, it's not like there are many werewolves about these days."

"Except here," Peter said. "Except now."

"True. But that's... unusual."

"Then there must be a reason."

Carys opened the bookcase, looking along the titles. "This place has always been associated with the wolf," she said. "Hence it's name. You know the legend of the du Bois family and the stories about the origin of the stones?"

Peter certainly did. He'd dreamed it – more than that, he'd *experienced* it.

"So people have known about werewolves for centuries," Carys said.

"Ah!" She had found the book she was looking for. She pulled over a chair to stand on and reached it down from a high shelf. The book was old, bound in leather and filmed with dust. She placed it carefully on the table and leafed through the thick, yellowing pages.

"It's a translation of a French book from the eighteenth century."

She turned the book so Peter could read it. The print was old and faded and the paper was dry and brittle.

That night, Antoine was walking in the forest close to his home as he was wont to do, and the moon was full and clear. As he walked, a wolf attacked Antoine and would have slain him but that Antoine never travelled without his sword. He smote the beast, and did sever the animal's forepaw, which was cut clean away and fell to the forest floor.

The wolf howled in pain and limped away, wounded. Antoine recovered his breath and cleaned his sword. He took the paw of the wolf and placed it in his bag to prove to others that the great beast was a danger and should be hunted.

Then Antoine went to the house of his friend Jules, who lived nearby, so he could rest and recover his strength, and tell his story.

But when he took the beast's paw from his bag to show his friend, the skin was smooth and it had become the elegant hand of a woman. There was a ring on the third finger of the hand, which bore a stone both men knew at once.

They took their swords and ascended to the bedchamber where Jules found his wife bandaging the stump of her wrist. And together Antoine and Jules did slay the beast.

"They killed her?" Peter said in surprise.

"Of course. As they saw it, she was a monster. But don't forget every werewolf story is also a tragedy. The wolf doesn't choose his nature – it's inherited, or caught from a bite. No one *wants* to be like this, and most of the time they're perfectly normal."

"I guess it's only a story," Peter said.

"Every fiction has some truth behind it," Carys said. She closed the book, climbing up on the chair again to put it back. "Ovid told a similar story," she said. "You know who Ovid was?"

"Roman poet," Peter said. "Dad bangs on about him sometimes. He was around just as BC became AD."

"There was another Roman writer called Petronius, I think," Carys said, "who told of a soldier who stripped off his armour in some sort of fit. His servant ran to a nearby farmhouse for help, and was told the dwelling had just been attacked by a wolf that was driven off and wounded."

"And that was the soldier?"

Carys nodded. "When the servant found his master again, the soldier had a sword wound in his shoulder. And don't forget that Rome was founded by twins who were brought up by a she-wolf."

"Now that *is* just a story," Peter said. "There have always been wolves in stories."

"Usually as the villains," Carys pointed out. "Think of *Red Riding Hood,* or *The Three Little Pigs*."

"Peter and the Wolf?" Peter suggested with a smile.

"Beauty and the Beast is the same sort of story too. We've always been afraid of the Big Bad Wolf."

Peter frowned. "Are you suggesting it's more than just

a fear of being attacked and killed?"

"Why just wolves? There are other animals that can kill. Wolves aren't even that dangerous to humans, not usually – remember what Janey said at the sanctuary? The fear stems from something deeper, more personal."

"The fear that we might not just die. We might actually become the thing we fear," Peter said.

"It's a thought, isn't it?"

They sat in silence for a while. Then Carys said, "I used to think they were all just stories, and that my grandad was the only one. That he was special. I guess that made things easier to cope with, seeing it like that."

"What changed your mind?" Peter asked.

"The weight of evidence. If they are all just stories, there are a hell of a lot of them. You know, werewolves were seen as such a serious problem in medieval France that they started a register. Every case had to be reported and logged, though a huge number must have gone unreported. Guess how many werewolf cases are registered in the hundred years from 1520?"

Peter had no idea. "Perhaps a couple a year, I suppose," he guessed. "And some of those would be mistakes… So maybe three hundred?"

"Not even close. Add a few noughts and you're there."

"How many?"

"Over thirty *thousand*."

Peter was surprised and shocked. "If only a fraction of those were actually true, that's still... a hell of a lot."

Carys was reaching down another book. This one was not so old. It had a plain cover, and Peter just caught the title on the spine: *The Werewolf in Fact and Fiction*.

"Here we are." Carys ran her finger down the text as she read. *"The English clergyman Montague Summers claimed the werewolf myth was reality. He described a creature possessed of all the characteristics, the foul appetites, ferocity, cunning, the brute strength, the swiftness of that animal..."*

"More medieval superstition?" Peter said, though he didn't for a moment believe that was all it was.

"Summers was writing in 1933," Carys said. "People still believed even then."

"And with good cause," Peter agreed. "But like I said – why here, why now? And what's it got to do with poor Annabelle Forrest? You know what I don't get?"

"Surprise me."

"Forrest himself is involved, right – in whatever is going on. I saw him."

"So?"

"So why's he got Dad doing a survey of the stone circle if he's conducting some sort of weird ceremony there? You'd think he'd want to keep it private. Off limits."

"But that's just it," Carys realised. "He has. Everyone knows that your dad's working up there and the locals have been asked to keep away so as not to interfere with the work."

"Of course – so Forrest knows he's safe when Dad and Abby and Mike aren't there. Maybe he arranged it so that Dad got called away when there was a full moon?"

"It's a possibility. And you asked "Why now?" Maybe that's the answer – it's only now that Forrest owns the circle. It was in the du Bois family for centuries before that."

"Why did they sell up?"

Carys didn't know. "They"ve not lived here for decades. Not since the Second World War, Grandad said. I think he knew old Lionel du Bois."

"He's older than he looks, your grandfather."

"Something to do with his condition, Mum says. But none of us really understands it."

Mention of her grandfather prompted Carys to check her mum was coping. While she was gone, Peter looked again at the book by the local historian, Arterton. There was a short section about the fabled 'lost' Rogue Stone. He showed it to Carys when she returned.

"I've seen it," he said. "It's not lost. It's in the cellar under Wolfstone Manor."

"They must have built the place round it," Carys said.

"How's your grandad?"

She made a face. Obviously he wasn't good. "I just wish..." She shook her head.

"Do you want to call it a day?" Peter offered. "If you need to—"

"No, no." She cut him off. "Mum's coping. She doesn't really want me there fussing and worrying. She gets very protective. Tell me again about the other lot."

"Sorry?"

"You said another lot turned up, in a helicopter, to this ceremony or whatever it was."

Peter repeated what he could remember. He described again the man they had called the Old One – with his limp arm and grey skin. "I just ran for it, hid in the woods. One of the wolves found me, but I fought it off."

Carys looked impressed, which was a first. "It didn't bite you?"

"No, I'm sure it didn't. It got a sharp branch through its paw." He demonstrated with his finger, poking it into his palm. "Then I got shot... Hang on!"

"What is it?"

Peter jumped to his feet. "They shot me with a dart. I pulled it out and put it in my coat pocket. I bet it's still there!"

"Careful!" Carys warned as Peter rummaged through his pockets.

They'd gone to his room, and he was emptying out his coat on the bed. There was a half-finished pack of Polo mints, scraps of paper and old receipts… And, finally, the small metal dart.

Carys picked it up carefully, holding it through a tissue. The back end of the dart was a glass vial. She held it up to the light and they could see there were several drops of clear liquid inside the small reservoir.

"Venom?" Peter wondered.

"Saliva, I'dguess."

"Like being bitten at long range." He peered closer. "What's that? Something's scratched on the glass."

"The manufacturer's logo? Might be a number. Looks like a figure of eight."

Peter carefully took the dart from Carys and looked for himself. It might have been a figure of eight, though it was angular – like two squares, one on top of the other. "I've seen this somewhere before," he remembered. "And recently." He thought hard. He could see the symbol, on a notice. Outside a building… "At the Lupine Sanctuary."

"Why would they have the same symbol?" Carys said. "Unless Janey and the others are involved somehow…"

"They do work with wolves," Peter pointed out.

Carys wasn't convinced. A few minutes with Peter's laptop proved she was right to be sceptical. The logo that looked like a squared figure of eight was actually the letters EI written over each other.

"Einzel Industries is the name of the company that sponsors the sanctuary's work," Peter said, scaning the screen. "As well as Forrest." He clicked through to a website for the corporation. "Based in Vrolask, wherever that is." There was a page of location information – the nearest airport was given as "St Petersburg (LED)".

"I recognise that too," Peter said, feeling suddenly cold. "I found an airline ticket, just the stub – the boarding pass – in Annabelle's room at the Manor. 'LED' was one of the airports. The other one was 'LHR', which is London Heathrow. That's quite a coincidence."

Carys was looking over Peter's shoulder at the screen. "More of a coincidence than you think," she said. "David Forrest had a plane ticket to St Petersburg. I saw it when I was cleaning his room the other day. That must be where he and his father have gone. And Vrolask – where this Einzel Industries company is based – is also where the other stone circle is. The one in Russia that's laid out exactly the same as Wolfstone."

CHAPTER 15

If Forrest had taken Annabelle to Russia, then there was nothing Peter could do to help her. Unless he followed them there, but that was hardly an option. He felt tired and suddenly he couldn't keep his eyes open any longer.

Carys obviously noticed. "I'll leave you to get some sleep."

"You don't seem tired." He wasn't sure if he was jealous or feeling guilty that he couldn't keep going himself.

"I knew I was in for a difficult night with Grandad, so I slept this afternoon. We've kind of got into a routine. I'll go and take over for a bit so Mum can get some rest."

Peter yawned. "I'm sorry I'm so useless."

"You're not useless." She smiled. "Not entirely. I doubt we can persuade Mum we need to go to Russia. But we should check out Wolfstone Manor again tomorrow."

The next morning was bright and sunny. Peter thought they'd get a lecture from Carys's mother about how the manor was private property and they'd be trespassing if they went up there. They didn't. Instead, she insisted on coming with them.

"I don't like what's happening here," Faye Seymour said simply. "Things aren't right. I can tell."

Peter half expected her to add that she'd cast the runes and dealt the cards and consulted the talisman of Mercury or whatever. But she did seem genuinely worried – which for someone whose father-in-law was a werewolf meant things must be pretty serious.

They walked so as not to attract any more attention than they had to. They talked about everything and nothing as they went.

Glancing back, Peter thought he saw movement in the trees that lined the footpath. But it was a good way back, and the sun was in his eyes. Probably nothing. But he couldn't shake off the uneasy feeling that they were being watched.

The feeling grew more intense as they approached the manor. In daylight, it was still forbidding, the detail lost in shadows. Peter showed them where he had prised away the board over the window, and they climbed inside.

Faye Seymour looked round in obvious distaste. "I suppose it's been empty for quite a while," she said. "But *really*..."

Carys sighed. "It's falling down, Mum. The whole place is a wreck, they're not going to be sending in the cleaners every week."

There was a tearing, creaking sound from behind

them. They all turned as the board over the window was torn away. A dark shape hauled itself up and through the window, landing heavily and crouching inside the room.

Peter felt a rush of adrenaline and fear. Carys gave a startled cry. Only Faye seemed unsurprised.

"I thought you were asleep," she accused.

Carys's grandfather straightened up. "What you doing?" he growled.

"Nothing. Just looking round," his daughter-in-law replied. "You can come with us, but don't touch anything." It was like she was speaking to a child.

"Du Bois lived here," Seymour said, looking round the dusty room. "Lionel and me go way back."

"Lionel du Bois is dead," Faye said gently. "He died a long time ago." She turned to Peter. "They were in the army together," she explained. "He gets confused about time."

Peter led the way to the tower.

"All gone now," Seymour said sadly. "Forrest doesn't live here."

"No, he doesn't," Carys agreed.

"Family seat for hundreds of years and he abandons it."

"That was the du Bois family," she pointed out. "Not Forrest. He's bought it recently. You remember – the new houses?"

"Gave me the pub he did. After..." His voice tailed off. "After..."

"What's he mean?" Peter wondered aloud.

"I don't know," Carys said.

"He's confused." Her mother shook her head sadly. "It wasn't Forrest who gave you the pub," she said to Seymour.

"Forrest, du Bois, all the same," he grumbled. "Lionel gave me the pub. To make up for what happened in the war."

"Up or down?" Peter asked when they reached the staircase.

They went up, to the room where Annabelle Forrest had been held prisoner – who knew for how long? It was exactly as Peter had left it. He showed them the notebook, and Faye picked up the shredded remains of the teddy bear. Her eyes were glistening and she clasped the toy tightly to her and looked around the room.

Carys stood in the doorway, her expression unreadable.

"You want to see?" Peter asked.

She shook her head. "This is *her* room. It just feels... It feels like we're intruding."

"We're trying to help," Peter told her.

"Even so..."

Peter showed them the plane ticket stub. "You think

Forrest has taken her to Russia now?"

"I don't know what to think," Faye said. "Oh, the poor girl." She placed the teddy on the bed next to the pillow. "How could someone..." She sighed and shook her head. "And now Mr Seymour's wandered off."

Peter couldn't remember if the man had even come upstairs with them. "He can look after himself, can't he?"

"I hope so," Mrs Seymour said.

"Can we go now?" Carys asked. She waited for Peter to follow her mother, then walked beside him back down the corridor to the stairs. "We'll find her," she said. "We'll do anything we can."

"I don't even know her," Peter replied. "But she asked me for help..."

"We don't know her either, but no one should be treated like that. Not for any reason."

"You think there was a reason?"

"There's always a reason," Faye said. "Maybe we'll find it in this cellar you described."

Remembering how the cellar vault had been lit by candles, Peter had suggested they bring torches. Sure enough, the candles were burned out now, twisted stumps of wax were all that was left of them. Illuminated only by the torch beams, the vault seemed even bigger.

The silver cage was empty, the door standing open.

Carys crouched down inside, examining the floor. Then she quickly stood up and hurried out. Peter guessed she was imagining how Annabelle must have felt.

A movement in the shadows made Peter turn quickly. Mr Seymour stood in the corner, looking back at him across the silent sleeping figures on the family tombs.

"Paintings," he said. "Portraits. Forrest."

"All the paintings have gone," Faye told him. "There used to be paintings, I remember – I came here once, with you and..."

"I saw paintings," Peter said in the ensuing silence. "Or, I thought I did. Through one of the windows. I thought I saw portraits on the staircase. Old and dark and dusty. Only, they're not there now, so I must have imagined it."

"Here," Mr Seymour said.

"No," Peter told him. "Upstairs."

The man was shaking his head. "Pictures *here*. Forrest pictures."

"Ignore him," Carys advised. "He won't be right for a few days yet. And even then..."

But Faye was shining her torch into the shadows behind where Mr Seymour was standing. There was something there, something pushed up against the wall.

"No, I think he's found something."

Carys and Peter made their way across the chamber.

"I see what you mean about the Rogue Stone," Carys said. "This must be it. This chamber is below the level of the raised terrace round the house, but I guess the stone's at ground level really."

She ran her hand over the rough surface. In the torchlight, the stone glittered like the stones in the circle.

"He was right," Faye called. "Look."

She shone her torch into the corner – it was the furthest part of the vault, and Peter had not ventured that far the last time. Two rows of pictures leaned back against the stone.

Seymour pulled a picture from near the front of one of the stacks, turning it so they could see. "Forrest!" he announced. "Du Bois."

"What's he mean?" Peter wondered.

Beside him, Carys gasped. "Don't you see it?"

Faye shone her torch at the picture. It was a portrait of a middle-aged man. He was standing in front of a bookcase. The pose was formal and obviously staged. But it was the man's face that drew Peter's attention.

In the full glare of the torchlight, despite the dust and the way the picture had darkened with age, Peter recognised the face. Or rather, he could see how similar it was to someone he knew.

"But that looks like Sebastian Forrest."

"David Forrest too," Carys agreed. "Look at the shape

of the mouth and chin."

Faye wiped away the grime from a brass plaque at the bottom of the frame. *"Edward du Bois,"* she read. *"1887."*

"Forrest," Mr Seymour said. "And du Bois."

"The same family," Peter realised. "That must be it. Don't you see? They changed their name. Sebastian Forrest didn't *buy* this house and the estate – he already owned it."

"You knew that, didn't you," Carys said to her grandfather.

He was smiling in the torchlight. "Forrest is a du Bois. Recognised him. I knew Lionel in the war. He gave me the pub."

"Is that true?" Peter wondered.

"Oh yes," Faye said. "Lionel du Bois owned the whole village. Most people are still tenants of the estate."

Mr Seymour didn't answer. He was holding the picture of Edward du Bois, angling it in the torchlight and peering at the detail. He set it down and picked up another picture – a portrait of a young woman this time. Again, he angled it to catch the light, moving it slightly back and forth.

"What are you doing?" Carys asked. "What is it?"

"The pictures never lie," he said. He picked up the portrait of Edward du Bois again. "Look."

They gathered round. Carys shone her torch full on the painted face. But Mr Seymour, resting the picture on the top of the others and holding it steady with one hand, reached out and moved the torch. He angled it so it shone across the paintwork rather than directly onto it.

Peter stared at the picture, wondering what he was supposed to be looking at. Then he saw it – the detail emerging like a lenticular image that you move slightly to make the picture change.

Here, the hand of Edward du Bois changed. The skin darkened and sprouted hair; the fingernails became claws. His face changed too – from the pale face of a man into the features of a wolf.

Carys caught her breath, almost dropping the torch.

"Are they all like that?" her mother asked in a whisper.

Mr Seymour put down the picture and picked up the portrait of the woman again. As Carys moved the torch, the woman's braided hair became matted and grey. Her youthful features twisted into the grotesque face of a wolf, its hairy jaw jutting forward in savage defiance.

"They didn't disguise what they were," Carys said.

"Perhaps they were proud of it," Peter suggested.

"Or simply accepted it." Faye gently touched her father-in-law's arm. "You knew Lionel du Bois – what do you think?"

"There's paper," the man said in reply. He put down the portrait, and moved more of the pictures to pull out a torn scrap of paper that had been caught between them. "Letter."

"Look at the letterhead," Carys said, shining her torch at it.

The letterhead was about all that was left. The paper had been torn across, but the Einzel Industries logo was intact. Below that was a reference number and a subject line:

RE: Wolfstone Meeting, 28th September

"That's next week," Peter said.

"Does it mean they're having a meeting about Wolfstone? About the Lupine Sanctuary, maybe?" Carys said.

"Or perhaps the meeting is actually here, in Wolfstone," Peter suggested.

"But who's going to be at this meeting? What's it about?" Faye asked.

"That's something you will never know," another voice announced.

The man stood at the foot of the stairs. The same man Peter had seen at the churchyard a couple of nights earlier. The ragged remains of the man's ear looked even more grotesque shadowed by the light from the torches.

The man blinked, his eyes red like the eyes of the wolves that had chased Peter through the wood.

Another memory – a wolf with one ear torn into a ragged stump…

The man's face twisted into a sneer. "By the time the wolves meet at the circle, you will all be dead." He hefted a crowbar, the dull metal gleaming. The end was curled into a sharp claw.

He moved like an animal – treading carefully, body swaying slightly as he stalked towards Peter and the others. Peter would have backed away, but there was nowhere to go. They were right in the corner of the vaulted chamber.

"We can get past him," Carys whispered. "He can't stop us all."

"If we all move together," Faye agreed. "You ready?" She glanced at Peter, then at Mr Seymour, who was watching the approaching man with calm intensity. She grabbed his hand. "Ready?" she repeated.

Mr Seymour nodded.

"Now!"

Carys was quickest, easily evading the man with the crowbar as he lunged towards her. The movement took him away from her mother and grandfather as they stumbled past.

The man's cold red eyes fixed on Peter as he raced across the vaulted chamber, torchlight dancing erratically as he ran. He could do it, he was past the man – he was safe. But with a howl of rage, the man hurled the crowbar at him.

There was a sudden sharp pain in his leg. The crowbar clanged onto the stone floor. Peter stumbled, kept going, tried to ignore the pain where the clawed metal had hit him.

The man's shoulder connected with Peter's stomach, driving him sideways. He crashed into the side of the metal cage, and found himself off balance – falling. He tried to stay on his feet, staggering backwards into the cage.

The man with the torn-off ear stood in the door of the cage, staring across at Peter. His mouth opened impossibly wide in a snarl of triumph.

Peter felt the cold, hard bars of the cage dig into his back as he tried to get as far away from the man as possible.

But there was nowhere to go. He was trapped.

CHAPTER 16

The torch beam was filled with the man's snarling face. His eyes were blood red discs. Saliva dripped from his jaws as he lunged at Peter.

The crowbar came out of the darkness, smashing down on the man's head. The effect was immediate and extreme. He slumped heavily to the floor, leaving Carys standing in the torchlight, crowbar in her hand. The clawed end was stained as red as the man's eyes.

"Don't just stand there," Carys yelled. "Come on!"

Peter slammed the door of the cage behind him. There was no way to secure it. He just hoped the man was out cold for a while. But even as he turned away, he thought he could hear him scrabbling to his feet…

The house was a blur. Light filtered in through the remains of some grimy windows and round the edges of the boards that covered others. Their torches danced along the walls and the floor as they ran.

It seemed further going out, as if the house had changed and stretched around them – keeping them tight in its dusty embrace. Finally they reached the room where they had come in. Faye Seymour clambered out of the window first, then Carys helped her grandfather out, with Faye ready to assist him on the other side.

Then they were running again, along the terrace. The paving stones were cracked and uneven, overgrown with moss and grass. Peter slipped, almost fell. He realised he was still holding his torch, though they were in bright daylight now, their shadows running alongside them across the wall of the house. He turned off the torch and jammed it into his coat pocket.

They'd almost reached the end of the house when a window exploded. The sound was incredible – splintering wood and shattering glass. Debris blasted across the narrow terrace in front of them. A huge wolf landed heavily in the midst of it, twisting towards them, fangs bared.

Peter skidded to a halt, catching hold of Carys. Faye grabbed her father-in-law. The wolf threw back its head and howled. Its jaws snapped closed again and it picked its way through the splintered wood and broken glass, muscles rippling beneath its fur. The sun was behind the creature, but even so, Peter could see that one of its ears had been torn away, leaving a scarred stump of gristle.

"How fast are they?" His voice was a dry, fearful rasp.

"Faster than us," Carys told him.

"We'll split up," Faye said. "It can't get us all."

"We're stronger together," Carys said.

Peter only just heard her beneath the sound of an angry growl that had started as a low rumble, and was building to a snarl of rage.

It wasn't coming from the wolf with the ragged remains of an ear, but from beside them. From Mr Seymour as he pushed Faye aside. His whole body seemed to swell as he padded forward, swaying from side to side like a hunting animal.

"Father – no!" Faye yelled.

Carys pulled her mother back. "It's too late. He can't stop it now. You know what he's like when he gets angry. When he's on the cusp."

Peter watched in horrified fascination as Mr Seymour approached the wolf. At first the animal seemed to welcome the challenge, tossing its head and snarling. Then it became wary. Finally, slowly, it began to back away.

But all Peter's attention was on Mr Seymour. The man's hands were spread wide, fingers stretched apart. Hair erupted from the backs of the hands. The fingers lengthened and curled. Claws sprouted from the fingertips. He rolled his jaw from side to side, as if easing it out from the rest of his face. A hairy snout split through the skin with a sound like tearing paper. Jagged teeth clenched together. Eyes reddened and receded into the fur that now covered Mr Seymour's face – covered his whole body. His jacket split suddenly down the seams. He ripped at his other clothes with sharp claws, shredding them as he fell forward onto all fours.

The two enormous wolves faced each other silently for a moment. Then the creature that had been Carys's grandfather let out an ear-splitting howl and launched itself from powerful hindlegs at the other wolf.

They met in mid-air. Claws raked down, splitting fur and flesh. Blood spattered across the paving slabs. The creatures became a single mass of matted bloody fur, teeth and claws. Rolling, clawing, tearing into each other.

Peter watched in horror, unable to do anything but shudder and hope. Carys was white-faced. Her mother's hand was clenched tight, knuckles pressed to her mouth.

It was difficult to tell which was which as they fought. One of the wolves had its jaws round the other's throat. Blood welled up, bubbling from the wound. With an almighty effort, the wounded wolf broke free and hurled itself back at its attacker. Claws bit deep into the flank of the other wolf.

The whole terrace was slick red. Both animals were tiring. One was bleeding its life out through its throat. Its howl was a gurgling cacophony of pain. The other wolf collapsed on its side – wounds gaping at the sky as light drizzle diluted the blood. There was a distant rumble of thunder.

The wolf with the bloodied throat had only one ear. Peter, Carys and Faye ran to the other animal. It turned slightly to look at them through bloodshot eyes. The pupils were like dark crescent moons. Its breathing came in irregular gasps. It reached out a paw, claws drawing back into the fur. The paw became a hand that grasped Faye's as the drizzle turned to rain.

He looked so old now, Mr Seymour. He lay in the thinning blood and the rain, staring up at her. Naked and shivering; one side of his chest torn away. Then his hand fell away from hers and slapped to the wet paving slab.

Across the terrace lay the body of another man – a man with straggly hair and a beaked nose and one ear reduced to a scarred stump. His throat was a red-raw mess, and his eyes stared sightlessly up at the gathering storm clouds.

The only sound was the pounding of the rain as it washed the blood from the terrace and the tears from Faye Seymour's eyes.

They stood for an eternity, just staring at the scene in front of them. Carys was shaking with the cold. It was only because he could feel her shoulders trembling that Peter realised he had his arm round her. Her head was pressed against his chest. He barely noticed. He'd just seen someone *die*. Two people – one of whom he knew. Not well, but the man was *dead*.

Finally, Carys's mother straightened up and wiped her eyes on the back of her hand.

"We have things to do," she said.

She had it all planned. It was only slightly complicated by the fact there were two bodies to deal with. But Faye said she'd always known that one day she would have to explain away her father-in-law's disappearance, though she'd always imagined he would kill himself while chained up in the cellar of the pub.

"We'll say his mind deteriorated to the point where he finally had to go into a home," she explained as they carried the bodies into the woods. "It's not like he's got friends who"ll want to visit. With wounds like that we can't just pretend he died in his sleep."

Carys and Faye carried Mr Seymour between them. Peter had the slight body of the man with the ragged ear over his shoulders in a fireman's lift. He tried not to think about it. Carrying a dead body. Stare straight ahead, he told himself. Try not to see the dead man's bloodied arm swinging with every step. The body became heavier as he walked. A dead weight, in every sense.

"I know a doctor, not a local, who… understands," Faye said. "He'll give us a death certificate in a few weeks."

"So we tell everyone he went into a home, and he died

there," Carys said bitterly.

"What else can we do?"

Faye already knew a good place deep in the woods. Peter offered to stay with the bodies while Carys and Faye went to get spades to dig the graves. He didn't really want to, but at least he knew it would give the other two some time alone together.

As soon as they had gone, he wondered what he'd say if anyone found him, sitting on a fallen tree next to two dead bodies. One with a gaping chest wound, the other with his throat ripped out. The rain was still falling heavily, but its effect was mitigated by the cover of the trees. At least it would have washed away the blood from the terrace by the house.

Everywhere he looked, Peter saw people watching him. Leaves that looked like a face; an arrangement of branches in the shape of a wolf; a shimmering of light through the moving trees that *had* to be an approaching police car... It took him a while to realise that he really was being watched.

She was standing behind one of the trees at the edge of the little clearing where Peter sat. Her face was so stained and muddy that it blended in with the undergrowth. Her long, fair hair was dark with the rain, hanging in matted clumps. One bare arm reached round the trunk of the tree, like she was holding on for comfort.

Peter stared in surprise, and the girl pulled back.

"It's all right, Annabelle," he called. "It's me – Peter. You remember? I tried to help you. Did you get away? Are you okay?"

He moved slowly towards her. One careful step at a time. She watched him warily, but she didn't pull away again. Her bare shoulders were dripping wet. Rain ran down her face. The grubby nails on the fingers that clutched the bark of the tree were ragged and broken.

"Peter?" Her voice was trembling as much as her body.

"You must be cold," he realised. "What happened to your clothes? Here – have my coat"

He took it off slowly, trying not to startle her. He was sure she was trembling as much with fear as with the cold and the wet. He held the coat out at arm's length to her. It was sodden, but it would help her keep warm. Once Carys was back they could take Annabelle to the pub, get her some more clothes, warm her in front of the fire...

She reached out hesitantly, her eyes never leaving Peter's.

He smiled reassuringly. "It's okay. Everything will be okay. I don't know what's happened to you, but I promised I'd help you and I will. I'll find out what's going on. All right?"

She bit her lip, and nodded quickly. She leaned forward, stretching out her hand. He thought she was going to hug him – maybe kiss him again.

He turned abruptly away at the sound of the car. He could see it approaching through the trees. The coat was snatched from his hand, and he turned back to tell Annabelle that she was safe now, that they'd look after her.

But she had gone. Peter caught a glimpse of her, struggling into his coat as she loped away into the depths of the wood.

CHAPTER 17

They didn't get back to the pub until it was almost dark. A retired couple who lived close to the church were covering the bar. They whispered sympathetically to Faye, assuring her they were coping fine.

"They often help out when it's busy," Carys told Peter. "When we came back for the car, Mum explained about Grandad being taken ill and having to go into a home."

They sat in the restaurant. The few people who were eating tonight were happy in the bar, and Carys muttered that the chef was taking it easy.

Faye Seymour sat with them, holding tight to a glass of brandy and sipping it only occasionally. Peter and Carys had coffee. They were all soaked through from the rain. Peter was shivering with both the cold and the shock.

"I'm sorry," Peter said at last, when the silence became unbearable. It seemed an embarrassingly weak and pathetic thing to say, but he meant it.

"Don't be." Mrs Seymour drained her brandy in a gulp. "Really, he'd had a long life. Maybe too long. It might have been better if he'd died years ago."

"You can't mean that."

Carys put her hand over Peter's, warning him not to pursue it.

"Was he very old?" Peter asked instead.

"He worked with Lionel du Bois in the war. That was when..." Faye stood up. "I need another drink."

It wasn't really a question, but Carys shook her head, and Peter also declined. The hot mug of coffee was slowly thawing him out from the inside.

He waited until her mother had gone, then said to Carys, "We need to go to Russia. More than ever, we need to know what Einzel Industries is up to."

He tried to sound determined and sure of himself. But having seen Annabelle in the woods he wasn't at all sure what to do. He was desperate to help her. But how?

The answers must lie in Vrolask, with Einzel Industries. Everything pointed there – the logo etched onto the dart, the air tickets at the manor, the Einzel Industries headed paper that mentioned the Wolfstone meeting. The fact that there was another elliptical set of stones at Vrolask, identical to the Wolfstone Circle...

He tried to explain what he was thinking. But he still didn't mention seeing Annabelle. Somehow, he felt he ought to keep that just between the two of them. He'd felt a bond, if only for a moment. He wasn't sure Carys would appreciate that, or understand how desperately he wanted to keep his promise to help the girl.

"We can't just drop everything and go to Russia," Carys told him.

"We have to do something."

"Why?"

He almost laughed at that. But at the same time she had a point. "Well, because..." he blustered. "Because your grandfather is *dead*, for one thing."

"So is the man who killed him."

"But he wasn't the only one involved in... in whatever's going on. It isn't over. They'll come back. They have some meeting set up for next week – that man said so. Don't you want to know what they're planning, who they are even? Forrest is involved, but apart from that we don't know anything."

He paused, but Carys said nothing. "Okay, maybe I'm overreacting," he went on. "But I've been shot at with werewolf venom, I've been attacked by wolfmen, seen people die..." He shrugged, running out of steam and emotion. "I promised to help Annabelle, and then I couldn't – I let her down. I just want to do the right thing, you know? To find out what's going on. I think it's something bad – *really* bad. And if it is..."

"Then we should stop it?"

"Well, yes."

Carys nodded. "I agree."

"What with?"

"All of it. Except for the going to Russia bit. I just don't see how it will help, okay?"

"Okay," he agreed reluctantly.

"So," she said, "convince me."

"We need to know more about this place, Vrolask. About the stone circle there, and Einzel Industries."

"Right, but first we need to change out of these wet clothes before we catch our deaths," Carys said. "Then meet me back here with your laptop, okay?"

Carys seemed to take an age. While he was waiting for her, Peter found a website for Einzel Industries, but it didn't tell him much. It was in Russian. He eventually came across an English language version, but that seemed only to be a short summary.

"You all right?" Peter asked when she did eventually appear.

Carys looked shaken and worried. Then again, Peter thought, he probably did as well. And with less of a reason.

"Sorry," she told him. "Mum had some stuff she wanted me to look at. So what have you found?"

"Einzel Industries is a large pharmaceutical company created out of a state-owned set of laboratories in the early

1990s," Peter summarised.

"With subsidiaries dealing in engineering, electronics, medical equipment..." Carys read off the website Peter was showing her. "Based in Vrolask, which we knew, and run by some guy called Einzel, which isn't really surprising." She motioned for Peter to scroll down.

At the bottom of the page were options to return to the original home page, and several links to other sites. Most of them were Russian government sites, or regulatory bodies. But one link said: "Vrolask Palace – Official Site".

"That's their address," Peter said. "Vrolask Palace. I thought they were just being posy, but maybe it's a real palace." He clicked on the link.

"Wow," Carys said. "Looks pretty real to me."

It was certainly impressive from the photograph.

Unlike Einzel Industries, this site seemed keen to cater for international interest. It had been translated into several different languages – including English, French and German. Peter clicked through to the main English page.

Now the headquarters and main laboratory of Einzel Industries, the Imperial Palace at Vrolask is steeped in history and tradition. It was leased to Einzel Industries in 1999, and the company has restored and preserved

much of the original architecture, while modernising selected areas. The stables and various outbuildings have also been redeveloped as laboratories and clean rooms, thus leaving the historic palace itself virtually untouched.

Originally built as a winter retreat for Peter the Great, the Imperial Palace at Vrolask was extensively renovated by Tsar Nicholas I. Unlike so many of the imperial palaces it survived the 1917 revolution almost intact.

The reason why the palace was not damaged, or even looted, may lie in the legends that surround it. Being so close to a circle of standing stones – unusual in Europe, though common enough in Britain – the palace has a mystical heritage. The locals fear the building and estates as much as they seem to shun the Vrolask Circle.

'Circle' is actually a misnomer, as the complete arrangement of stones must have been an ellipse – a shape unique to these standing stones, save for one other obscure example in the English Cotswolds. The ellipse is, however, incomplete, as many of the stones have long since disappeared. Indeed, those closest to the palace are absent even from the third century engraving that now hangs in the Irminski Gallery.

The renovated palace itself is a fine example of the

excesses of nineteenth-century Russian imperial style and extravagance. It is ironic, therefore, that the most extravagant of these excesses was actually an original feature dating back to at least the seventeenth century: The Crystal Room.

"Crystal Room?" Carys said out loud as she read to the end.

"Whatever that is," Peter said. But there was something in the way she had said it that made him look up. "Is it important?"

She frowned. "I don't know. But just now, with Mum..." She shook her head. "No, probably nothing," she decided.

"Well, the palace looks impressive enough," Peter admitted. *"Further Information,"* he read, looking down the links at the side of the page. "Let's see if that's more helpful."

For more detailed historical information about the Vrolask Palace, contact the Russian Heritage Agency. Or why not include Vrolask on your Eastern European tour? As part of their leasing agreement with the Russian State, Einzel Industries opens the palace to the public on a limited number of days every month. Tours are available in various languages. You are advised to book your tour through an authorised agent, as transport to and from Vrolask is limited.

There were links to several travel companies. There was also a map.

"It really is in the middle of nowhere," Carys said.

Peter zoomed in on the map. "You can just see the circle, look. And there's a railway line. It heads to St Petersburg one way, and towards Poland the other."

"You planning a holiday?" Faye asked.

Peter had not heard her coming up behind them.

"Er, maybe," he hazarded.

She peered over his shoulder. "Vrolask. You still think there's something to be learned there?"

"I do, actually. I don't know what, but it must be important." He went back over the arguments he'd used with Carys, who nodded and occasionally backed him up.

"And the stone circle there is supposed to be exactly the same as the Wolfstone Circle," he finally finished.

"Maybe," Faye conceded. "But even if it is, that doesn't necessarily mean anything."

"What about the poison dart?" Carys said. "The headed paper that letter about the meeting was on? The plane tickets?"

Her mother pressed her hands down on the air,

quietening them. "Okay, okay. There may be some connection. But we don't know what. It could just be to do with them sponsoring the Lupine Sanctuary. Maybe they have a meeting coming up about that. Forrest would be invited along. And he'd probably visit them at their posh palace to discuss it all."

"But why is a pharmaceutical company paying to reintroduce wolves to Britain?" Peter argued.

"Lots of companies sponsor all sorts of things that are nothing to do with their main business."

"But isn't it at least worth finding out?" Carys said.

"I want to know what's going on," Faye countered. "Of course I do. But I've already lost..." She sighed. "I'm not letting either of you get into danger."

"I think we're already in danger," Peter said. "Anyway, we're old enough to decide for ourselves."

"You are not!" Carys's mother snapped. "While you're under my roof, you're in my care. And without your father's permission there is no way I'm letting you go on some jaunt half-way across Europe – any more than I'm letting Carys go."

"She's right," Carys said, with a sigh of resignation. "Let's face it, the whole thing's a crazy idea."

Peter didn't know what to say. He kind of agreed with her. But all the same, it felt like the last hope of discovering the truth had been ripped away from him. He was annoyed and disappointed. Annoyed that he was so helpless and that the only plan he could come up with was, as Carys said, crazy. Disappointed that she didn't at least put up a token argument on his behalf.

He felt abandoned and alone. He closed his laptop.

"You're right," he said. "Crazy."

* * *

Rough shaking and an urgent voice in his ear woke Peter. He felt like he'd only just fallen asleep – it couldn't be morning already. Someone turned the light on.

"What time is it?" he asked blearily.

"Nearly one," Carys hissed. "We need to get going. Hurry up and get dressed. I won't look."

"Going? Where?"

"I brought a small rucksack. Just pack the essentials. We only want to take carry-on. Have you got your passport with you?"

He sat up in bed, convinced he must still be dreaming. But Carys looked solid enough. She was wearing jeans and a heavy coat, as if she was on her way out.

"My passport? It's at home. You don't need a passport for the Cotswolds!"

"Don't worry, we'll pick it up on the way. I need to phone the number through. There's a place I found that can get us a visa in twenty-four hours, though it costs a bit."

She pulled the covers back from the bed impatiently, gesturing for Peter to get up.

"Come on, we haven't got all night. I told Mum I'd need a lie-in after everything that happened yesterday, but even so she'll miss us by lunchtime. And she'll miss the car before that."

Carys turned away as Peter struggled into his clothes. "I don't have a clue what you're talking about. Where are we going?"

She turned back, caught him pulling up his trousers, and looked away again quickly.

"Are you always this slow? We're going to Russia, of course. To Vrolask."

CHAPTER 18

Carys let Peter sleep in the car, but his head was spinning as he tried to work out what was going on. Eventually he decided it was easier to pretend he was still in bed, dreaming, and he drifted off into a light sleep.

There was no sign of Dad at home. No sign he'd even been there, except that the post had been picked up and put on the kitchen table, unopened. Dawn was breaking as Peter climbed back into the car and flourished his passport at Carys. She took it from him, opening it with one hand as she dialled a number into her mobile with the other.

"Who's this?" she asked when she got to his photo.

"Good question," Peter said. He wanted to tell her that it was an old photo. And taken on a bad day. Which was why he looked like a startled adolescent rabbit. But her call connected and she waved him to silence.

"I've booked a flight to Berlin where we can pick up the visas," Carys explained, once they were on the move again. "From there we go direct to St Petersburg. After that it's a bit more tricky."

"Right. Tricky." It sounded tricky already to Peter.

"But I checked the days the Vrolask Palace is open to the public and the next one is the day after tomorrow, so there's a special train. If we make the connections we should catch it. I got us seats through the travel company the website linked to. So we're booked on the tour."

"Great. What tour?"

"Of the Vrolask Palace. Remember the website sent you off to a travel company to book a tour? So I booked a tour."

"Simples," Peter said in a mock Russian accent.

"Expensive," she countered. "You owe me. Or rather, you owe Mum. When she gets her credit card bill, she'll do her nut."

"She'll do her nut before that," Peter murmured.

Carys glanced across at him. "I'll call her from the airport when we've checked in. She'll get over it. Probably."

"You reckon?"

Carys shook her head. "No. She'll be livid. But what can she do?"

She *was* livid. Peter could hear Faye Seymour's voice through Carys's mobile. Guiltily, he moved away and rang his dad. He was glad to get voicemail, and left a brief message saying he had gone away on a short trip with Carys and that her mother had the details. He texted Abby and Mike with a similar vague message. Then he texted

Mum, just to say hello.

They changed planes in Berlin, where Carys picked up their visa documents.

"We're down as students, and I said we're researching Russian art and architecture, and only just discovered about the tour of the palace. It seemed too good to miss."

As soon as they were in the air, Carys produced a book from her rucksack.

"What's that?" he asked.

"You're a student now. It's homework. This is the real reason we're going. At least – it's the real reason *I'm* going. I'm still not sure exactly why *you're* here."

"For Annabelle," he said simply. He felt a lump in his throat as he said it. A flash of images – the deserted bedroom, the ripped teddy bear… Annabelle at the window of the tower like Rapunzel calling for help… Then Annabelle trapped in the cage – the smell of roses and her lips pressed against his face… And finally, the girl in the wood – bedraggled, afraid, alone.

"Annabelle," Carys said.

"I promised to help her."

"By going to Russia?"

"By going to Vrolask. Everything we find out seems to lead back there. Maybe I'm clutching at straws, but I don't know what else to do. What else *can* I do? I thought you wanted to help me."

"I hoped *you* wanted to help *me*," she said sharply.

"What do you mean? What have I done now?"

She handed him the notebook. It was well-thumbed, with a cardboard cover. The yellowing pages were breaking from the spine. The handwriting was faded, but clear and neat.

"Mum showed me this yesterday. She'd read it before, of course. But I'dnever seen it. It's Grandad's journal. Or one volume of it anyway. I read the others too, but this one's the important one. It tells you what happened to him, why he was like he was... *That's* why I'm going to Russia."

"How do you mean? What's it say?"

"Read it, and you'll see. As soon as I saw that mention of the Crystal Room at Vrolask... Just read it. I want to understand what happened to Grandad."

Peter didn't know what to say to that. So he just took the book.

It's what you don't know that kills you.

But I do know this: the next 24 hours could change the course of the war.

Am I exaggerating? I certainly feel like I have the whole future of the world in my hands. Not just me of course - Acer is in charge. And Boffin's the man who first discovered the terrible secrets of Castle Wolfenburg.

I keep this journal to take my mind off little things like that.

Boffin has briefed us on the background – the why. He told us about the Nazi experiments – as much as he knows, as much as his colleagues in the Special Operations Executive have managed to discover. It sounds incredible – incredible but grotesque. Inhuman. Devilish.

WOLFENBURG – 1943

The room was made of glass.

The walls, ceiling, even the floor was polished glass or crystal. It had a strange milky quality, like quartz. The light of the candles positioned in glass-shelved alcoves was magnified and echoed all round the room, and the whole place seemed to shimmer. Only one of the many alcoves didn't contain a candle. Instead, a sword handle projected from the glowing wall, the blade visible as a shadow thrusting deep into the crystal.

In the centre of the room stood the SS officer – the only dark shadow in a world of shining crystal. The light threw his gaunt features into stark relief. His jutting chin, thin nose, the arrogant set of his jaw. His eyes were dark, set deep within hollow sockets. His hair was cut short and swept sideways.

The man's voice was a deep rasp – full of hate and anger. It was a voice used to giving orders.

"Welcome to my lair."

It took Copper a moment to realise he had said it in English.

The man's next utterance wasn't in any language. He threw his head back and roared – a tremendous, guttural burst of sound. Saliva dripped from his mouth. His whole face seemed to shimmer and crawl in the glowing light. Like something was trapped under his skin, and trying to rip its way out. The man's eyes had taken on a red tinge. The gun clattered to the floor and the man spread his arms, his hands clenched like claws. His teeth glinting and yellow. The death's-head emblem on his lapel glowing angrily.

Claws.

Teeth.

Death.

Another roar. The creature in the SS uniform hurled itself at Copper, snarling with rage and anticipation. Claws raked down towards him. Elongated jaws snapped hungrily at his throat. The pervasive glow of the crystal was blotted out by darkness – by black uniform, dark fur and death.

Just as the claws were about to shred Copper's face, the creature fell backwards. Acer's arms were locked round its chest, heaving it away. The creature fell, pinning Acer beneath it. For a moment, it seemed to Copper that Acer was also changing – becoming a creature like the SS colonel.

"Find a weapon," Acer gasped. "Anything silver."

"Silver?" Copper struggled to his feet.

"There must be something."

With a roar, the creature broke free of Acer's grip and hurled itself again at Copper. He dived to one side, felt the claws catch in his uniform, tearing at his sleeve. His eyes had adjusted now. He could clearly see the long table in the centre of the room, the chairs alongside it – all made from the same glowing crystal. Like amber, lit from within.

The walls shimmered so that they seemed insubstantial, like they were actually made of light. Only the hilt of the sword was stable and steady.

The sword.

The creature seemed to realise what Copper was thinking. It bounded across the room towards the silver handle projecting from the wall. But Copper was closer. He raced for the alcove, grabbed the handle and pulled.

For a moment, the sword remained stuck, like the legendary sword in the stone, but then with a creaking protest, it moved. The creature was almost on him. Copper wrenched the sword from its crystal sheath. He swung it in the same movement – a great arcing blow. The crystal blade glittered and shone.

The animal's claws skittered on the smooth floor as it tried to avoid the blow. It almost succeeded. Almost…

The sword struck it in the shoulder, biting deep. Copper felt the blade connect with bone and judder to a halt. The creature fell, tearing the sword from Copper's grip. The enormous wolf fell on its injured shoulder. Copper heard the shattering sound as the sword blade fractured. The scream of animal pain.

Acer was there already, grabbing at the hilt of the sword and pulling it from the creature's shoulder. He paused, sword raised, the crystalline tip of its blade broken off in a ragged line. Inside the crystal ran a thinner, finer blade of silver. The whole length of the blade was slick with the creature's blood.

"Finish it off!" Copper yelled, running to help.

The creature groaned in pain.

Acer stabbed down. But the creature rolled aside at the last moment. Sparks erupted from the floor where the silver core of the blade struck. Shards of crystal flew like broken glass. The creature cried out again. But the sound of its pain was blotted out by Copper's own cry as a sliver of the sharp crystal tore into his leg. It burned like ice, and his leg gave way beneath him.

Acer raised the sword again, turning to pursue the creature.

"Kill it!" Copper yelled. "Kill the thing. It's an

abomination."

But his last word was lost in the roar of the explosions. The whole room shook around them. A crystal chandelier crashed down onto the translucent table.

Acer grabbed Copper, hauling him to his feet. "This place is finished. Let's get out of here."

But the doors were jammed shut, refusing to move.

"There's no other way out. This is our tomb." Copper cried.

Acer was looking round. "The wolf – where did it go?"

"Wolf?" It seemed an inadequate description. "I don't know."

The floor trembled under their feet as more charges went off in the castle above. Acer dragged Copper with him, supporting him, as he followed a trail of red to the side of the room. It disappeared into the wall.

"Another door?" Acer wondered. He handed Copper the broken sword. "Hang on to this. If we meet the wolf again, we'll need it."

Copper took the sword. He leaned heavily against the smooth wall, gasping for breath as Acer searched for a way to open the door. Finally he found an indented groove that served as a handle and swung open a section of the wall. Grinning, he turned back to Copper.

"Looks like we have a way out after all. Bring the sword.

If we don't need it, you can give it to Boffin. A souvenir – he'll be fascinated." The grin became a frown. "Are you all right?"

"I got hit by some of that crystal," Copper said. "But there's something else you should know. That creature – before you dragged it away and I got the sword…"

"Yes?"

Copper swallowed, his mouth suddenly dry. "When it came at me the first time," he confessed, wiping blood from his throat. "It bit me."

Peter finished reading 'Copper's' account. He closed the book and leaned back in his seat. The sketched pictures were almost as unsettling as the text – an upright wolf in German SS trooper's uniform, the stark forbidding castle with the craggy mountains behind it, a rough plan of the maze of underground tunnels through which Copper and Acer had escaped to return to the beach rendezvous and then the submarine that returned them to Britain...

He was aware of Carys watching him.

"So it happened in a room made of glass?" he asked.

She nodded. "That's when he was infected. Grandad was 'Copper' of course. And Acer was actually Lionel du Bois. Or so Mum says. She says that when they got back, du Bois changed his name to Forrest."

"Why?" Peter wondered.

"A patriotic gesture. Before the war, du Bois spent a lot of time in Germany. He was said to be a friend of Himmler, but maybe that was all bluff. And we now know that du Bois was the best person to lead the raid. He had unique knowledge of what they were supposed to be searching for."

"The Nazi experiments, whatever they were."

"Right," Carys agreed. "So they destroyed the place, and when they got back, du Bois set Grandad up at the Red Fleece. I guess he blamed himself for what happened to Grandad."

"He sounds like a hero," Peter said. "But that doesn't seem to fit with the current Mr Forrest." He handed the notebook back to Carys. "And this room they found. Made of glass... When we read up on the Vrolask Palace it mentioned a Crystal Room."

"It could just be a coincidence. But I doubt it. That's why, as soon as I found out about it, I booked the visas and tickets. Do you..." She looked away. "Do you really think Annabelle Forrest is in Vrolask?"

"No. I did. But now I'm sure she's still in Wolfstone." He ought to tell her he had seen Annabelle. But it was awkward – why hadn't he mentioned that earlier?

Carys interrupted his thoughts before he could decide

what to say. "So, like me, you're just along to find out what you can? You don't have some grand plan?"

"Discover what Einzel Industries is up to, how it ties in with Wolfstone and everything that's going on there. Once I know that, then I can start thinking about a plan. If it's involved at all." Now he was actually on a plane flying to Russia, Peter was wondering what he was really doing. A good idea in the middle of the night or the heat of the moment didn't always translate into something sensible in the cold light of day.

"Oh it's involved all right," Carys said. "Here's a company that's making vials of wolf venom, sponsoring a wolf sanctuary, setting up some mysterious meeting at Wolfstone, linked to Forrest and his family, and headquartered in a palace that has a Crystal Room just like the Nazi scientists had under the castle where they did their werewolf experiments. Whatever they're up to, it isn't good. Whatever they're up to, I'm going to stop them." She wiped her hand across her eyes. "No one should go through what Grandad did. No one should suffer like Mum had to." She turned to look out of the plane window. "One way or another, it stops."

The train from St Petersburg to Vrolask was pulled by an old steam engine.

"Diesel probably freezes in the winter here," Carys said.

They met the rest of their tour group at St Petersburg station, Carys checked the print-out of her emailed instructions. There were about a dozen of them in all, mostly Americans on a set tour. Peter and Carys were the youngest by a long way. A tour rep with a fixed smile ushered them onto the train, which had separate compartments with a corridor running alongside. Carys and Peter found a compartment to themselves.

The phone signal came and went, so Carys called home from the train when she got a chance. From the side of the conversation he could hear, Peter could tell that Faye had calmed down. She seemed more worried about how much the long-term parking at Heathrow would cost than whether Carys and Peter were safe.

They settled in for a long journey, heading west towards Poland. The landscape soon became bleak and grey, and the windows steamed up from the cold outside.

"What were the Nazis doing?" Peter asked after they'd sat in silence and stared at the misted windows for what seemed like for ever.

"There are some hints in a couple of the other journals." Carys ran her finger down the window, drawing a rough outline of a castle like the sketch in the notebook. "Nothing specific that I saw, though."

"Experiments, obviously," Peter said. "But were they

experimenting on, well – on werewolves? Or just trying to create them?"

"They took people from the local village. Not volunteers. Just young local people. About our age." She drew jagged mountain peaks behind the castle. They looked like sharp teeth. After a moment, she wiped her hand across the glass obliterating the picture. "It was horrific."

"The journal mentioned kids going missing in the night. Genetic experiments," Peter said. "Those poor people. But then there's that SS colonel who bit your grandad. Maybe he was a volunteer, or maybe he was ordered to take part. I wonder what happened to him."

"Probably crawled off to die in one of the tunnels somewhere." The window was already misting up again. "I hope it took a long time."

Vrolask was a small industrial town with no hint of a phone signal. Before Einzel Industries arrived, it had settled into dilapidated obscurity.

"We shall shortly be arriving at the Vrolask Palace," the guide announced from the front of the minibus. Her name was Ludmilla and she was a severe-looking, middle-aged woman.

The minibus turned through huge ornate gates. The driveway curved gracefully round a vast lake, and ahead of them was the Vrolask Palace.

Peter had seen the picture on the website, but that did nothing to convey the scale of the place. It was an enormous ornate stone structure with more windows than Peter could easily count. The Vrolask Palace certainly dwarfed Wolfstone Manor.

Stone steps led up from the terrace, where the minibus parked, and into the wide hallway. Inside was even more impressive. The whole group looked around wide-eyed. The floors and walls were lined with polished marble. The ceiling was painted to look like the sky. Giant crystal chandeliers were almost lost in the enormous space.

A security guard checked their names off on a list and examined passports. Ludmilla explained that they had to submit details of everyone on the tour in advance. Peter and Carys were obviously lucky to have made it.

Ludmilla led them down the hallway, her heels echoing on the marble floor. Finally they all trooped into an enormous ballroom. At the far end was a raised platform. Standing there, staring down at the tourists, one black-gloved hand gripping the top of the stone balustrade was a man.

Peter went cold. His legs were suddenly weak and he felt light-headed. He grabbed Carys's arm for support.

"What is it?" Carys whispered.

Peter hardly trusted himself to answer.

"We are most fortunate and honoured today," Ludmilla was saying, "that Herr Einzel himself, the chairman and chief executive of Einzel Industries, is here and has graciously agreed to greet his guests."

There was a smattering of applause. The man on the dais acknowledged it by raising his arm. His good arm. Because his other arm hung uselessly by his side. Under the harsh light of the chandeliers, Herr Einzel's skin was even more grey, his features even more sunken and emaciated than when Peter had last seen him. He wore a light-grey suit rather than the long, dark leather trench coat but there was no doubt at all that it was the same man.

"That's *him,*" Peter whispered, his mouth dry with fear. "That's the Old One."

CHAPTER 19

Herr Einzel's eyes were as grey as his skin. They lingered on Peter for a moment, but then moved on. He welcomed his 'guests' to the Vrolask Palace and promised them a unique experience. He spoke briefly about the work his company did in pharmaceutical research. The introduction was confident and brief.

The guided tour of the palace took in the more impressive state rooms. Some areas were off-limits, as they were used as offices or laboratories by Einzel Industries. But Peter paid little attention. He was desperate to talk to Carys, but that would have to wait until the tour was over and they were alone again. The ornate splendour of palace rooms seemed to merge until he could not remember one from another.

Then they came to the Crystal Room.

"The Crystal Room dates back to a time when the villagers believed that the palace and its occupants were cursed," Ludmilla explained as she led them along yet another wide corridor. Windows on either side gave views of the formal gardens outside. The sun was an orange disc hovering above the horizon.

"In the nineteenth century, the villagers even tried to burn down the palace. They marched on it with burning torches."

"Flaming peasants," Carys whispered, making Peter smile.

"Described as the Eighth Wonder of the World, there was nothing quite like the Crystal Room anywhere else in all the Russias... In all the world," Ludmilla announced proudly. She had stopped outside a set of large double doors that were braced with silver. "And here it is."

So saying, she threw open the doors and stepped aside to allow the tourists in.

The room was an empty shell. The walls were bare stone, scored and scratched with the marks of the tools the Nazis had used to prise away the crystal. Like claw marks down the walls.

The other tourists murmured with disappointment as Ludmilla explained how the retreating Nazis had taken the crystal. "But close your eyes and imagine how it was," she went on. "Imagine this whole room lined with crystal – even the floor and the ceiling. And it didn't stop there. The large central table and the chairs, even the chandeliers, the fittings were all fashioned from crystal."

Now the tourists were more interested, walking slowly around the room, trying to get an idea of what it might have been like.

"And not just any crystal," Ludmilla told them. "It was a milky, quartz-like crystal that glittered as if backed or suffused with silver. With the hundred flickering candles that lit the room, the effect must have been quite startlingly beautiful."

Carys nudged Peter, looking pointedly across the huge room.

"I've seen it," he assured her.

Set into one wall, built into the structure itself, was a standing stone. The surface glittered in the harsh electric light that had long-since replaced the candles and chandeliers.

"Just like in the cellar room at Wolfstone Manor," Carys said.

Ludmilla joined them. "Beautiful, is it not?" she said. "It is called the Lonely Stone. Perhaps it was always here, or it is possible that the stone was brought from the Vrolask Circle to be a focal point. Most of the stones, sadly, have been removed over time."

"Was it covered by the crystal walls?" Carys asked.

Ludmilla shrugged. "Exactly how the room looked, we shall never know." She turned to include the other tourists in her explanation. "Vrolask was in the direct path of the German advance in Operation Barbarossa when Hitler sent his troops on their misguided and ill-fated invasion of Russia."

The few Germans exchanged glances at this, but they made no comment. They probably agreed with the sentiment, Peter thought.

"Again – remarkably – this palace was left virtually intact," Ludmilla said. "But when the German army retreated, they did take one trophy with them. This Crystal Room – in its entirety. The liberating Russian soldiers found just this chamber of stone, stripped of the famous crystal. As you see it now."

"So, what happened to it, miss?" an American lady asked.

"Perhaps the crystal was broken up. It must have been very fragile. Certainly, no part of the room has ever been seen since the Germans retreated. All we have left to help us imagine its strange beauty and power are a few eyewitness descriptions, the myths of the Sword of Destiny, and one poor-quality black and white photograph that hardly does the legend justice..." She shook her head sadly. "After so many years, it is inconceivable that any trace of the magnificent Crystal Room will ever be found..."

Ludmilla moved them quickly on. It was getting late, and she insisted they would want to see the grounds before the light faded.

Peter knew exactly where the Crystal Room had ended up – it was described in Carys's grandfather's journal. But there was one question he was keen to ask. In the event, Carys beat him to it.

"What's this 'Sword of Destiny' you mentioned?" she asked.

They were making their way back through the palace towards the main entrance. Ludmilla explained as they walked.

"The Sword of Destiny is a legend, a myth, a story. It was said to be made from the same crystal as the rest of the room."

"But you said the crystal was fragile," Peter reminded her. "Could you actually make a sword out of it?"

"Some accounts suggest the crystal encased a silver blade."

Peter looked at Carys, and saw she was staring back at him. She gave the faintest nod. The sword described in the journal. The sword Acer had used against the wolf.

"It was this sword that Count Alexander Grishko apparently used to dispatch his dinner guests," Ludmilla told them. There was a murmuring of interest from the group, and she paused in the entrance hall to finish the story.

"Legend tells how the count would invite villagers

he suspected might be witches or demons, warlocks or devils, to dine with him in the Crystal Room. If they refused, they were burned by Alexander's soldiers. If they accepted, Alexander watched them carefully, for any hint of demonic behaviour."

One of the American men laughed. "No demon would be stupid enough to give himself away."

"It is just a story. But it is said that the room had the power to reveal a monster, to draw out its true form. And at the first sign of change, their host – the count – would strike the villager's head from their shoulders with a single mighty blow."

"Well," the American said, "I guess that as trial by ordeal goes, it's probably as scientific as the ducking stool."

"A silver and crystal sword designed to kill demons and monsters," Carys said to Peter. "Interesting, don't you think?" She leaned closer. "There's something else you need to know. Something Mum told me. She said I could show you the journal because…" She broke off.

"Because – because what?"

But Carys was staring past Peter. "What's going on there?"

The tour group backed away as two uniformed security guards escorted a woman to the door. The guards were practically dragging her along as she shouted back over her shoulder.

The woman pulled an arm free from one of the guards as she passed close to Peter and Carys. She was middle-aged, her face lined with worry and hardship. Her greying hair spilled out from underneath a cotton headscarf, and her clothes were faded and patched. She clutched at Carys, speaking quickly and urgently, her eyes wide and her cheeks streaked with tears.

Carys looked at Peter, shocked and anxious. Then she shook her head. "I'm sorry," she told the woman. "I don't understand."

"What's going on?" the American man who'd joked about ducking stools demanded.

"Local woman," Ludmilla said. She spoke quickly in Russian to the guards who were propelling the woman towards the door. She reached back at Carys, but was pulled quickly away.

"She is upset," Ludmilla said as the woman disappeared through the main door. "She worked here, but has lost her job. She is angry. She worked in the kitchens, but was found stealing food. There really is no need for that; Einzel Industries feeds all its employees very well."

"And their families?" Carys asked.

Ludmilla ignored the question. "Now, please, you must see the palace grounds. They are quite spectacular." Flustered, she ushered them outside.

An elderly American woman caught Carys's arm as she and Peter followed the others. "You were right to ask about the families," she said quietly.

"What do you mean?"

"I speak a bit of Russian. That woman wasn't complaining about losing her job."

"What then?" Peter asked.

"She was asking about her son. "I know you took him," that's what she said. "I know what you will do to him, to my only son. I just want him back." She wasn't angry, she was desperate. And she was scared."

The tour of the grounds was by minibus. Ludmilla pointed out the stable block, the lake, and various outbuildings and interesting features of the grounds. A steam train stood in a railway siding, thick smoke billowing from its funnel.

"Einzel Industries has its own branch line," Ludmilla explained. "No passenger service, I'm afraid, or you could have come right into the grounds. It is for shipping out products and bringing in supplies."

Peter and Carys sat at the back of the minibus together. They were more interested in what they'd seen already – Einzel, the empty Crystal Room, the woman who wanted her son back – than what they were seeing now.

"Missing children," Peter whispered. "Like your

grandfather said in his journal. All that stuff about how it must feel if your child disappears."

"You think Einzel is doing similar experiments?" Carys asked.

Peter didn't know what to think. But just the suggestion made him feel sick.

Ludmilla was telling them all that there would be a small buffet supper back at the palace before everyone went their separate ways. Some were staying at a local hotel before continuing their tours. Others were on the night train back to St Petersburg. Sadly, they would not have time to stop and examine what remained of the famous Vrolask Circle.

Peter wiped at the window to try to get a better view. He could make out just a few stones. One lay on its side. There were gaps where others had been removed…

"It looks like a broken-up version of Wolfstone," Carys said, peering over his shoulder.

"Did someone mention wolves?" Ludmilla said.

Peter and Carys exchanged glances. But before they could answer, Ludmilla went on.

"You may have heard about the pioneering work Einzel Industries is sponsoring to reintroduce wolves to Great Britain." She smiled indulgently at Peter and Carys. "I am afraid that the Lupine Sanctuary is not open to the public, but we have over a hundred of the animals here being prepared for their journey first to Poland to acclimate them."

"Acclimatise," Carys muttered. "The word is acclimatise."

But Peter knew the disgust he could hear in her voice had nothing to do with Ludmilla's vocabulary; she shared his revulsion at the thought of what might really be going on at Einzel Industries.

Peter and Carys were last off the minibus. A small group of people had stayed on-board and were now heading back to their hotel for dinner, rather than stay for the buffet. Ahead of them, Ludmilla shepherded the other tourists into the palace.

"I wish we'd had a better look at the stones," Carys said.

"Let's go now, then."

"You're kidding, right?"

Peter shook his head. "No one will notice. They'll just think we're ducking out of the meal, like those guys." He gestured to the minibus pulling away behind them. "And if we're caught, so what? We're on a tour. The circle's part of the tour, it's open to the public. We're just getting a closer look."

The light was fading fast by the time they reached the circle. Just like the Wolfstone Circle, had once been a flattened ellipse, open on the side facing the Vrolask Palace. But there were only half a dozen stones left – irregularly spaced, leaning at drunken angles. One of them had fallen over completely. Lights still burned in the palace and in the office and laboratory buildings. The sun was low on the horizon, the crystal in the stones making them glitter just like their twins back in England.

"It's amazing," Carys said. "Like some giant just picked bits of the circle up from Wolfstone and dropped it down here."

"Be good when it's finished, then." In his mind's eye Peter could imagine the completed circle here in Russia. And he could see himself inside the circle as the robed figures dragged their victim towards him…

"Hang on, I want to try something."

"Looking for the Leprechaun's crock of gold?"

Peter crouched down beside one of the remaining stones. He was sure this was where he had seen the robed figure bending down in the Wolfstone Circle.

"When they'd brought Annabelle to the circle, one of them did something under this stone. Or the equivalent stone. I saw him." He didn't mention he'd seen the same thing in his dream.

"Probably tying his shoelace."

Peter fumbled round at the base of the stone, but he

couldn't feel anything.

Unless…

His fingers found a hole in the stone, just below the level of the grass. The ground was cold, and he wasn't sure whether he'd really found something or just lost all sensation in his fingertips. But he pressed and pushed.

"Sorry," he said at last, straightening up. "I thought there was something. It felt like a lever. But there's nothing."

Carys didn't answer. She had her back turned to him, staring into the middle of the circle.

"What is it?"

She still didn't answer. A gaping hole had opened in the middle of the circle. A deep, dark circular pit.

"Did I do that?"

"It just opened up. The ground dropped away. There must be some sort of cantilever mechanism to swing it aside, under the grass. I think…" She swallowed. "I think there's something in there."

The light was fading fast, and the pit was shrouded in shadow, but Peter could make out a darker shape lying at the bottom of the pit. The sides were shored up with wooden struts. The floor was flagged with cracked and pitted stone slabs – a disc of rock, like his dad had said the survey found at Wolfstone.

Lying in the centre of the pit was the body of a woman. Blood was pooling round her body, and her greying hair spilled out of a sodden headscarf. She was dead.

CHAPTER 20

"Let's get away from here," Carys said. Staring at the body in the pit – she'd seen the same woman alive and frightened just a short while ago. She felt as scared as she ever had. "Close it up and let's get out."

They closed the pit and hurried back to the main entrance, hoping they hadn't been missed.

"Let's just get on the minibus," Peter said. "Get back to the station. Then we can decide what to do. Who to tell. D'you know enough now about what happened to your grandad?"

"As much as I want to." She was wishing they'd never come. But it was too late now. Could they simply go home and forget any of this happened?

In any case, the minibus was still gone.

"What do we do now? Wait here until it comes back?" Carys said.

"Better to join the others. We don't want to attract attention."

"We could talk to that American woman. Tell her what's happened."

"And get her killed too?"

"I'm just thinking out loud, okay?" Carys snapped. Immediately she regretted it. "Sorry. But as soon as it's back, we get that minibus to the station and get on the first train to St Petersburg."

"Deal," Peter agreed. "But we said we'd put a stop to this – to whatever's happening."

"And how do we do that? Try to burn the place down like the peasants did?"

Peter looked for a moment like he was considering it. "We should tell the police or whoever," he said at last. "Let them sort it out. There's a body – they'd have to do something. As soon as we're well clear of this place we'll make sure something's done. But for now, let's behave like nothing's happened, right?"

Carys nodded. She forced a smile. Everything was certainly not all right, but Peter had a point – they needed to carry on as if it was.

Their plan survived only until they were in the large hallway. Two security guards emerged from the shadows and walked towards them. There was no mistaking the menace in the way they moved.

"I don't like this," Carys murmured. "They're the two who took that woman away."

The guards continued to advance. The chandeliers threw multiple shadows across the floor – distorted patterns in the vague shapes of the figures.

The figures had jutting jaws, and hunched shoulders.

They were the shadows of advancing wolves.

Carys turned, but another guard stood in the doorway behind them, cutting off their retreat. The man's eyes burned red. He opened his mouth to reveal sharp, yellowing teeth. Then, with a snarl of anticipation, he leaped towards them.

The guard morphed in mid-air. Claws erupted from his outstretched hands. His face was the image of a wolf.

Carys stood frozen to the spot. Then Peter's rucksack slammed into the guard, knocking him sideways.

"Don't just stand there!" he yelled.

The guard was already getting back to his feet. The two guards from inside the palace were running now. Peter grabbed Carys's hand and pulled her through a doorway off the hall. He slammed the door shut behind them. Something heavy crashed into the other side.

There was a large conference table surrounded by upright chairs, and beyond that was another door. Together they charged across the room. Carys heard the door behind her open. She didn't look back.

Out into another, smaller room, then through and back into the corridor from the hallway. Carys wondered if Peter had any idea where they were going. Or he was just running, like she was. She couldn't hear the guards following, but they didn't slow down.

Finally, they reached a set of doors that Carys recognised. "In here!"

"You sure?" Peter rasped, out of breath.

"You want a debate?" she demanded.

Peter didn't answer. He followed her into the empty stone-lined chamber – the Crystal Room.

"It's just that there's no other way out of here," he muttered.

He was right. If the guards found them, they'd be trapped. "We wait till they"ve gone, then head back to the main entrance, okay?"

"If you say so." Peter smiled thinly. "I don't have a better idea."

They listened, but couldn't hear any sound from outside. Best to give it a few minutes, they decided.

"So how did this Crystal Room make them change into their true form?" Peter wondered.

"I guess the crystal somehow captures and retains the moonlight. Forces the human to change into a wolf."

"Ludmilla said the room made monsters show their true form, or something," Peter agreed. "Maybe that's how the stones in the circle were used."

"Moonlight on the wolf," Carys said. "So a werewolf

brought into this chamber in human form would be forced to change, to reveal it's true nature. Unless it was powerful enough to resist somehow."

"Then the count killed them with his crystal sword."

"The silver is the key," Carys said.

"You mean like silver bullets?"

"Silver is a magical defence," Carys told him. She was glad to be on a subject she knew at least something about. "It has healing properties too, you know."

"Yeah, I read about that somewhere. Do you think it's safe to head back and see if the minibus is there yet?" Peter wondered. "We should be okay, if it's just those guards looking for us. You think they know we found the body?"

"I don't see how they could." But another thought had occurred to her – one she didn't like. "We were on the list of visitors. What if Einzel or someone recognised our names? I mean – you recognised him, after all."

"It would explain why Einzel bothered to talk to a bunch of tourists. He was checking us out. But in that case, we can't risk rejoining the tour. Everyone will be hunting for us."

"They'll be expecting us to head back to the main entrance," Carys pointed out. "Maybe we can find another way out, and get back to the station."

"This place is huge, we'll be lost in no time," Peter said.

"Let's just keep going in a straight line until we get to an outside wall, then find a door." She hoped she sounded more confident than she felt, but she couldn't see another option. "How hard can it be?"

It was late and the building was almost deserted. There was no sign of the security guards. With luck they were hunting elsewhere. The whole place was quiet, but that just made them even more cautious, creeping along deserted corridors, holding their breath. All the time expecting a wolf to snarl out of the next doorway, or drop from the ceiling above them...

Soon they found themselves in the newer part at the back of the palace that had been updated by Einzel Industries. The whole interior style changed. They moved from panelled walls and marble floors to functional paintwork and industrial carpet. There was a clinical feel and smell to the place.

Carys wondered who had ever thought it would be cost-effective to adapt the old palace to become hi-tech laboratories and sterile facilities. But there was something else here that Einzel wanted – the circle and the Crystal Room – what little was left of them.

"We must be close to the back of the palace by now," Peter said quietly.

Carys hoped he was right. Her nerves were stretched so tight she felt she might snap at any moment and scream the place down.

There was a noise from nearby – someone coughed. Carys looked back, but the corridor behind them was empty.

Now there were voices, someone laughing. It came from ahead of them.

"Quick – in here!" Peter hissed, heading for the nearest door.

He pulled it open, and they darted inside.

The voices were still audible, though muffled. Whoever it was had stopped outside the door.

"They might come in here," Carys whispered. "We need to move."

They were in a reception area, with a raised desk beside another door. Through the next door was a much larger room. It looked like a hospital ward. Carys just stared.

"Oh my God," Peter breathed.

There were half a dozen metal-framed beds. Bags of dark fluid fed down plastic tubes to the wrists of the patients – if they were patients. Electronic heart monitors traced peaked lines across screens. More screens noted temperatures and other data.

"Is this… blood?" Carys wondered, nervously touching one of the plastic tubes. She felt sick, wanted to get away as fast as she could.

"We should keep moving," Peter said.

The next room was almost identical. "How many of them are there?" Carys wondered. All the "patients" seemed young – no older than she was. Male and female.

"I don't think Einzel is just experimenting on wolves," Peter said.

Carys couldn't help but remember reading the description in the journal of the experiments at Schloss Wolfenburg. Her grandfather had taken several pages after describing their escape on the submarine to explain what the Nazis were doing. Men into werewolves.... Genetic experiments of a horrific nature – all those years ago... She looked down at the young man lying in the nearest bed. He looked so peaceful.

"That woman..." she said slowly.

"Said they'd taken her son." Peter finished the thought for her. "We can't know if he's in here, though."

"We don't know anything for certain," Carys had to agree. "Maybe this is just some clinical trial. For a new drug or whatever." She didn't believe it for a moment, but was it possible?

"Yeah, right." Peter gently lifted the unconscious boy's hand, angling it so Carys could see his forearm. So she could see the perfect square grafted onto the skin. A grey-brown patch of fur, like a wolf's.

A door banged shut in the distance.

"Come on," Carys urged. "We don't want to get caught. And certainly not here!"

Peter hesitated, still holding the sleeping boy's hand. Maybe he was thinking about Annabelle Forrest. Again. What was it about the girl that had got to him so badly? Carys gently lifted the boy's hand from Peter's grasp and let it flop back onto the bed.

"We can't help him now. We have to get away if we're to put a stop to this."

If they had any lingering doubt that what they had seen was to do with the experiments, what they found in the next room dispelled it.

The figures in the beds were humanoid wolves.

Carys stared in horror at the nearest. Its hirsute face was incongruous against the starched white pillow. Saliva dribbled from the jutting snout. As she watched, the creature's eyes snapped open, and it stared up at her. She jumped back. The wolf tried to sit up, snarling angrily. But it was strapped down with thick plastic bands across its arms and legs and chest. It strained desperately against them.

"Let's get out of here."

But they only got as far as the last bed.

The figure that lay there was not a wolf hybrid. It was

human – a boy of about their age. Tubes connected to the back of one hand, feeding into a system of valves and more tubes that ran to the beds where the wolves were strapped down. The other hand was wrapped in a blood-stained bandage.

"Oh my God," Carys breathed.

The boy on the bed was David Forrest.

"What's *he* doing here?" Peter said, aghast.

"Never mind that – we have to help him!" She didn't know what she was doing, but she pulled out all the tubes she could see.

David's eyes snapped open and he stared up at them in disbelief. "What the hell?" He sounded weak and confused.

"It's all right. We'll get you out of here. But we have to hurry, there are guards looking for us."

Carys was more careful with the tube into the back of David's hand. He winced as she pulled it out.

"What's going on?" he demanded.

"You tell us!" Peter said.

But before David could say anything, the figure on the next bed let out a howl. It was a mournful sound. More a cry of pain and distress than of anger, Carys thought.

The wolf was struggling to sit up. It stared at Carys, its eyes boring into hers. She stared back, transfixed, surprised at how human it seemed. Was there something still there, some vestige of the person the creature had once been? It tilted its head, and a tear spilled from one of the eyes and caught in the fur of its cheek. Then it slumped back on the bed.

"You help David," Carys said to Peter.

"What are you doing? Are you mad?"

Maybe she was. But she couldn't just let these creatures lie here, strapped down while Einzel's scientists did God knows what to them.

"Leave them," David said weakly. "They're just animals."

She rounded on him, surprised by her own anger. "They're not animals. They're just like *you* would have been. You want to get away from here? Fine – so do they."

"They'll kill you!"

She hesitated, looking again into the creature's eyes. They were wide with fear, but also just the faintest trace of something else. Hope.

"No," she said. "But they might kill whoever did this."

She fumbled with the straps, feeling under the edge of the bed for a buckle, found it, and snapped it open. The single buckle released all the straps, and the creature threw them off, rising up with a roar.

It stood facing Carys – much taller than she was. It could

kill her with a single blow. But instead, it gave a grunt and a nod, and lumbered away to the next bed. It didn't bother looking for the buckle, but ripped at the straps with its claws, shredding them.

David sat on the edge of his bed, watching – pale and weak.

"Please, just leave them," he said. "Let's get out of here."

Peter hurried to help Carys as she moved to another bed.

"You're right," he said. "And maybe we're in time. Maybe they can change back. We might be giving them a chance."

Carys wiped her eyes. "That's more than Grandad ever had."

Some of the creatures were so weak they couldn't move even with the straps undone. Others roared and howled, pacing the room. Carys could feel their pent-up anger and fear. She was not surprised when the first of the creatures – the one she had freed – smashed its huge hairy fist into the monitoring equipment beside its bed. The screen exploded in a shower of sparks.

In moments, the others were smashing everything in sight.

"Can you manage?" Carys asked, hurrying back to David.

She helped him up from the bed, and David swayed

unsteadily on his feet. He was shaking with emotion – fear and anger. "We have to stop them!"

"You kidding?" Peter said. "Even if we could, why should we? They'll trash the place. Put an end to all this."

He was having to shout to be heard. Carys flinched as an explosion behind them sent more equipment flying. Liquid from drips and broken bottles pooled on the floor.

"We have to leave," she shouted.

There were sudden cries from the next room – a rattle of gunfire, then a scream. Glass smashing, and then the flickering light of flames cast shadows of the creatures across the walls.

They ran, Peter and Carys supporting David as best they could. Whether by luck or good judgement, they managed to find a way through the maze of rooms back to the main corridor. Peter led them on in the direction they'd been going before. David shook off their help and ran with them. His face was slick with sweat, but he seemed to be recovering.

A group of armed guards ran towards them. Carys braced herself, ready to fight for her life.

But the guards ran right past – heading for the sounds of destruction coming from behind them.

More guards raced towards them.

Peter called out, "He's hurt – they got him! What's the

quickest way out?"

If they didn't speak English, they understood what he was asking. One of the guards paused long enough to point down a side corridor.

Here, they soon found a fire exit. Without pausing, Carys crashed through the exit door and out into the cool of the night. A klaxon sounded behind them – an alarm triggered by opening the door. But it was swallowed up by the mayhem inside. An explosion, then more gunfire. Flames licked out of a window further along the building…

"Keep running," Peter shouted.

"Where to?" Carys demanded. "They won't let us get away now. They'll be watching the station!"

"Just keep running."

"He's right," David said. "Maybe we should give ourselves up. Do a deal with Einzel."

"Is that what you did?" Carys said. Was that why he was here? "If so, look how it turned out."

"We'd end up in that laboratory," Peter agreed. "If they ever manage to put it back together again."

"They won't," Carys said. The place was trashed – it had to be. And the fire was taking hold. Soon Einzel would be looking for a new headquarters. "But if they catch us, they'll kill us." She was surprised how casually she said it. She was elated now, not frightened. If just one of the creatures they had freed got away from here and returned to human form when the effects of the experiments wore off, then it was worth the journey.

"So what are we going to do?" David said.

"Find another way out of here," Carys told him.

"Like what?"

"Like I don't know."

"There is one way we could get away without being found," Peter said. "Just so long as we're not too late."

She was too breathless to ask what he meant. They stumbled onwards, away from the burning palace. An inhuman roar split the air, and Carys looked back over her shoulder.

She saw a huge, misshapen form struggling out from one of the palace windows. Wreathed in smoke, backlit by flames, it stumbled forward, head back, roaring at the sky. At first, the figure seemed to be a huge, upright wolf, but then he assumed the shape and size of a teenage boy. For a moment, perhaps, he was human.

Then smoke drifted across, blotting out Carys's view.

CHAPTER 21

"You have to be joking," Carys said. "We don't even know exactly where it's heading."

"Poland," David told them. "They ship consignments to Einzel's subsidiaries there... But Carys is right – this is crazy."

"You got a better suggestion?" Peter asked. "*Any* suggestion at all?"

They lay on the cold, hard ground watching as the last crates were loaded onto the train. The engine was wreathed in steam. Men were running along the length of the train. One of them checked a clipboard at each wagon while others climbed inside. There was an urgency to it all – prompted, Peter guessed, by events at the palace. The fire cast a red glow over the landscape, and the air tasted of smoke. Sirens wailed in the distance, but getting closer. A helicopter almost deafened them as it flew low overhead.

"Searching for us, do you think?" Carys asked.

"Getting the hell out," Peter said. "I think that's Einzel's helicopter."

As soon as the men were out of sight, Peter, Carys and David ran for the nearest wagon.

The door slid open easily, and they hauled themselves inside. Peter heaved the door closed behind them, praying no one had heard. Moonlight filtered in-between the wooden boards that made the sides and roof. A door at each end gave access to the adjacent wagons. The air was heavy with a rank, feral smell that cloyed at the back of the throat. It was so intense that Peter almost opened the door again.

"We'll get used to it," Carys said. "I hope. Once we're moving we can open the door and let the smell out."

"They probably transport cattle or something in here," David said.

"Not cattle at the moment," Carys said.

The cargo was packed in wooden crates. They were stacked several deep, but there was still plenty of room to move around. It was too dark to make out details of the crates or read what was printed on the sides.

"Pharmaceuticals, probably," David said.

Moments later, there was a clanking jolt and the train began to move.

"We were just in time," Carys said. "Too late to change our minds now."

Peter hauled open the door again, grateful for the cold breeze on his face. He gulped it in, then slumped down on the hard wooden floor beside the others, exhausted.

"What the hell are you two doing here?" David Forrest

asked. "I mean – I'm grateful, obviously."

"Never mind that, how did *you* get here?" Carys asked.

"I came to see Einzel. God I was stupid. I had no idea how much danger I was in."

"So why would you think he could help you?" Peter asked. "He's the Old One, isn't he?"

David looked up sharply. "You know about the Old One?"

"I was at the Wolfstone Circle when he arrived in that helicopter. When they... well, when they did whatever they did to your sister."

"That's why I came," David said grimly. "I thought maybe Einzel could help me – could help Annabelle. Instead..."

Carys was looking intently at David, her eyes narrowed. "We know your father is a du Bois," she said. "And we know what that means. So tell us about the wolves."

David gave an exhausted sigh that could have been from frustration or relief. "When I was five years old, my father killed the thing he loved most in the world. That was when I first found out about the wolves.

"The full moon had passed, but we were still on the cusp. He thought he could control it, just like his father had. Just as, until that night, he *had* controlled it. I don't know what happened, what went wrong. Maybe he lost concentration for a moment. But he changed – right in front of me and Annabelle, he *changed*.

"Mother knew about the wolf in him. She must have known the risk. But by then she felt she was safe, and that we were safe too.

"She was wrong. So when I was five years old, I watched my father change into a wolf. I watched him tear my mother to pieces as she stood between us and him. And Annabelle and I watched him change back, and see what he had done.

"From that moment, I think, he decided that controlling the wolf was not enough. He had to destroy it. He could have killed himself, and maybe he tried. But that wouldn't save Annabelle and me. That was what he really craved – a cure that he could pass on to his children, just like he passed on the curse that afflicts us.

"Oh it doesn't afflict me yet. Maybe it never will. I don't know. It comes later in life, after adulthood has taken hold. For girls it's sooner – which is why the quest for a cure was so urgent. Girls mature faster. Father had to find a cure before Annabelle reached adulthood.

"She knew what was happening, but she couldn't control it. That takes years of practice. At the first sign that her time was approaching, Father kept her confined at the manor, though I didn't know anything about that. Not until Peter told me what was happening up at the circle. But it was all too late by then anyway. Dad had spent the family fortune on research. He was desperate for more money – he was so close, he said. The housing development should have provided the funds he needed. But the market collapsed, and with it, our hope.

"Until he met Einzel. The Old One. It's said that he's lived longer than any of us, and the Forrests – the du Bois family – are very long-lived. It's a side-effect that's a blessing and a yet very much part of the curse. Who wouldn't want a long life? But at such a cost...

"Einzel was also searching for a cure. He and father pooled their resources. The ancient knowledge and traditions of the du Bois family, and the cutting-edge technology and expertise of Einzel Industries. They used the wolves, taking blood samples, comparing their DNA with father's and others afflicted with the curse. That's why father sponsored the Lupine Sanctuary. That's why Einzel has wolves here, and plans to ship them to Britain...

"But it was all too slow. All too late for Annabelle.

"Father got desperate. He went back to the old ways, and used the Wolfstone Circle. The legends and myths are disjointed and incomplete, but he knew the circle was an ancient place of healing. Being on du Bois land, so close to Wolfstone Manor, it had to offer a solution.

"Einzel was horrified. He thought the circle would just

make things worse. Any ceremony was likely to scare Annabelle rather than cure her. And once scared, she would change. Too much emotion, and she might change permanently. It can happen.

"But father was determined, and he was so *sure*. The silver in the stones, the way they are positioned, the pit beneath, the legends... To him they all seemed to say that the circle offered a cure.

"He didn't know how much time he had, but he was determined to use the circle. He hired your father, Peter, to find out as much about the circle and its history as he could. The more he knew, the better he'd be able to deploy whatever healing powers the circle offered. The greater the hope that Annabelle might – just might – be spared the curse.

"But the change came too fast. It can be a sudden process. Annabelle didn't have time. Your dad's research had barely started. And so father was forced to act before he really understood what he was doing. Einzel came to stop him, to warn him that what he was attempting would just make things worse. But he was too late. Annabelle is gone. It's too late for her now.

"And I'll be next. Who knows how much time I have left?"

"But that wasn't a cure, it wasn't *treatment*," Peter said. "It was like a blood transfusion or something. Einzel wasn't helping – he was turning you into one of his creatures."

"Dad and Einzel fell out the other night. After what happened at the circle with Annabelle. Father's become obsessed, and I don't think Einzel trusts him any more. I thought I could persuade Einzel to carry on helping, maybe do some research on the Vrolask Circle. Since he set up Einzel Industries here, he must think it's important."

"And instead he wired you up to the wolves," Carys said. "Nice guy."

"It was worth a try. Anything is worth a try. You've seen what will happen to me if..." He broke off, breathing heavily. Finally he said, "You still haven't told me what you guys are doing here." He paused to take a deep breath, then added, "Not that I'm complaining." He managed a smile.

Between them, Peter and Carys gave David a quick summary of what they'd discovered. Carys made no mention of her grandfather's journal, but they described finding Annabelle's room and the crypt at Wolfstone Manor. Then they told him how Carys's grandfather had died.

"Stapleton," David said. "Dad left him to keep an eye on the manor – and Annabelle, I suppose. Nasty piece of work."

"Not any more," Peter said. He shuddered at the memory.

David flopped back against a crate. "God I'm exhausted.

Sorry – I think they took blood or something. I'm totally whacked."

He wasn't the only one. Now that they were safe – or as safe as they could be, Peter could hardly keep his eyes open. Carys looked wiped out. She saw him starring at her and smiled back.

"We should get some sleep too," he said.

"Tell me about it."

The floor was hard and uncomfortable, but Carys didn't seem to mind, and was asleep in moments. She lay close to Peter, and he could hear her breathing as it settled into a rhythm. Peter watched her. She looked so calm and carefree. He wondered what she was dreaming about – did she dream about him? Yeah, like that would ever happen.

He drifted off into a dreamless sleep of his own almost without noticing. He dozed and woke and dozed again. By the time Peter woke properly, pale, warm sunlight was streaming through the doorway. There was still a musty, damp, feral smell, but the cool breeze through the open door had dispelled the worst of it.

Carys was already awake, standing at the open door and staring out. She turned as Peter stood up, her finger to her lips. She pointed to where David lay asleep. He was curled up like a dog in its basket. His bandaged hand was close to his face, as if he was about to lick his wounds.

They were passing through fields of parched grass. In the distance, smog shrouded concrete buildings. A factory, perhaps, or a small town. Peter glanced at his watch and saw they'd been travelling for eight hours – how could he have slept for *eight hours*? He must have been exhausted.

"Maybe we should wake him?"

She shook her head. "There's something I need to tell you. I don't want David to hear."

That sounded ominous. "Oh? Why not?"

"I'm not sure."

"You don't trust him?" Peter wasn't sure he trusted David either. He didn't know why. But there was something niggling at the back of his mind.

"I just wonder why everyone else was strapped down in that place," Carys said.

"And David wasn't. But he was out cold."

"He woke up quickly enough. Why didn't he just walk away?"

They both looked over at where he was sleeping.

"It's probably nothing," Carys said. "Maybe I'm just being paranoid."

"That goes for both of us. After what we've been through, maybe we *should* be paranoid."

She forced a smile. "I guess it isn't every day you trash a Russian palace."

"I guess not. So – what did you want to tell me?"

"It's about the crystal sword."

"The one in the journal."

She nodded. "Grandad mentioned it again in a later volume, according to Mum."

"So?" He couldn't imagine where this was going. "What happened to it?"

They sat side by side, their backs against one of the large crates, looking out across the passing fields.

"They took the sword with them, Acer and Copper," she said. "Mum said there's a note in the next volume, where he talks about Lionel du Bois giving him the Red Fleece. He says what they did with the sword."

"It was broken. You'd think they'd just chuck it away, or give it to a museum or something."

"Pretty close, actually. You remember the expert, the historian on the submarine?"

Peter did, though he couldn't recall the man's codename. "Was it 'Brains' or something like that?"

Carys smiled. "It was Boffin."

"They gave him the sword?" It made sense. "Then unless we can find out who Boffin was, we're not going to get our hands on it."

"I think David's father knows who Boffin was."

"Could be," Peter agreed. "Lionel du Bois probably

knew. You think David knows too, is that it?" He glanced back at the sleeping figure further down the wagon.

"So you don't?"

"Of course I don't. How would I know?"

Carys seemed to consider her answer carefully. When she did reply, it was with a question of her own. "What's your dad an expert in?"

"He's a historian, you know that. He's published books on ancient Egypt and medieval superstition. He lectures on everything from the Bronze Age to the Elizabethan theatre."

"But he's not the greatest expert on stone circles?"

"Well, no," Peter admitted. "He's the head of department, but I guess it's not really an area he specialises in. Abby's pretty clued up on Avebury and Stonehenge and all that."

"I started trying to tell you before..." Carys began, hesitantly. "Mum thinks there's another reason why Forrest approached your dad. I mean, specifically your dad."

"Because of the journal? Something to do with the crystal sword?"

"That's right. Because Boffin's real name was Doctor Henry Crichton. That mean anything to you?"

Peter stared at her. It couldn't be true, could it? But suddenly a lot of things made a lot more sense. "Henry

Crichton was Dad's father," he said. "He was my grandad."

How much did Dad know, if anything? Instinctively, Peter checked his phone, but there was still no signal.

"So you must know where the Sword of Destiny is."

They both turned sharply. There was an edge to the voice that Peter had not heard before. David was sitting up, watching them intently. He got to his feet and padded towards them.

"You were listening," Carys said.

"All the time."

The crate behind Peter's back shifted slightly. Like something inside it had moved. He pushed himself away from it and stood up. "Well, for your information, I don't know where the sword is," he said. "I've no idea what happened to it."

"But your father knows."

"Possibly. Does it matter?"

"Does it *matter*?" David clutched at the air in front of Peter, the stained bandage wrapped round the palm of his hand.

"Okay, sorry if it's important to you," Peter said. "You think Einzel can use the crystal to find a cure, or something? To stop you ever becoming a wolf?" Unless… A cold chill was spreading down Peter's back. "What happened to your hand?"

"Nothing."

"It's obviously not nothing," Carys told him.

"Something Einzel's people did, then. I don't know."

"Show us," Peter said. But he wasn't sure he wanted to see, to admit it – even to himself. He knew what was under the bandage.

David met his gaze. He raised his hand and slowly teased off the bandage with his other hand. A chunky gold ring on his free hand caught the light as he moved.

"Looks painful," Carys said, though her voice was devoid of sympathy.

"It's fine," David said. "It's healing."

The bandage dropped away to reveal a ragged crust of blood in the middle of his palm.

"Just an accident," he explained. "I..."

But Peter interrupted him. "You impaled it on a branch," he said. His mouth was dry, he was suddenly cold at the realisation... the memory: The wolf leaping at him. The broken branch in his hands. The wolf trying to avoid it. The paw slamming into the sharp wood. Blood showering from the wound.

"You've already turned," Peter said. "It's too late to cure you."

"You know nothing," David said. "Of course I can be cured, but you're as bad as my father. You really think Einzel's trying to find a way to stop us turning into wolves?"

"So what *is* he doing?" Carys demanded.

In answer, David reached out and grabbed the side of one of the crates. With a sudden snarl of exertion, he ripped the wood open – to reveal the animal lying asleep inside.

To reveal the wolf.

"They're sedated. But they'll wake soon. This is what Einzel is working on. And I'm helping him. Father wouldn't help me – he made that very clear at the circle the other night, before Einzel arrived. He'd arrange a whole ceremony in the hope of curing my sister. But for me – nothing. For me it was too late, he said. So I went to Einzel and offered him my help."

"Your help?" Peter echoed. "How can you help Einzel?"

"The curse is hereditary. But for Einzel's wolves, the infection dies with them."

Peter glanced at Carys. She gave him the merest hint of a nod – that was why she had not inherited the werewolf curse from her grandfather. The difference between the naturally occurring werewolves and those that had been *manufactured*.

David seemed not to notice. "When you found me," he went on, "I wasn't getting infected blood from those creatures. They were getting *my* blood. So you see, I didn't need to be strapped down. *That's* what I signed up for. That's what I want. I want to be cured of being *human*."

The crate behind Peter and Carys shifted as something

moved inside. The musty animal smell was getting stronger again. A muffled snarling, scraping, scratching came from inside.

"And you think the crystal sword will somehow help?" Carys asked. She took hold of Peter's hand, pulling him gently with her as she backed away from David.

"The tiniest fragment is all you need," David said. He held up his good hand. The gold ring glinted as it caught the light. With his other hand, he carefully turned what Peter had thought was a coin set into the ring. The gold disc opened, tiny slivers of the metal folding back on themselves like the iris of a camera lens. Inside nestled a shard of broken crystal.

"My new toy. Just enough," David said softly, "to store the light of the full moon until you need it. Just enough, but not too much, mind. We mustn't overdo things."

The crystal was glowing gently. The light from it played over David's features as he brought his hand close to his face.

David's voice was a dry, guttural rasp. "They might be sedated, but it's wearing off now. They come when they are called. And they will wake at the cry of their master." His words became an unearthly howl of triumph.

As his mouth stretched open, the skin was ripped apart, another face tearing through: the snarling, savage face of a wolf.

CHAPTER 22

Carys pulled Peter back as claws raked through the air inches away from him.

David tilted his head back and let out an almighty roar. The fur round his neck shivered. His shirt split open and he shrugged off his coat. From all around, other voices answered – howls and barks from within the crates as the wolves inside were awakened by the call.

The crate behind Peter exploded. Splinters whipped past his face as the wolf inside tore its way through the thin wooden panels. Carys screamed. Peter realised he was yelling too. But their voices were lost in the noise of the shattering crates.

Carys heaved open the door at the back of the wagon. Peter followed her and dragged it closed behind them. There was a bolt at the top, and he shot it home. The door shuddered as something slammed into it on the other side.

They were outside the train, on a narrow platform at the back of the wagon. Peter could see the coupling to the wagon in front in the gap between this platform and the next. Below that, the ground rushed past in a blur.

Carys leaped easily across to the next wagon, landing

lightly on its platform.

"Come on!" she shouted, her words whipped away by the noise of the engine, the howl of the wind and the muffled cries of the wolves.

The gap was only about a metre, but Peter couldn't bring himself to jump. What if he missed? What if he fell? The ground sped past below him… He pressed back against the door they had just come through. It shook again. The wood began to splinter.

He took a deep breath, and jumped. But too far – colliding with the door to the next wagon and staggering back. One foot dropped into space and he felt himself falling.

Carys grabbed Peter's arm and wrenched him back. He gasped his thanks, but she was already pulling open the door and dragging him through.

The next wagon was identical to the one they had left – including the wooden crates. They were stacked along both sides, leaving a narrow corridor that led to the door at the other end.

"They're in every wagon!"

"Let's hope not," Carys told him. "Come on!"

Several crates were shaking, breaking apart. Claws sliced through the wood as Peter and Carys ran between them. Wolves struggled to free themselves, paws scrabbling. Peter felt warm, damp fur touch his neck. Claws scraped at his face.

The door behind them burst open just as they reached the next one. Peter turned – and saw an enormous wolf bounding down the corridor of shattered wood. Several more wolves poured into the wagon behind and leaped from the broken crates.

He dived through the door and slammed it shut. Turned, leaped for the next wagon and landed easily beside Carys. "We can't do this for ever."

"I know. We'll run out of train. We must be nearly at the engine."

There were not so many crates in this wagon. Just half a dozen. But already wolves were breaking out of two of them.

Carys grabbed splinters of wood and used a larger piece of broken plank to hammer them round the edge of the door, wedging it shut.

"We have to make a stand somewhere," she shouted above the howling of wolves and splintering of wood.

"Why here?"

"What if the next door's bolted?"

She turned to face the wagon. The first wolf was still shaking its way out of a crate. Carys raised the broken plank like a club.

"We can't fight them off," Peter pointed out.

"Then what? You got a better idea?"

"Yes," Peter told her. "Help me with this."

Together they heaved open one of the loading doors at the side of the wagon. Together they dragged the nearest crate to the doorway. Peter and Carys heaved the crate through the door and watched it tumble away down the sloping embankment. The wood split apart to reveal nothing more than a mass of boxes and cartons.

But there was no mistaking the wolf in the next crate; it was almost out and they kicked the crate across the floor. Peter braced himself against another, almost intact crate, and pushed with both feet. The crate shot through the door. But the wolf was already leaping free. Its paws scrabbled on the floor just inside the doorway as it tried to drag itself back in.

Carys and Peter heaved another crate through the door. The crate collided with the wolf as it tried to climb back in. Crate and wolf disappeared in a melee of fur and wood.

Peter turned back just as a wolf leaped at Carys. There were three crates left. Two were intact. But one was a shattered mess. The wolf had broken free and launched itself through the air with a howl of rage.

Carys stood frozen with fear. The animal hurtled towards her.

Peter was closer than the wolf. He dived at Carys, wrapping

his arms round her legs in a rugby tackle. She slammed to the floor as the wolf flew through the space where she had been. It landed hard on the wooden boards behind them. Its claws bit into the floor, but it was travelling too fast to stop and skidded forward – out of the open doorway.

Winded, Carys crawled out of the way and lay panting and coughing as Peter dragged the last few crates to the door. They didn't seem as heavy – more cartons and boxes, probably. "No point in taking chances."

When they were gone, he flopped down next to Carys, exhausted.

She grabbed his hand and held it tight. "Thanks."

"Might be a bit early for that," Peter said.

He had to shout over the sound of the hammering on the wagon door. The wood was shuddering under the onslaught. As they watched, claws pierced the wood – ripping and tearing it away.

Peter got up and staggered over to the open side door. "You fancy jumping?"

"No. We just threw a couple of angry wolves out there, remember?"

"Good point. Next wagon, then?"

"And do it all again? Any wolves in there will be awake and free by now."

"Then we need to jam that door shut too."

"That'll trap us in here until they break in," Carys said.

But she helped Peter slam makeshift wedges into the gap between the forward door and its frame.

"We're not trapped if there's still a way out."

Carys shook her head. "You're not serious about jumping? God knows how fast we're going. If we're lucky we'll just break our legs and lie there in agony until the wolves find us."

Peter was standing in the open doorway. He held on to the frame and leaned out, looking up rather than down. The wind tore at his hair and jacket. He clung on tight.

"How about climbing?" he yelled.

Carys stared back at him. "You are totally and utterly mad, you know that, don't you?"

"We can do it. And it's so crazy that when they get in here, David and the wolves will think we jumped."

"Even if they don't catch our scent, then what?"

"We lie on the top of the wagon until the train gets where it's going, or slows down enough that we really can jump off."

Carys stared at him, hands on hips and head to one side. From behind her the sound of the wolves attacking the door increased in volume and determination.

"You go first," she said.

Reaching up, Peter managed to grab hold of the lip of the roof where it overhung the side of the wagon. He pulled himself up, battling against the wind rushing past as the train sped through the landscape. There were trees now – the beginnings of a wood.

Carys grabbed his feet and pushed him upwards. He managed to get his hands, then his forearms onto the roof. Fortunately the surface was rough and he could grip the rusty metal and drag himself up.

As soon as he was on top, he turned and reached back down. Lying on his front, the roof was cold and scratched his stomach, even through his coat and shirt. The wind was even stronger on the exposed roof, blowing him backwards and sideways.

Carys caught hold of his hands, and Peter heaved her upwards. He could feel himself slipping under her weight, and tried to grip with his feet. She reached up over him, pulling at his coat as she desperately tried to get on to the roof. He could feel her slipping back, so Peter grabbed the waistband of her jeans. Somehow he managed to get a grip on her legs and drag her up and Carys collapsed on the roof beside him.

"You all right?" he shouted, the wind whipping his words away.

She nodded. "Just never do that again, okay?"

Peter crawled to the back of the wagon, peering carefully over the edge of the roof. Several wolves stood on their hind legs, pummelling the disintegrating door below with their massive hairy paws. Others watched from the platform of the next wagon, gathered in the doorway, snapping their jaws in anticipation. One wolf threw back its head and howled.

Peter crawled back quickly to avoid being seen. He was moving against the wind now, heading towards the front of the train. It felt like his hair was being torn out by the roots.

"They're nearly through," he said, his hand cupped from his mouth to Carys's ear, so she could hear him. "With luck they'll think we've jumped. But if not…"

She nodded. "We have to get moving. Maybe we can make it to the engine and stop the train."

They crawled forward. The wolves would be in the wagon below very soon, if they weren't already. They mustn't make any noise that might be heard inside. They clawed and scrabbled frustratingly slowly into the wind until they reached the front of the wagon. Again, Peter peered over the edge.

And again, there were wolves on the platform below.

Carys was looking too. They both edged back. Peter opened his hands and shrugged, asking, "What now?"

Carys leaned close. Her breath was warm on Peter's cheek as she said, "We have to wait till they get into the wagon. Then we can jump across."

Peter cupped his hand to Carys's ear to reply. "Against the wind?"

"This is your idea, remember."

They had to time it exactly right. As soon as the wolves were through the door, Carys and Peter moved back along the roof. There wasn't time to climb down to the platform, jump across and climb back up again. They'd almost certainly be seen.

So instead, they had to jump the far wider gap from roof to roof.

Holding hands, they stood up, leaning into the wind. Now it came to it, Peter hesitated. Was it such a great idea? But what choice did they have?

"Let's do it!" Carys yelled.

Heart thumping, holding Carys's hand tight, he ran. It felt like a dream where you run and run and get nowhere. But gradually they gathered speed as they battled into the wind. At the last moment, right at the edge, they jumped. Peter's free arm flailed in the air. His other hand was torn from Carys's grip.

He thumped down belly first on the roof of the next carriage, the wind knocked out of him. Carys landed beside him, but further back – sliding away as her legs hung over the edge. Peter grabbed for her hand again – caught her by the wrist and managed to hold on to her.

Slowly, he eased her back up onto the roof.

"I'm not doing that again," she said as she collapsed against him.

"Me neither. So let's hope we don't have to."

They crawled along to the end of the roof. There was one more wagon between them and the engine. The wood was getting thicker now. Branches whipped at the sides of the wagon and along the roof. Several times they had to duck down below a branch and feel it scrape along their backs.

There were no wolves on these platforms. Relieved, Peter dropped down. He turned to help Carys down beside him. They jumped easily to the platform of the front wagon, and cautiously opened the door.

Inside it was hard to see. The sunlight was all but cut off by the thickening trees of the forest. As their eyes adjusted to the light, they saw that the floor of the wagon was strewn with splintered wood from several broken crates. But mercifully the wolves were gone.

They ran through the wagon, and carefully opened the last door. The dark shape of the tender rose up in front of them. There was a ladder set into the metalwork, leading up to the top of the coal heaped inside.

"There's nowhere else to go," Carys said. "And maybe the driver doesn't know what's in his cargo."

Peter thought he could hear the wolves howling angrily in the distance. But perhaps it was the wind whipping past the train as it sped through the trees.

Climbing the ladder was easy compared with the journey they'd already made. But as Peter reached the top, smoke and steam stung his eyes. It was difficult to see through the acrid smog. The coal was hard and sharp-edged under his hands and knees as he made his way along the top of the tender.

The smoke cleared for a moment – just in time for Peter to see that the pile of coal dropped away. He clambered carefully down, hands and clothes black with soot and coal dust. Carys was close behind him.

When they reached the floor of the tender, they were both relieved at how far they'd come, and each managed a smile at the state of the other. Carys's features, usually so pale and delicate, were smudged and blotchy. Her hands looked like black gloves.

"Sooty and Sweep," Peter joked.

She grinned, and wiped a dusty finger down his nose.

Ahead of them, the light from the fire broke through the smoke and steam. It cleared as they moved towards the engine. Soon they were beneath the cloud of smog belching from the engine's funnel. The driver was looking through the front window, watching the track ahead.

The fireman shovelled coal from a small pile at the back of the footplate into the open furnace. Their overalls were almost as sooty as Carys and Peter's clothes.

Neither of them noticed Peter and Carys watching. The driver's attention was now on the various dials and controls, handles and levers.

"We're slowing down," Carys shouted above the sound of the engine.

She was right, the noise of the wind had lessened. The wheels were squealing on the track below as the driver pulled at the brake.

"Because of us?" Peter wondered. "Or have we arrived?"

As he spoke, the fireman slammed the door of the furnace shut, and turned. He stared right at Peter and Carys, his jaw open in astonishment.

The driver turned too.

Like the fireman, he had the face of a ravening wolf.

CHAPTER 23

Carys backed away into the smoke and scrambled back up the coal. Peter was right behind her. The climb was steep. The coal shifted under their feet and they slipped down almost as fast as they climbed up.

Somehow Carys made it to the top. She turned. One of the wolves was climbing up after them. Peter was still scrabbling his way over the shifting mountain of coal. The wolf reached out and grabbed at Peter's leg, dragging him back.

Carys was too far away to help. She couldn't reach Peter's outstretched hand. Instead, desperate, she grabbed a lump of coal and hurled it with all her strength.

The coal caught the wolf on the shoulder. It cried out – a howl of anger, surprise and pain all merged into one unholy sound. But it held on to Peter's leg.

The next lump of coal hit the wolf full on the jaw. At the same moment, Peter kicked out with his free leg. The wolf let out a screech of agony at the double impact. Peter tore free, and somehow managed to make it up to the top of the coal to join Carys.

"Thanks!" he gasped.

"Don't thank me yet," Carys told him. "Look."

She pointed along the train behind them. Through the smoke and steam, they could see three wolves bounding along the roofs of the wagons, heading straight for them.

"We're trapped between them," Peter said, looking back down at where the upright wolf that had grabbed him was recovering and climbing up the coal again.

"Well done, Einstein."

The train jolted as it slowed. The shudder made one of the wolves lose its footing, and it skidded across the roof of the nearest wagon, almost sliding off the edge. Which gave Carys an idea – it was desperate, but what choice did they have?

"Come on," she said, getting to her feet, feeling the coal shift under her.

"What? Where to?" Peter demanded.

She forced a grin, hoping she'd seem more confident than she really was. Because she felt terrified. "We're going to do what you suggested before – and jump for it," she said.

Peter stared at her in horror. "Right," he said. He looked from the wolves bounding along the wagons to the creature clambering up the coal, as if weighing up the alternatives. "Okay."

The train jolted again. A mass of steam erupted from the engine as the brakes came on. Peter and Carys were lost in a sudden fog. Carys felt for Peter's hand, and gripped it tight.

"Now!" she shouted above the noise of the screeching wheels.

Together, they leaped into space.

The ground appeared as the last wisps of steam faded and the air cleared. Undergrowth and bracken raced towards them.

The ground slammed into Carys's feet. Her legs buckled under her and she rolled. Peter's hand was torn from her grip. Branches of a tree whipped at her face and body and she rolled, trying to lessen the shock of impact.

She finally tumbled to a stop, bruised and battered. She closed her eyes, just for a moment, getting her breath back. When she opened them, a shape appeared right above her, and she cried out.

"Hey, hey, hey!" It was Peter. "We have to get out of sight. The train's stopping. We were lucky with the steam, but it won't take them long to realise we jumped."

They ran through the forest. Daylight penetrated the canopy of trees in scattered puddles, dappling the forest floor. The noise of the train receded, and was replaced by a distant howling and barking.

"We're covered in coal and smoke," Carys whispered. "Maybe it's masked our scent."

"Or maybe they"ve got better things to do now they"ve arrived. Wherever we are," Peter said.

Carys shrugged. "Somewhere in Poland?"

"Maybe we can work it out," Peter suggested. "If we know how many hours we were travelling, and can guess the average speed."

"Yeah, because we're both experts at estimating train speeds." She was tired and scared, and that made her scratchy and irritable. He was trying to help, and they were both in this together. She was cross, but in truth, there wasn't anyone else she'd rather be in this with. "Let's just see where the train stopped."

"Is that a good idea?"

"If it's a station, there might be people. Other trains to get away from here."

"Fair enough. That is a good idea."

They made their way back towards the railway track, keeping low to the ground and as quiet as possible. Following the track, they found the train had stopped in a clearing. The trees thinned until the area was completely open. In the distance, ragged mountains thrust up into a dull grey sky.

The train was wreathed in smoke. The driver and fireman stood close to the engine, lit from behind with an eerie orange glow from the furnace.

At the edge of the clearing, several more figures stood on guard between Carys and Peter and the train. They wore dark uniforms and carried guns and were constantly alert. Carys caught their musty smell and crawled back into the bracken, beside Peter.

"More of them," he said quietly. "Two types of creature."

"Wolves and werewolves," she agreed. "The wolves must be on their way to the sanctuary at Wolfstone."

"Are they in different stages of the same process?" Peter wondered.

"It's Einzel's doing," Carys said, though she didn't know what Einzel had actually done. It wasn't good, that was for sure. But it could wait. "I don't see another way out of here."

"We're in the middle of nowhere," Peter agreed. "No station, no town, nothing. Why are they unloading the wolves *here*?"

"They must have some way of transporting them on to the next stage. This might be just where the train tracks stop."

They broke off as the nearest guard turned and looked in their direction. His red eyes glinted hungrily in the light from sun shining between the peaks of the mountains. He snapped his jaws, yellowed teeth clicking together. There was a faint crystal gleam from a ring on his hairy finger – a ring just like the one David had worn.

Carys didn't dare move. The guard was coming towards them, looking round all the time, sniffing the air. Did he know they were there? He gave a low, throaty growl of anticipation.

David appeared out of the drifting smoke from the engine, back in human form. He hurried up to the wolf-guard, just a few metres from where Carys and Peter lay hidden in the undergrowth. His face was a contorted mask of rage.

"The Old One wants the wolves recalled," he snarled. "I'drather let them hunt those two down and tear them apart for what they did at Vrolask. But he doesn't think they'll get far. After all, where can they go?"

The guard looked at David. His expression was impossible to read.

"Just call them back," David said.

Carys pressed deeper into the undergrowth as the guard turned towards them. She could smell the cold, damp of the grass and leaves – fresh and clean after the stench of the railway wagons. Peter's leg pressed against hers as he shifted position slightly, warm and reassuring.

The guard threw his head back and let out a long, low, mournful howl. It was answered almost immediately – wolf calling to wolf. Then the sound of something running through the undergrowth. The wolves were coming.

Carys could feel the ground vibrating beneath her as the wolves approached. They ran past, either side of her and Peter. One leaped over them, hurrying to answer the guard's call.

She risked raising her head slightly, and saw the wolves bounding past the guard, following David as he turned and ran ahead of them. His legs kept the same rhythm as the animals as he disappeared into the distance, the wolves close behind him. The wolf-guard turned to watch them go.

Carys glanced at Peter, and found he was staring back at her. "What?" she mouthed.

Then a phone rang. It seemed incredibly loud, as if it was right by Carys's ear. She felt a sudden stab of fear and horror as she realised it *was* right by her ear. Peter was desperately fumbling in his pocket, trying to turn the sound off.

The wolf-guard turned back in their direction, walking slowly towards the noise.

Finally, Peter managed to turn it off. "Sorry," he mouthed. He looked pale, and Carys guessed she looked just as afraid.

The guard stood silhouetted against the low, red sun. He had stopped when the noise cut off. The creature was close enough that Carys could have stretched out and touched his boots.

It grunted, turning to look one way, then the other – its sense of smell confused by the acrid smoke drifting from the engine. Then it stood staring out across Peter and Carys for what seemed like an age. They lay perfectly still, holding their breath. Finally, the guard gave another grunt, turned and walked away.

Carys waited until they had crawled back well out of earshot of the guard before she opened her mouth to tell Peter he'd almost got them both killed.

But he spoke first. "Sorry – I almost got us killed. Should have put my phone on silent. But hey – at least it means we have a signal."

"Who was calling?" Carys demanded. "Because it wasn't exactly the best moment."

"Voicemail." He held the phone between them so they could both hear the tinny filtered sound of his father's voice.

"I'm back at Wolfstone. The good news is the funding's all sorted. The bad news is... well, you know the bad news because it's *you,* isn't it?" There was a theatrical sigh. "Faye has told me what's happened. I don't believe a word of it... Well, I don't know. I do and I don't. Look – just call. And tell Carys her mother's worried sick." There was a long pause, and Carys thought the message had ended, but then Peter's dad added, "We're both worried sick. Just call, okay?"

"Well," Carys said, "I've got nothing better to do right now. What about you?"

"We could send a text, but there's no way of knowing they got it," Peter said. "So, what do we tell them?"

Carys shrugged. "Just do what I always do. Lie, and say we're fine."

Her own phone still had no signal, so they called the Red Fleece on Peter's.

Carys's mum spent a few minutes telling her off for not keeping in touch, like it was a school trip or something. The fact that there had been no phone signal didn't seem to count as an excuse. Peter's dad joined them on the call, and already seemed resigned to the fact that his son had disappeared to Russia, to hunt werewolves with a teenage girl he'd met only a few days earlier.

Before long he was telling them that Abby and Mike's findings at the circle seemed to support some of what Carys's mother had told him about what had been going on.

"There's rather more solid and hairy evidence here," Peter said.

Carys glared at him. But Peter's dad didn't seem to pick up on that.

"We sent the bones from the graves we found for analysis. Seems the skeletons were mutated – consistent with a transition to lupine anatomy, I'd say."

"Werewolves," Peter whispered to Carys.

"I know," she whispered back.

"They were shot in the back with silver-tipped arrows, as we know. So the working supposition is that they were trying to escape from the circle. If it was a place of healing, then it seems they didn't want to be healed."

"The cure might have been worse than the ailment," Carys's mother added.

"Getting it in the back with an arrow certainly was," Carys agreed.

The signal was getting choppy. Peter's dad's voice was fading in and out and they missed bits of what he said.

"We'll have to go," Peter said. "You're cutting out. The signal's pretty dodgy here. Dad, this might sound daft but do you have a crystal sword lying about somewhere?"

They could hardly hear his reply. "Sword? Why… when he… want to know?"

"Didn't get that," Carys said, as loudly as she dared.

There was silence from the other end.

"Dad – are you still there?" Peter asked. "Look, if you can hear me, that sword is *important*. The wolves are after it. And don't trust Forrest – or any of them. Okay?"

Still nothing.

"We'll be back soon, I hope."

Carys was about to tell her mum not to worry. About to say, "I love you, Mum." But the phone cut out, and there was just a steady tone.

"We're on our own again," she said. "You think he heard – about the sword?"

"We don't even know if he has it."

"So what's the plan?"

"Get home. God knows how. It looks like we're in the middle of nowhere."

"There must be something here," Carys reasoned. "Or else why did they come?"

"New plan," Peter decided. "Explore, find out what's going on. *Then* go home."

"Easy," Carys told him.

A faint, damp mist was permeating the forest. It hung close to the ground and smelled of soot and salt. Ahead of them, a clanking and wheezing told them the train was preparing to leave again. With a hiss of steam, the train backed slowly into a siding. Several of the wolf-guards changed the points over so the train could return the way it had come. The clearing filled with noise and smoke as it departed.

When the smoke cleared, Carys could see that the clearing was actually at the edge of the forest, on a plateau, overlooking a bay. With the smell of the train dissipating, she could smell the salt of the sea. She could hear the distant waves breaking on the shore. A roadway curled away into the distance, hugging the coast further along. Beyond the road, the mountains were now revealed as cliffs, rising ominously above the water as the sun dipped lower, elongating the shadows of the trees.

Now for the first time, Carys noticed the ruins. Obscured by the train and the smoke, they hadn't seen the stunted stone walls and broken ground. The remains of a flagged floor stretched into the distance. A flight of stone steps rose into nowhere. Rubble and debris lay strewn across the plateau, grass and ivy growing over and through it. Whatever large building had once stood here, it was long gone.

"What are they doing?" Peter wondered.

The wolf-guards were raising what looked like rectangular screens. They positioned them round the middle of the ruins, forming a semi-circle. The screens slotted into spaces cut into the ruined floor. More guards were erecting scaffolding at the edge of the ruins. They hoisted huge lights into place.

"It looks like a film set," Carys realised.

"Except those are mirrors," Peter pointed out. He was fiddling with his phone, and Carys hoped it was on silent.

One of the screens to the side of the ruin caught the sunlight and reflected it straight at Carys and Peter, dazzling them for a moment. Then a screen slotted into place, and the light was angled above them.

"You see the shape they're making?" Peter whispered. "Remind you of anything?

Carys saw at once what he meant. The shape of the flattened semi-circle; the positioning of each screen.

"The Wolfstone Circle."

"Vrolask, too," Peter said. "So that's three identical circles – except they're not circles. And the one in Vrolask is pretty much gone."

"But why here?" Carys said. "There's some sort of ruin, but this doesn't look like an ancient sight – not stone-circle ancient. Medieval, maybe, but no older than that."

Peter held his phone so she could see the screen. "I've got a signal. It's not great, but it might be enough."

He had the maps app open. A flashing dot showed their current position. The map around the dot was slowly appearing in blocks. It showed a vast expanse of sea and the top of northern Poland.

"I'll zoom in," Peter said. "Get a place name or something."

Carys searched through her rucksack for Grandad's journal. "We're on the coast," she said. "And I've seen those cliffs before. I remember the shape."

"You've been here?"

"No. I saw them in a drawing. A sketch."

She riffled through the pages until she found what she was looking for. She held the book out for Peter to see. A sketch of a castle, large and forbidding. But behind it, the cliffs of the bay formed the same distinctive shape.

Peter held up his phone as the map appeared fully.

Right next to the flashing dot showing where they were there was a word. A place name.

Wolfenburg.

CHAPTER 24

A car was approaching along the coast road. It wound its way up towards the plateau where Schloss Wolfenburg had once stood. Its headlights cut through the gathering dusk.

"Someone important," Peter guessed.

The wolf-guards were working quickly now, perhaps to get the lights and mirrors erected before the car arrived.

"Never mind that," Carys whispered, "it's a way out."

"Good point. Let's see where it's going."

The car had almost reached the top of the plateau when it stopped. There was the sound of a mechanism – a heavy, metallic noise. Then the car drove on, and disappeared from view. It looked as if it had driven right into the side of the cliff.

"Where did it go?" Peter asked.

"A lot of the castle was underground. Remember, in the journal, they had to go down into the cellars to find the labs and that crypt and the Crystal Room? That area might have been protected from the blasts. Maybe it's still there..."

"Surely the whole place would have collapsed into it," Peter said.

"Then where did the car go?"

"Who knows?" Peter said. "And how do we get in? I don't fancy trying the front door."

They sat at the edge of a wooded area, in the shadow of the trees and went through their options. There weren't many.

"We can try to sneak past the guards, which is going to be difficult," Carys suggested. "Or wait for the car to come out again and try to hijack it somehow, or hide inside. We could wait for another car, if there ever is one, or just walk away and hope we find civilisation before we starve to death or die of exposure."

That was pretty much it, Peter thought. "Which do you fancy?" he asked.

"None of the above."

"Then we need to think of something else. You got the journal?"

Carys took it out again. "You think it might help?"

"There must be something, some clue in here that we've missed. Something that will help."

Carys leafed through the brittle, yellowing pages. "I don't know what."

"Me neither," Peter agreed. He was clutching at straws, but the journal was the closest thing to a guidebook that they had.

They read slowly through the whole book again. Nothing. Carys turned back to the start.

"You know what's missing?" she said. "There's nothing

about how they escaped after they planted the explosives and got out of the Crystal Room."

"He'd just been bitten by a werewolf," Peter pointed out. "He probably didn't remember much."

"They blew the place up, though, so how did he and Acer get out?"

It was a good question. But at the crucial point in the narration, there was just a blank page with a faded pencil sketch. A series of lines joined into an enclosed shape, and another dotted line curved over some of it.

"He had time to doodle," Carys said. "He must have written all this on the way home, anyway. It's not like he was keeping notes during the raid."

"But he couldn't describe what he couldn't remember," Peter said. "Unless..." There was something about the random lines. Maybe they weren't so random after all – the enclosed shape looked a bit like... "Hang on."

"What is it?"

He turned back to the beginning of the section – the sketch of the castle, and a rough plan of its layout. The plan was the same shape. "It's not just a doodle," he said. He flipped between the two pages. "Look – it's a map."

"Another sketch of the castle – so what?"

"So, what if that dotted line shows how they got out?"

Carys took the book from him and examined it carefully.

"It's possible," she agreed. "You know there are times, just a few, when I'm glad I brought you along."

They made their way carefully round the site of the ruined castle. They kept to the trees, though the wolf-guards seemed preoccupied with the lights and mirrors.

Soon they reached a point where they could see where the car had gone. The edge of the plateau gave way sharply, and they were looking across to where the road entered the original castle. The remains of the gatehouse were built into the side of the cliff – a cliff made of shattered debris created when the had walls tumbled down.

The gateway had been opened up and scaffolding and metal props had kept the roof from collapsing across the road again.

Two wolf-guards in their dark uniforms stood either side of the gateway, guns over their shoulders.

"You're right," Peter said quietly. "They"ve excavated right under the castle."

"Looking for the labs – for the Nazi experiments," Carys said. "But how did they know there was anything there?"

"Maybe they're putting their own labs in," Peter suggested. "They need somewhere to keep the wolves."

"To 'acclimate' them." Carys nodded. "So here's the plan – find a way inside, see what they're up to, then get out."

"In the car," Peter added, though he knew it wouldn't be easy. "So if that dotted line is a way in, it should be..." He turned to get his bearings. "Should be that way."

They looped round to the cliff, and clambered down towards the sea. There was a narrow path about halfway down. It was slippery from sea spray, and in places had crumbled away completely. Bracken and brambles overhung it, so they had a choice of either pushing through and getting scratched, or tumbling over the edge.

"Is it far?" Peter asked. He didn't dare look down. The tide was in, and the waves were crashing against the base of the cliff. He pushed a branch out of his way and eased past.

"Not very. Assuming this map – if it is a map – is anything like accurate."

"And assuming the way in is still there," Peter muttered. After all, the castle itself was all but gone. But they didn't have a choice – they needed the car to get away.

They edged on round the narrow path. Finally Carys stopped.

"I think this might be it."

She pulled back a mass of foliage to reveal a dark hole in the side of the cliff. It was too regular, the edges too straight, to be natural. Peter got his phone out and the pale glow of the display lit a muddy stone floor, but not much more. A brighter light cut through the gloom above as Carys produced a small torch. The walls of the passage were lined with ancient crumbling bricks.

"Always come prepared," she told him.

"Always? If you think I'm ever doing anything like this again, you are seriously deluded."

The passage was cold, damp, claustrophobic. With every step he took, Peter felt more and more like the walls and the roof were pressing in on him.

"Your namesake was found not that far from here," Carys said as they made their way along the narrow passage.

"What do you mean?"

"Peter the Wild Boy."

"Yeah, very funny." He had no idea what she was talking about. He tried not to think of the weight of earth and rubble pressing down on the roof of the passage – of what would happen if it collapsed while they were still inside.

"No, he was real," Carys said. "He was found in the early eighteenth century."

"A wild boy?"

"They called him Peter. Don't know why. But he was found fending for himself in the woods. They said he was raised by wolves."

"What happened to him?" Peter wasn't all that

interested, but it took his mind off where they were, and the danger they were in.

"King George I took him in at his court in London. He was a sensation."

"As "Peter the Wild Boy"?"

"That's right. He refused to dress. Slept on the floor. Ate with his fingers. And he never learned to speak."

"Can't see the attraction," Peter said.

Carys slipped on the damp floor, and clutched at Peter's arm. He caught her, holding her hand.

"Thanks… Maybe they felt sorry for him. He lived at court for years. Grew up there, until the king pensioned him off. He gave him a farm in Hertfordshire."

"Maybe he felt at home with the animals."

She was still holding his hand. "Maybe. There was a waxwork statue of him in the Strand for a while. Even today, people still leave flowers on his grave."

"And you think it's funny we have the same name?"

"I'm not teasing you." She sounded surprised.

"So why are you telling me this?"

"Because…" She looked away. "Because I'm scared, and if I'm talking I don't have time to be so frightened. All right?"

Peter squeezed her hand. He wanted to tell her he was scared too, but would that just sound like he was trying to please her? He was saved from having to say anything by a noise ahead of them.

"What's that?" Carys hissed.

"Not sure," he whispered back.

They stood silent and still, straining to hear. It was a faint, mechanical sound. Irregular but insistent. As they moved along the passageway, it grew slowly louder, until it was reverberating round them. The ground trembled. Then, abruptly, the noise stopped.

"I don't think we need this any more." Carys turned off the torch. Sure enough, there was a pale glow from further along the passage.

The way ahead was blocked. The roof had collapsed, filling the passage with rubble. But the light and the noise were filtering in from a hole in the wall close to where the roof had caved in. The gap was narrow, but they managed to squeeze through into another, wider corridor.

Fallen masonry and broken stone had been cleared to the sides. Metal stanchions held the remains of the roof in place. Lights were strung along the length of the corridor – bare bulbs attached to thick, dark cable. It was painfully bright after the gloomy passageway.

"They're excavating," Peter realised. "Digging their way back into whatever's left.

"This is where the labs and the experiments were,"

Carys whispered. "That must be what they're after. But how did they know?"

"From Sebastian Forrest, maybe?" Peter suggested. "If his father told him about the raid."

The noise started up again – and now they could hear that it was drilling.

"They're still excavating." Peter had to speak loudly to be heard over the noise.

They went cautiously, ready at any moment to duck into whatever cover they could find. There were piles of debris, alcoves, side corridors. But they stuck to the main route, heading towards the sounds of excavation. The drilling stopped again, and was replaced by a scraping sound.

They reached an arched doorway. One wooden door was jammed closed, the wall beside it bulging out. The lintel above had slipped down. The other door had been wrenched from its hinges and was leaning back against the wall.

The room beyond was virtually intact, though layered with debris. Two rows of metal-framed beds lay under blankets of dust and shattered stonework. Equipment lay broken on the floor. Glass crunched under their feet as Peter and Carys picked their way across the room.

Carys gave a gasp of disgust. Peter wasn't surprised. He felt weak and sick. He tried not to look at the beds. The light was poorer in here, but even with just a couple of bulbs strung up overhead, he could see clearly what lay on them.

The bodies were dry, decaying husks. Skeletons poked through the flimsy remains of sheets and hospital gowns. Sunken eyes stared out of parchment-wrapped skulls. Several of the bodies still had tufts of hair clinging to the brittle bones and translucent skin. All of them were misshapen – jutting jaws, elongated limbs, claws emerging from the ends of gnarled fingers…

"Let's get out of here," Carys hissed. "We've got to find that car."

Peter wasn't about to argue. They hurried on through to the next room. The doors were standing open, so they saw at once the figures standing in the chamber beyond – and froze.

The chamber looked exactly as the journal described it, and it was almost intact. Peter guessed that the vaulted ceiling had angled the blast of the explosives away from it. The raised altar in the centre had collapsed and the remains were strewn with fallen stone, but the floor had been cleared. Bright lights stood on metal poles, illuminating the work at the doorway on the far side.

And in the middle of it all, stood Einzel , hands clasped behind his back, his left shoulder hunched, watching the work. Pale dust spattered the shoulders and back of his dark leather trench coat.

Two of the wolf-guards held a massive drill, ramming it into a pile of fallen rubble. The sound of the drill shook the floor and echoed around the chamber. The room filled with a fog of dust.

After a few moments, the drilling stopped. The guards pulled the drill away, and two more wolf-guards shovelled the fallen debris into wheelbarrows. They carted it away, through another door. The wolf-guards with the drill set it down, and clawed at the pile of rubble, digging their way through.

Peter strained to see better. "What are they looking for?" he whispered.

"The next room," Carys whispered back. "Remember?"

Peter edged back into the laboratory. "Time we were going."

"That corridor must lead back to the car. I guess that's how Einzel got here. He probably flew to somewhere nearby and had the car waiting for him."

They hurried back through the lab, trying not to look at the bodies.

"But why does he need the Crystal Room?" Peter wondered as they emerged back into the corridor.

"They want more of the crystal, like in David's ring."

"So how does he even know where to find the Crystal Room?"

The answer came from ahead of them. "That's something you can ask Herr Einzel yourselves." It was a voice they both recognised at once.

David Forrest stepped out of one of the dark alcoves. Beside him, a woman dressed in a dark business suit raised a pistol, covering Peter and Carys. Her blonde hair was cut to her shoulders and her eyes were a cold ice-blue.

"You are so predictable. Caught like rats in a trap." David smiled at the woman with the gun before introducing her. "Let me introduce you to Einzel Industries" public relations director. Irena has the rather tricky job of explaining how the laboratories in Vrolask got burned down yesterday." He stepped forward, raising his hand to strike Peter.

"No," the woman said. "There's no need for that."

David froze, hand raised. It was obvious who was in charge.

"Einzel wants the boy alive and unharmed," she continued. "So if he tries anything, I will kill *her*." She moved the gun so it was aimed at Carys.

"She'll do it too," David smirked. "Tough bitch."

Irena ignored him. "As for why we need the Crystal Room…" she went on, "well, if you are really unlucky, we'll show you."

CHAPTER 25

Einzel looked back over the shoulder of his limp arm, as Irena and David led Peter and Carys into the chamber.

Bloodless lips drew back to reveal sharp teeth. "Vandals," he hissed. "Have you any idea how much damage you have caused?"

"Lots, I hope," Carys snapped back.

Einzel's grimace became a smile. "Then you will be disappointed. I was already closing down the laboratories in Vrolask. You achieved nothing!"

"That'll be why you're so upset then," Peter said.

David's fist slammed into his stomach and he doubled over in sudden pain.

"Leave him," Irena said.

"After what he's done? Both of them – they humiliated us, and they're still laughing!"

"Leave him," Einzel agreed. "Oh they will suffer for what they have done, but not yet. When the time is right. When they can be of some use, repairing what *little* damage they have done. If they have made work for anyone, it is Irena."

"I have already issued a press statement about the accident and fire," the woman said. There was a hint of pride in her voice.

David gave a disgruntled sigh. "They know about the Crystal Room," he said.

"I doubt that."

Einzel turned back to the excavation. The wolf-guards were attacking the last of the rubble with pickaxes. They hammered them into the debris, ripping out chunks of stone and clouds of dust, grunting and snorting with the effort.

"Carefully, my friends," Einzel warned. "We must not damage what lies behind those doors."

"Why not?" Carys demanded. "You just want to break up the crystal to put in those rings you all wear. You're going to smash the room up anyway."

"How little you understand. We have enough crystal for the rings, and for the lights we're setting up outside to replicate the stones at Vrolask. You saw them, I'm sure. David tells me you came by train. I applaud your resourcefulness."

"Listen," Peter said, "you've had your gloat. We're no use to you, and no threat. So why not just let us go?"

Einzel turned to stare at Peter with what looked like pity. So close to him, Peter could see the fine tracery of lines across his aged face – like cracks in the glaze of ancient porcelain.

"Everyone has a use. People are nothing more than

a commodity. David here did not know how useful he could be when he came to me. He wanted something from me, but I have been able to take so much more from him."

David smiled proudly, taking Einzel's comments as praise. "Anything I can do."

"And Irena," Einzel went on, ignoring David, "she thought she was working in public relations. But now she appreciates the benefits of joining us. The *real* benefits. And in return she makes problems like a small fire at an obsolete laboratory fade into obscurity."

"My father served Herr Einzel for many years," Irena said. "Now I am glad it is my turn."

"Your turn to become a wolf, that is?" Carys asked wryly.

"To live like those things," Peter gestured to the wolf-creatures clearing away more of the rubble. "That's no kind of life. Not really."

"You understand so very little," Einzel breathed. "If, as David says, you know what lies behind the doors we shall soon uncover, then I must assume you know what happened here, during the war."

"The experiments. The raid," Carys said. "We know everything."

"You do not even know who I am," Einzel told her. "How could you? And as for the Crystal Room, well – you might know where it is, you may remember the legends, but you do not know the whole story and what it implies. If you did, you would never have dared to come here. You would have taken your chances with my wolves in the forest outside."

"So tell us the whole story," Carys said.

Einzel turned to look at her. His grey eyes narrowed as he considered her question. "Why not?" he decided at last. "It's just an exercise in public relations, after all." He nodded to Irena, then turned away again, apparently losing interest.

She seemed happy to oblige, leaning back against the stone altar, gun held across her body. "Once upon a time," she said, "there was a count who had a beautiful daughter. He loved her very much… All the best stories are about parents and children, don't you find?"

There were wolves in Russia in those days. Wolves, and worse-than-wolves. Soon after his daughter was born, Count Grishko lost his wife to a wolf – to a worse-than-wolf. He determined that he would not lose his only daughter too, vowing that he would rid the land of the beasts.

The count consulted the wisest men of the area. He sent for the most learned scholars in all the Russias. He asked them how to protect his child, and they all told him the same thing: that there is no certain way to protect a beautiful girl. Because girls become women, and women will not be ruled by their fathers any more than men will be ruled by their mothers.

So the count kept his daughter locked in the highest tower of his palace at Vrolask, and he let no one see her except her serving maid.

Until one day, a young huntsman came to the palace. He brought a deer that had been savaged by a wolf, and he presented it to the count. He told the count that he had found the deer close to death on the Vrolask Estate. He had driven off the wolf, but could not in good conscience keep the deer, so he had come to return it to the count. Impressed with such honesty, the count invited the huntsman to dine at the palace.

That moonless night they feasted on venison from the deer, and they talked long into the night. When they had eaten and drunk much, the count asked the huntsman if he knew any sure way of keeping the wolves at bay.

"You are worried about your daughter," the huntsman said. "I have heard she is very beautiful, and you have consulted the wisest men in all the land on how to keep her beauty safe and pure."

"Without success," the count confessed. "No one can tell me a sure way of protecting her."

"If someone could," the huntsman said, "what would you give him by way of reward?"

"I would make him rich," the count said. "Can you

help me?"

The huntsman laughed. "I want no riches, but I can tell you the surest way to keep your daughter safe. In return, I ask for only one, small thing."

The count agreed, and the huntsman told the count to construct a special room in his palace. He showed the count where to quarry stones that contained the tiniest fragments of crystal – crystal that captured and retained the moonlight. The same stone as had been used in ancient times to construct the Vrolask Circle outside the palace. He taught the count's craftsmen how to extract and work the crystal, though he never saw or touched it himself.

And under the huntsman's guidance, the count constructed a room lined with the crystal. The crystal walls were built around the furthest stone of the Vrolask Circle – the Lonely Stone – just as the count's finest silver sword was also lined with crystal.

When the work was done, the count sent for an old woman from the village, who was said to be a witch. The count bade her dine with him in the Crystal Room. Just as the huntsman had promised, the moonlight from the crystal worked its power on the old woman. As she ate, she changed – she transformed into the hideous beast that she really was. The crystal revealed her hidden nature, and the count took his crystal sword and severed her grotesque head from her hideous body.

Then the huntsman, hearing that the Crystal Room was complete, claimed his reward. He asked only for a kiss from the count's daughter. He took the girl in his arms and kissed her on the lips. And, having never seen a man so handsome as the huntsman, she kissed him back.

The count's daughter grew more beautiful with each passing season. But any suitor for her love had to dine with the count in the Crystal Room. They were allowed but one meeting with the daughter, and each one she thought less handsome than the huntsman. Each one she scratched with her elegant fingernails to see if their blood was red, or if the beast might be revealed beneath the skin.

And each and every man, besotted with her beauty, dined with the count in the Crystal Room. Each and every man died there when the infection within him was manifest in the cruel moonlight stored in the walls. Each became a ravening beast, and each had his head struck from his body by the count.

Until one day, when she was come of age, the count's daughter asked her father to show her the Crystal Room, where so many of her suitors had met their fate. The count unlocked the door and showed her the room. The room he had constructed to keep her safe from the wild beasts.

As soon as she crossed the threshold, as soon as she saw the beauty of the crystal and the glow of the scattered moonlight, the count's daughter began to change. He watched in horror as his beautiful daughter became disfigured by the revelation of the beast within her.

Then the count took the crystal sword from where it hung on the wall of the Crystal Room. And he plunged it into his own heart.

For who can know what might be revealed when you scratch open the skin? Who can tell when the infection of the beast and the heat of desire might be passed on, not by a scratch or a bite, but in a simple kiss?

From that day on, the count's daughter and the huntsman ran free in the woods around the palace, and loved happily ever after. For while a wound may heal and memories may fade; a kiss can last for ever.

"The huntsman bit the girl's lip when he kissed her, of course," Irena said, lips drawn back over her own teeth in a cruel smile.

Carys glanced at Peter before asking Einzel, "Are you the huntsman?"

Einzel had been watching them both intently as Irena related the story of the count and his daughter. At this he gave a guttural laugh.

"Don't be absurd! It may explain the Crystal Room, but it's just a fairy tale."

David sniggered. But it didn't seem absurd to Peter. "So how do you come to have pieces of crystal for your rings if you haven't excavated the Crystal Room yet?"

Einzel nodded slowly. "Ah, I see the logic. You think that, as the huntsman knew how to refine the crystal from the raw stone, then I must be the huntsman."

"Or someone with his knowledge," Carys agreed. "We know most of the stones at Vrolask have gone."

"Logical." Einzel smiled thinly. "But wrong. The stones were taken from Vrolask hundreds of years ago, which does present its own problems of course." He gestured to one of the wolf-guards still clawing rubble from the blocked doorway. "It has taken decades for me to acquire this site. Years to excavate it to this level. The ruins of the castle above had to be cleared away almost completely. Then I could open up various routes in, like the passage I assume you used to get here."

"They did," David said. "Just like you said."

Carys was surprised. "You knew about that?"

The wolf-guard was helping Einzel out of his long coat. Once it was removed, they could see that his left arm hung limp and emaciated at his side. With his good hand, he unbuttoned his shirt.

"Is it wise to show them your weakness?" Irena asked.

"My weakness is our strength," Einzel retorted.

"Tonight," he said to Carys and Peter, "at last we shall break into the Crystal Room."

The wolf-guard helped Einzel out of his shirt. One whole side of his chest was sunken and tinged blue like a huge bruise. The colouring was deepest and most pronounced at the shoulder. He turned slowly, exposing his back.

"The Crystal Room," Einzel went on, "that I brought out of Russia for Reichsführer Heinrich Himmler."

"*You* brought it out of Russia?" Peter gasped.

"Didn't you ever wonder why we call him the Old One?" David asked.

"But that's impossible," Carys replied.

"I can assure you it is not," Einzel said. "I was one of the first volunteers for Himmler's experimental programme. The Reichsführer himself shook me by the hand and explained the plan of how we would be the first of an army of wolves. Unstoppable. Bluitzkrieg taken to the next level. Then he kissed me on each cheek, and told me how indebted the Fatherland would be for my sacrifice. But it was not a sacrifice at all. It was an honour." He drew himself up to his full height. "You asked me how I knew the Crystal Room was there, my answer is: because I rebuilt it there, in 1942."

"So long ago," Irena breathed. "If only we could reproduce the experiments."

"Longevity is a problem," Einzel conceded. "But we each have our cross to bear. For me, it is this."

The skin on his back was as discoloured as his chest. It was paper thin, almost translucent. And through it, Peter could see the broken-off end of a blade, embedded deep in the flesh. A blade made of silver, encased in pale glass-like crystal.

"Doesn't it hurt?" Peter asked.

Einzel gave a short laugh. "Constantly."

"That's how you knew about the passage," Carys realised.

"It is how I escaped the explosion when the British destroyed this castle." Einzel motioned for the wolf-guard to help him back into his shirt. "Two of the commandos attacked me in the Crystal Room. I was wounded, and the tip of the sword remains in my shoulder. Poisoning me, as you can see. Yet it gives us strength."

"The crystal for the rings," Peter said. "They take it from *there*?"

"But the blade works itself ever deeper, and it is harder to get to now without invasive surgery."

"Why not have it removed completely?" Carys asked.

Einzel buttoned his coat. "I am told the operation could kill me. And I keep it as a constant reminder of who I am, and of what happened here. Of why I must succeed. Where better to keep the most precious resource that we have than concealed inside my own body?"

As the digging continued, Einzel dismissed David. Irena led Peter and Carys away. One of the wolf-guards went with them, grunting with anticipation. He jabbed his gun into Peter's back to keep him moving.

"Soon you will know what it's like when your own body turns against you," Irena said.

"What do you mean?" Carys demanded.

They stopped outside a heavy wooden door off the main corridor. There was a small square window set in the top of the door, criss-crossed with bars. Irena kept them covered with her gun as the guard drew back heavy bolts and pushed the door open.

Irena smiled. There was a grotesque contrast between the smiling beauty of the woman and the savage snarl of the upright wolf standing beside her.

"We will need to test the Crystal Room," she said. "We must be sure that an infected human will be transformed by its power."

"But we're not infected," Peter protested.

"No," she said quietly. "Not yet."

The cell door slammed shut behind them. The bolts scraped across. The only light filtered under the door and through the small barred window. Peter could make out

Carys's face in the gloom. She looked scared.

"It'll be all right," Peter said. He felt stupid as soon as the words were out of his mouth. They both knew it wouldn't.

"What in Heaven's name are you two doing here?"

They both turned in surprise. A figure sat on a bench at the back of the cell, barely more than a silhouette. But Peter recognised the voice, and he was just as shocked.

"Mr Forrest!"

"What is this?" Carys said. "A family reunion?"

As his eyes adjusted to the dim light, Peter saw that Sebastian Forrest looked older than he remembered. His face was drawn and lined, dark rings under his eyes.

"You know David's here, right?" Peter said.

Forrest laughed, but the sound held no joy. "I followed him. Thought I could persuade him that what he was doing – what Einzel is doing – is madness." He shook his head sadly. "His mother might have talked some sense into him, but I couldn't." He turned away and his shoulders heaved in a silent sob.

"And with David's help, I guess Einzel no longer needs you," Carys said.

"That's right. We do not, as you may have realised, see entirely eye to eye."

"Is that why you're locked in here with us?" Peter asked.

"Or..." A horrifying thought occurred to him and his stomach lurched. "Are *you* going to infect us – turn us into wolves?"

Forrest shook his head. "Not if I can help it. And Einzel's methods are a little more scientific than scratching and biting these days. I imagine he will inject you with his latest potion. A refined venom extracted from saliva."

"And why do they want to test the Crystal Room on us?" Carys said. "Do you know?"

"I can only imagine," Forrest said, "that it's because everyone else here is already a wolf."

"Including you and David," Peter said.

"He's been duped. Suborned." Forrest's voice was laced with bitterness. "David's young and impetuous. The young always think of themselves before anyone else. I'm sorry," he added, "that was an ungenerous generalisation."

"What is wrong with him – Einzel, I mean?" Peter said.

"You mean the megalomania, the sadistic delusions, or the argyria?"

"The what?" Carys said.

"I mean that bruising," Peter explained. "His withered arm. It can't just be because of the crystal blade."

"It's argyria," Forrest said again. "From the silver at the heart of the sword. It poisons the body, giving it that grey-blue tinge. Silver can promote healing, but it is also a poison – especially to people like myself and Einzel. That's the irony of course, it's slowly killing him. But too slowly."

"Very slowly, if he really is the Nazi that my grandfather and your father fought," Carys agreed.

"You know about that?"

"Grandad kept a journal."

"But it doesn't tell us everything," Peter said.

"He didn't know everything, and neither do I," Forest told them. "But I do know that my father led the raid. He pretended to be friendly with Himmler before the war."

"Pretended?" It sounded to Peter like a rationalisation after the fact.

"On the orders of the secret service, such as it was in those days. He was using Himmler to try to discover what Hitler and the rest of them were planning."

"I'm guessing it didn't do them much good," Carys said.

"I really couldn't say," Forrest replied. "But more to the point, while my father was using Himmler, Himmler was also using him. He took genetic material, as we'd call it now. Blood samples. Himmler knew the truth about the du Bois family, and tried to persuade father to help him set up his obscene experiments."

"But he didn't?"

Forrest shook his head. "He escaped back to England. Soon after that we were at war. Father kept track of what

Himmler was up to as best he could. When it looked like they might even succeed in creating wolf-soldiers… Well, you know what happened. Lionel du Bois organised the raid in 1943 that destroyed this place. Operation Velvet Claw."

"And got my grandad infected."

"Yes. He always felt very guilty about that. He gave your family the pub, to try to assuage that guilt. After the raid, my family changed their name to Forrest, and we moved away from Wolfstone. Partly out of guilt, partly to muddy the waters so any German agents in Britain would find it harder to find us, and Himmler – hopefully – would lose track of us."

"I guess it worked for a while," Peter said.

"Except," Carys went on, "Einzel survived. And now he's carrying on the Nazi experiments."

Forrest nodded. "That's true. And he has the same problem that the German scientists ran up against. Longevity."

"Yes," Peter remembered, "he said something about that. But he's *ancient.*"

"And he doesn't know why. He assumes that the Nazi experiments were ultimately successful and he was given the gift of a long life."

"Is that true?" Peter asked.

"Who knows? There doesn't seem to be any other reason, unless it's the effect of the crystal and silver buried inside him. But whatever the case, he can't reproduce it. Genetic werewolves, like myself and my family, are naturally very long-lived. Your grandfather too," he said to Carys.

"Not any more," she said quietly.

"Ah." Forrest nodded. There seemed to be genuine sadness in his voice. "I'm sorry."

"Not your fault," Carys told him. "I hope."

"Certainly not. But unlike Einzel's followers, he had a long and full life. Again, that could be because Einzel is long-lived and infected him, or because, as you know, he had a piece of the crystal lodged in his leg. The people that Einzel turns to the way of the wolf, and the wolves he transforms into proto-humans, they don't live anything like so long. So far he has been unable to transfer the gift of longevity, and instead they seem to inherit the lifespan of an ordinary wolf."

"How long is that?" Carys wondered.

"It varies of course, but about eight years is normal."

"I'm guessing that's a bit of a problem if you're trying to get recruits to the cause," Peter said.

"I imagine he's making them promises he cannot yet keep."

"So what's your solution?" Carys asked. "What do you think he should be doing?"

"Like Einzel, I was looking for a cure. But something to *expel* the wolf from us, not to bring it out and make it dominant. Not that it matters now," he said sadly.

"Why?"

"Because it's too late. Far too late for me, and for my son. And now that Annabelle..." His voice choked off and he turned away. "Now he has Annabelle. I've lost both my children in just a few days."

"Sorry – who has Annabelle?" Peter demanded.

"Einzel has her. She's already turned; her time has come. And he has her imprisoned in the wolf-pit beneath the circle back at Wolfstone, to ensure my co-operation with his foul plans. Prolonged exposure to the crystal in the stones themselves, focused by the shape of the circle, will turn her permanently into a wolf. I've lost them both. Failed them both."

"But – that's not true," Peter blurted out. "That's not where she is."

"What?" Forrest was on his feet, advancing on Peter. "What do you mean?!"

"Just that Annabelle isn't in the pit under the circle," he said. "She got out – she escaped."

"How do you know?" Forrest grabbed Peter's shoulders, shaking him. "Tell me!"

"All right, all right!"

"Let him go!" Carys pulled Forrest's arms away.

He stepped back. "I'm sorry. It's just – my *daughter*..."

"I've seen her," Peter told him. "Since the ceremony in the circle where you tried to cure her."

"Without success."

"Peter's dad thinks the Wolfstone Circle was used like the Crystal Room," Carys said. "It forces a werewolf to change and reveal it's true form. That's the sort of "healing" it was for, not actually to cure the ailment, but to reveal who was a monster so they could be killed."

"We aren't all monsters," Forrest said quietly, but his voice was trembling with emotion. "You're sure you saw Annabelle?"

"In the woods," Peter explained. "She was freezing. I gave her my coat."

"You never said," Carys told him coldly. "You said you thought she was still in Wolfstone; you didn't tell me you'd actually *met* her."

"It was while you and your mum were… busy. With your grandad."

She nodded, biting her lower lip. "Okay."

"Anyway, it wasn't a meeting. She ran off," he told Forrest. "She's free."

Forrest sighed. "None of us are free."

"Certainly not in here we're not," Carys agreed. "You will help us?" she said to Forrest.

"Knowing that Annabelle is alive and safe, I'll do

whatever I can to stop Einzel."

Peter hoped that Forrest was telling the truth. Could Einzel have caught Annabelle since Peter saw her in the woods? It didn't seem likely. But anything was possible. He shuddered at the thought of what they might do. The girl's beautiful, frightened eyes bored into his memory.

The scrape of the bolts snapped him back to reality. The cell door swung open, light from the corridor spilling into the small room.

Irena and two of the wolf-guards stood in the doorway. She stepped inside, hands clasped behind her back.

"It is time."

"You've opened the Crystal Room?" Forrest asked. He seemed surprised.

"Almost. Herr Einzel felt you should be there to see it."

Forrest smiled thinly. "How thoughtful. I imagine we're all in for a treat."

"Oh yes," Irena agreed. She turned to stare at Peter. "Especially you."

The two wolf-guards moved quickly, each grabbing one of Peter's arms. They gripped him so tightly it was all he could do not to cry out in pain. His heart lurched – what was happening?

Irena was holding what looked like a gun. Except there was a small glass jar attached to the underside. In it, Peter could see a clear, viscous liquid. Fear turned to pain, and he cried out as the gun jabbed into his arm. He felt the injection through his coat and shirt, hammering into the muscle at the top of his arm.

CHAPTER 26

At once, Peter sagged. Forrest grabbed him by the shoulder to stop him collapsing to the floor.

"What have you done?" Carys demanded, her vision blurred by sudden tears.

Irena raised an eyebrow, but did not reply. She turned to the two guards. "Bring them."

Carys and Forrest managed to support Peter between them. He seemed to be recovering slowly, but his forehead was slick with sweat. Irena led the way out of the cell and along the corridor.

"Wolf venom," Forrest said quietly to Carys. "They want to try him out in the Crystal Room, to see if it has infected him."

"Like the count's daughter scratching her suitors," Carys said. "Or the huntsman's kiss?"

"He'll be all right, provided we can keep him in human form for long enough to get the poison out of his system."

"Grandad wasn't all right," Carys said.

"He was inside the Crystal Room when he was infected. His metabolism changed at once, and irreversibly."

Back in the vast chamber with the raised altar, the

doors to the Crystal Room had been cleared. A wolf guard scraped away the last of the rubble with a shovel.

"You haven't opened it yet?" Forrest asked.

"We wait for Einzel," Irena told him. "He must be here when we open the doors. He wants to see the boy change."

"I bet he does," Carys muttered angrily.

"Easy," Forrest warned under his breath.

"What – what's going on?" Peter pulled his arm away from Forrest, trying to stand on his own.

Carys held on to his other arm, but gently – letting him stand unsteadily on his own.

"How are you feeling?" she asked.

"Like I've got flu or something. Headache. And I'm burning up inside." He was shivering uncontrollably.

"Your body is fighting the infection," Forrest said. "That's a good sign."

"It will make no difference," Irena said. "As soon as the Old One is here we will open the doors, and the Crystal Room will change you for good."

Forrest rounded on her angrily. "There is nothing at all *good* about it!"

In answer, one of the guards thumped the butt of his gun into Forrest's back. The man sank to his knees in pain.

Irena pointed at Forrest. The ring she wore was identical to the one David Forrest had, glinting in the light from the lamps trained on the impressive wooden doors.

"You will be silent," she snarled. "And you'll stay where you are. We already know what will happen to *you* when you enter the Crystal Room."

"Really?" Forrest seemed amused as he pulled himself back to his feet. "Some of us can resist it, you know. Oh, not the real light of the fullest moon, but the glow of the crystal. My father did not change when he entered the Crystal Room all those years ago. He could tolerate it, at least for a while."

"Are you saying the crystal doesn't work?" Carys asked.

"No, it works all right. I'm just saying..." Forrest smiled. "I guess I'm saying, don't be surprised by what we might or might not find when those doors are opened." He leaned closer to her. "Be ready," he mouthed.

Einzel strode into the chamber. He stood in front of the wooden doors, nodding with satisfaction. "Excellent," he whispered. Then he stepped aside. "Very well. Open them!"

Carys watched with trepidation as two of the wolf-guards pulled on the doors. The wood creaked and strained as they heaved on the huge metal handles. Slowly, the doors swung open, scraping over the remaining rubble.

"Bring him!" Einzel pointed at Peter.

Another wolf-guard grabbed Peter and pushed him

forward. Carys grabbed at his hand, and felt how cold, clammy and sweaty it was. Then it was wrenched from her grip as the wolf-guard shoved Peter forward.

She expected to be dazzled by the light from within. Carys had her hand up to shield her eyes. But there was nothing. Blackness. She glanced at Forrest, and he met her eyes for a moment. He had just the trace of a smile and gave the faintest nod of reassurance.

The doors opened back fully. Light shone in from the lamps set up outside. Einzel gave a cry of astonishment and stepped through the doors.

Into an empty room.

Irena turned to look. Her smile froze as she too saw the room beyond the doors. An empty room lined with plain, dark stone.

"It's the wrong room," she said. "We've opened the wrong room!"

"No!" Einzel shrieked, turning back from inside. His face was a washed-out grimace of anger in the spotlights. "You think I don't know – don't remember?! It was *here*." He turned a full circle, as if trying to find the smallest shard of crystal still clinging to the stripped walls. "It – was – here!"

"Now," Forrest whispered urgently to Carys. "Be ready, and help Peter!"

"What?" she started to ask, but he'd already turned away.

Irena was staring at Einzel as he continued to rage, pacing round the empty stone-walled room.

Suddenly, in a single swift movement, Forrest lunged for Irena's hand. Not the hand holding the gun – her other, free hand. He grabbed it, and she turned in surprise.

She seemed to realise what Forrest was doing at the same moment as Carys did. He wasn't going for her gun – he was after her ring. Forrest prised open the top, and the light from the crystal inside splayed out across his face.

Irena snarled with anger, bringing the gun round. But Forrest's massive paw slapped it from her grasp. The gun clattered against the wall. Before it hit the floor, Forrest had closed the ring again and flung Irena away from him.

He grabbed Carys's arm, and ran.

Carys was dragging Peter. He stumbled after them. The wolf-guards turned in confusion, one of them stooped to help Irena to her feet. Another was inside the chamber with Einzel. But the third brought his gun up. Bullets chiselled into the floor round Carys's feet. Chips of stone flew from the walls as more bullets bit. She closed her eyes, hoping Forrest knew where he was going, hoping she could keep hold of Peter.

Peter staggered, and she cried out, thinking he'd been

hit. But he stumbled on, regaining his balance and running with renewed strength. Maybe he was recovering – pray God he'd be all right.

They passed the altar in the main chamber and carried on through. Peter was strong enough to shove the doors closed behind them. They kept running. The gunfire was muffled by the doors. Carys opened her eyes again – and saw the huge misshapen shadow of the wolf on the wall beside her as she ran. The wolf dragging her to safety. The wolf that had been Sebastian Forrest.

They raced along corridors, dashing between the pools of light that cast grotesque, blurred shadows across the walls. Clambering over piles of rubble. Squeezing through gaps where the walls had collapsed. Slowly, away from the effects of the crystal, Forrest was returning to his normal self. His shirt had been shredded when he changed, his jacket was split across the back and his trousers ripped. The ends of his shoes were torn open where sharp nails had erupted.

Carys lost track of where they went. They just ran, dodging back and forth down passages and corridors. Some were well lit, others almost completely dark. Finally they slumped against a wall, breathing heavily. All three of them strained to hear the sounds of pursuit. But there was nothing.

"You think we're safe?" Peter gasped.

"Not for long," Forrest replied, his voice still a guttural growl. "But let's deal with you while we have a moment."

Peter backed away as Forrest reached out. He grabbed Peter, dragging him close, pulling off his jacket and ripping open his shirt at the shoulder.

"You'll have to do it," he told Carys. "Obviously I can't."

"Do what?" Peter demanded. "What's going on?" His teeth were chattering as he tried to speak.

But Carys knew what Forrest meant. She gripped Peter's upper arm. A bruise was appearing round the swollen puncture mark where Irena had injected him. She squeezed either side, and clear liquid wept out.

Peter winced with the pain, but she kept squeezing, forcing out as much of the poison as she could and wiping it away with her sleeve. Finally, when nothing more was coming out, she took a deep breath, and clamped her mouth round the wound. His skin was smooth and burning hot. The taste of the poison was bitter and sharp.

She spat it onto the floor, rubbing at her mouth with the back of her hand.

"Thanks," Peter said quietly.

"That is so gross. You ever get wolfified again and you're on your own."

He nodded weakly. "Deal."

"Now that's done," Forrest said, "we have to get away from here. There's a small airfield about three miles away. We just need to follow the road. If we can get there, I have a plane waiting. If..." He hesitated, looking back down the passageway where they were hiding.

"What?" Peter prompted.

"If I can't be with you, then tell the pilot I sent you."

"Will he believe us?" Carys asked.

Forrest smiled grimly. "We all look a state. He'll believe you."

Forrest was right, if Carys looked anything like Peter, then they were both obviously exhausted. Their clothes were torn and stained, covered in grime and dust from the excavated rubble.

"Let's hope Einzel and his friends are more worried about their precious Crystal Room than finding us," Forrest said. He led the way back down the passage. "It looks lighter this way."

"I guess the more lights, the closer we are to heart of things," Peter said. "And to the way out."

Carys was relieved he seemed to be recovering. And it was a good point – he wasn't daft. In fact, without Peter she'd be dead by now. Several times over.

"What happened to the Crystal Room?" Carys asked. "You knew it was gone, didn't you?"

Forrest nodded. "My father came back after the war. He wanted to make sure the castle really had been destroyed. But it was clear that the cellars and basements were largely intact. Just buried."

"So he dug them out?" Peter asked.

"He dug out the Crystal Room," Forrest said. "Made sure it couldn't be excavated – as you saw. Then he had the site covered over again. He hoped no one would ever find this place."

"What did he do with the crystal?" Peter wondered.

"Smashed it to bits, probably," Carys said. "But he reckoned without Einzel."

"We all reckoned without Einzel," Forrest told her.

From then on, they spoke rarely, and in whispers. Occasionally they heard voices. Once they ducked into the shadows behind a pile of rubble as a wolf-guard hurried past them. It paused, sniffing the air, before moving on, oblivious to Carys and the others crouching so close. All the time, Carys was terrified that they would be found – then brought before Einzel and ripped to pieces by the wolves.

But somehow they made it back to the passageway.

A huge uniformed wolf stood guard at the opening. Carys could hear its throaty breathing.

"Stay back," Forrest whispered.

They pressed further into the shadows. Forrest reached down for a chunk of stone, and hurled it – not at the wolf, but off down a side passage.

The wolf turned at once, unshouldering its gun. With an angry snarl, it set off to investigate. Forrest, Carys and Peter made it to the passageway before the wolf returned, hiding in shadows as it glared into the gloom.

Carys almost laughed with relief as they neared the end of the passage and she felt the breeze on her face. Peter was pale and close to exhaustion, but he was relieved too. He leaned on Forrest for support.

"Head for the road," Forrest said. "Any trouble, and I'll deal with it."

Carys wasn't about to argue. They made their way uphill and through the woods. Before long they were back at the ruins of the castle. The mirrors were all set in position, and there was no sign of anyone. The dimmed lights stood as stark, black silhouettes against the grey sky.

"We can cut through the ruins," Forrest said. "The road's on the other side." He fixed first Peter then Carys with his steel grey eyes. "We're going to be all right."

"Course we are," Carys told him.

"Can we get moving?" Peter said. He was shivering again, and looked in a bad way.

They were halfway across the ruins when the lights came on. Beams stabbed through the darkness, reflecting off the mirrors in a criss-cross of brilliance that met on the far edge of the ruins of Schloss Wolfenburg. Out of the light came a figure, walking slowly towards them – a man.

As he approached through the light beams, his form changed. His back hunched, hair sprouted from his body, his jaw elongated. Claws broke from the ends of his hands and feet and his whole posture changed. His cruel smile became the snarling rage of the wolf.

Carys glanced at Forrest. The man was transfixed by the sight of the approaching wolf – by the sight of his son.

And he too was changing. Caught full in the glare of the lights, Sebastian Forrest was once more transforming into the wolf.

Peter was breathing heavily, his head down and shoulders hunched. As he looked up at Carys, his eyes were blood red. He gave a snarl of pain.

"Oh no!" She grabbed Peter, pushing him out of the light.

Together they stumbled across the ruins. Peter was still breathing heavily, but his eyes were not so red – had she caught him in time? Had she halted the transformation? She thought she'd got all the poison out, but there must have been some – a tiny amount – already in his bloodstream.

She hoped it wasn't enough to trigger a transformation. Hoped his body was fighting against it, and would win. But if he didn't have time to deal with the infection, then the lights could condemn Peter to a life like her grandfather's. She wouldn't wish that on anyone, and especially not...

"Father!" The sound was a roar of both satisfaction and anger.

"You don't have to do this," Sebastian answered, the wolf transformation almost complete. "It doesn't have to be this way."

"Oh yes it does. It was always going to end like this."

The wolf that was David Forrest hurled itself at its father. Claws split the air. The artificial moonlight was torn by the howls and snarls of the two animals. One attacked, the other tried only to defend itself – unwilling to fight back.

"They'll kill each other," Peter said between chattering teeth.

The two wolves were locked together, rolling across the broken ground, snarling and roaring at each other. It was horrifying and gruesome. The larger was already a bloodied mess. It turned its head to stare across at Carys and Peter. For a moment, all was still. The large, sad, bloodshot eyes bored into them.

Then a massive paw slashed across its face, knocking the creature's head to one side and spraying red across the nearest lamp.

Peter was sagging. Carys pulled his arm round her shoulders, supporting his weight as best she could. She struggled to drag him away from the fight – how far to the road? And how many miles to the airfield? A single glance back told her Forrest would not be making the flight.

"Come on," she told Peter, feeling his weight increase as his legs buckled. "Stay with me – don't give up now. *Please.*" She blinked back the tears as she dragged him away.

Behind them, the two animals fought on in the crimson-stained moonlight.

CHAPTER 27

It was all a blurred nightmare to Peter. How Carys got him to the airfield, he had no idea. He remembered the hard gravel of the road under his feet. He had fallen, pulled himself upright, leaned on Carys, and somehow reached the small plane.

He remembered Carys shouting at the pilot. "He's not coming – can't you understand that? The man is *dead*!"

Peter tried to say something, tried to tell the pilot that Carys was right. Forrest was as good as dead when they left – his son was ripping him to pieces. They heard the howls of triumph and roars of pain as they stumbled down the road. Then the awful silence.

Lights across the airfield – headlights coming straight for them.

"That could be him now," the pilot said. "We wait for Mr Forrest."

Bullets rattled against the outer skin of the plane. Peter remembered the exact tone the pilot used when he swore, but not what he said.

Carys belted him into a seat. The pilot worked frantically at the controls, and suddenly the plane was moving. Slowly at first, then picking up speed. More shots hammered into the fuselage. The window next to Peter crazed like a cobweb.

Then the plane pitched backwards, and the rumble of the tyres across the runway became the mechanical sound of the undercarriage retracting. The jolting of the ground became the turbulence of the air. The headlights were pinpricks of light far below, fading into darkness as Peter faded into sleep.

He woke strapped in to the seat on the plane, and smiled at Carys. She smiled back – then her expression froze and blurred again as he fell back into the pit of oblivion.

When he woke again, he was in a car.

The time after that, in bed.

"Back with us, then? How are you feeling?"

Peter struggled to sit up. "Dad? I had the strangest dream."

"Really?" Dad was sitting on a chair beside the bed. He smiled, but it was a smile of relief as much as amusement. "You think?"

"Yes, I..." Peter's voice trailed off as he saw he was in his room at the Red Fleece. "Or, maybe..."

"More of a nightmare, from what Carys says. I'll tell her you're awake."

"Is she all right?"

"Faye only sent her off to get some sleep a couple of hours ago. She's been sitting here for the last couple of days. So if I don't tell her you're awake, she'll have seven kinds of fit."

"Sorry, Dad. I know you were worried."

"Just a bit. Well, quite a lot actually. At least you called."

"I should have told you what we were doing. Did you understand about the sword? Do you have it?"

Professor Crichton smiled and nodded. "Had to dig it out of a crate of your grandfather's old junk in the attic. It's polished up nicely, I have to say. I put it in the bookcase in the restaurant, with the other research."

"You brought it here? Can I see it?"

"Later. When you're feeling better."

"I want to see it," Peter said. He was surprised how sharply the words came out.

Dad seemed taken aback too. He paused in the doorway. "When you're feeling better, I'll show you the sword. Or what's left of it. I promise. I always wondered why your grandfather was so fascinated by it. I guess now I know. He never spoke much about the war or what he did. To be fair, I didn't really ask."

"You gave me a fright," Carys told Peter a few minutes later. She looked tired, but otherwise all right.

"We've both had enough frights to last a lifetime."

"True enough. But it was worth it."

"Was it? I'm not sure what we achieved."

"Apart from you getting ill, we did loads. We know what Einzel is trying to do. And we know Forrest was trying to stop him. And with the Crystal Room gone, and his laboratories burned down, his plans must be on hold if not completely scuppered."

"Let's hope so."

"I doubt he'll bother with Wolfstone any more now Forrest is out of the picture. How are you feeling?"

"I'm fine," Peter told her. But he could feel himself slipping back into sleep.

"It'll take a while for your body to recover. Just stay in bed till you're sorted, okay?"

"Okay," he breathed. His eyes closed and he imagined he could feel Carys's lips brush against his cheek as she whispered. "Sleep well."

But maybe he was dreaming again.

He was woken by the sound of a car outside. The room was in darkness. Thin strips of light seeped in at the edges of the curtains. Peter felt hot again, and his pillow was damp with sweat.

He pushed off the covers and padded over to the

window. His pyjamas seemed hot and clammy, sticking to his body like a second skin. His vision was blurred, out of focus.

"Did you bring it?"

The voice sounded clear. It was coming from outside. He reached between the curtains and pushed open the window. It was Carys.

The reply was also clear – a woman. He knew the voice but couldn't place it.

"It's here. With my laptop."

"Let's hope we don't need it."

Peter drew back the curtains. There was a Land Rover parked outside. Carys and the woman were standing beside it. He recognised her; it was Janey from the Lupine Sanctuary. They walked towards the pub, disappearing under his window. A few moments later, Peter heard the main door close.

He was feeling better, standing in the cool draft from the open window. The near-perfect disc of the moon seemed huge, lighting up the whole bedroom. He stared up at it, trying to make sense of the patterns across its glowing surface.

The glow reminded Peter of the crystal inside David Forrest's ring. That in turn made him think of the sword. He felt a sudden urge to see it – to see it now. He was thirsty too, so he could get a drink from the kitchen at the same time.

Before he knew it, Peter was closing his bedroom door gently behind him and making his way slowly and carefully towards the stairs. He wondered what time it was. Carys was obviously up, but he didn't want to wake anyone else.

The only illumination came from moonlight filtering through occasional windows. Peter stopped, listening. He thought he'd heard something – maybe an echo of his own footsteps, like the click of claws on the bare wood floor.

There was something else. A soft susurrating sound. He held his breath... No, nothing – just his imagination. He continued along the corridor – and there it was again. Like a purring, or a low growl.

There was something behind him, in the shadows. Peter quickened his pace. He glanced back over his shoulder.

A shadow on the wall. It was almost level with him – a patch of darkness in the shape of a wolf. He quickened his pace, and it followed, always at the edge of his vision. At any moment he knew it could leap out at him. But where was it?

Down the stairs. The creature was so close he could hear its steady, rasping breathing. Its shadow cut suddenly across the floor in front of him as he reached the bottom of the stairs. Enormous, hirsute, poised to strike.

He ran. The sound of the creature's paws smacking into the floorboards was so close now. The scrape of its claws on wood. Its growls of anger as it gained on him.

He caught a glimpse of the thing itself in the glass panel of a door as he raced past. Dark, with fierce red eyes staring back at him. Claws pummelling the air in front of it, inches from Peter.

He saw it again in the glass panels of the door to the restaurant. So close it must catch him at any moment. He couldn't outrun it. He had no way of fighting it.

Unless – the sword! He crashed through the restaurant door. The room was bathed in moonlight shining through the windows. The bookcase was ahead of him. But he'd never make it.

He dived to one side, expecting – hoping – the wolf would go past him. But it must have guessed what he was planning. It was in the room somewhere. He could still hear it. He crawled towards the glass-fronted bookcase at the far end of the room.

In the glass of the windows, he saw the creature working its way slowly along, towards the same end of the room. It moved cautiously on all fours, muscles rippling under the heavy fur, looking round all the time. Hunting.

He looked straight at it, facing his fear. And at the exact same moment, the wolf looked back at Peter.

No way could he reach the bookcase now it had seen him. He'd been stupid to think he could. Instead he leaped to his feet and raced for the door. He tried to shout for help, but all that came out was a howl of fear.

The wolf was running alongside him. Keeping pace. Between Peter and the window, red eyes staring malevolently, hungrily back at him as he ran.

A shape in the doorway. A figure.

He tried to shout a warning, but he hadn't the breath.

Carys stepped into the room. She was holding a gun. Raising it. Aiming.

But not at the wolf. She was aiming it right at Peter. He skidded to a halt, shaking his head. Shouting at her that it was *him*. Shoot the wolf instead. But his voice was drowned out by the roar of the creature.

The sound of the shot was like an explosion in the back of Peter's brain. He felt the savage sting of pain in his shoulder and fell backwards.

Reflected in the window, the wolf mirrored his movements.

And the moment the world went black, Peter realised that he had not seen the creature at all. He'd seen only shadows and reflections. Shadows and reflections of *himself*.

* * *

Carys lowered the gun. It slipped from her numbed fingers and fell to the floor.

"I'm sorry," she murmured, her whole body shaking with emotion. "I'm so sorry."

She sank to her knees beside the body of the creature she had shot. Carys hugged Peter's body to her, rocking slowly back and forth as she wept.

CHAPTER 28

Burning silver. It cut into Peter's wrists and ankles where he was shackled to the wall. The chains rattled and clanked as he fought to be free of them. But it was no use.

"Grandfather tried for decades to escape from those, and he never succeeded."

His head was pounding. His vision blurred. He felt like he had the most almighty hangover.

"Carys?"

The word came out as a roar of pain and anguish.

Then he felt something soothing. Cold and wet, close to his shoulder. His upper arm burned almost as much as the where the silver manacles touched his skin.

"Don't get your hopes up." Another voice – Faye Seymour, close to Peter. She was bathing the top of his arm. "We may be too late, but I think he's responding."

His vision slowly cleared. The stark, bare light of the cellar was blinding but gradually he was able to see. His head sagged forwards on his chest and he looked down at the stone floor. Down along his own body.

And he screamed.

A howl of anger and fear.

"What's happened to me?" he gasped. The words were barely recognisable.

"The injection that woman Irena gave you," Carys said. She was standing close in front of him, her face streaked with tears. "I thought we'd got the poison out. There must be some still in there, and then when the moonlight..." She turned away, the words choked off.

Peter stared at her, willing her to turn back, to let him see her face. Even if she couldn't bear to look at his.

"This wolf's blight poultice should draw the poison out," Carys's mother said. "If we're not too late. The moon isn't really full until tomorrow night. There's a chance, if you weren't changed for too long and there isn't much poison in your system..."

Another figure stepped into his field of vision. "We won't give up on you," Peter's dad said. "Just stay with us. We'll get through this."

He felt his father take his hand – and Dad's own hand seemed so small and weak.

The pub was closed. Faye had put up signs outside the car park and let the regulars know that she was taking time out to get her father-in-law settled in the care home.

So the only people sitting round one of the tables in the bar were Abby, Mike and Janey from the Lupine Sanctuary.

Carys brought them coffee.

"Mum's making breakfast," she said as she put the tray of mugs down. "She says it's best to keep busy." She'd also told Carys to leave Peter and his father alone. It wouldn't help, she'd said, having Carys moping about down there with them and getting in the way.

"I can't believe this is happening," Mike said.

"Which bit of it?" Abby asked.

"Any of it. The whole thing's bizarre."

Janey thanked Carys for the coffee. "How is he? I mean…" She shrugged. "I don't know what I mean, actually."

"Mum gave him a drink made from infused wolf's blight. It looks like he's over the worst of it."

"Wolf's blight tea?" Mike made a face. "How's Matthew bearing up?"

"His son's a werewolf," Abby said. "How do you think he's bearing up?"

Janey shook her head in disbelief. "I just don't understand what's happening here. I mean, I work with wolves – but this is something else."

"It's a good job you were here," Abby said.

"Carys called me."

"I was worried about Peter," she explained. "I mean, I thought – I *hoped* – he was all right. But it seemed sensible to ask Janey to bring a tranquiliser gun. Just in case."

"I nearly didn't. I wasn't convinced by your story about seeing a wolf. I checked and were none missing from the sanctuary."

"How can you be sure?" Mike asked.

"They're microchipped. I've got an app link to the GPS system which shows where each of our wolves is. I brought my laptop too, to show you and put your mind at rest," she told Carys. "If only it'd been that easy."

"Well, like Abby says – thank God you came." Mike grinned. "Otherwise we'd be fighting poor Peter off with a replica arrow."

"With what?" Carys asked.

"Mike's made a replica of the arrows we found at the circle," Abby said. "He's annoyingly proud of it."

"It's very good," Mike protested. "With a silver head and everything. Well, let's face it – it'd be that or a broken crystal sword."

"A what?" Janey said.

"Long story," Carys said quickly. "It's an antique relic that Professor Crichton brought back with him. It's all connected. Somehow."

"Right. Sounds like the tranquiliser gun is your best bet then."

"If we can hang on to it," Carys said. "It looks like Peter's on the mend. Mum thinks he's over the worst and the effect shouldn't be permanent. But if he has some sort of relapse – I mean, it's a full moon tonight."

"No problem." Janey drained her coffee. "God knows what I'll tell Josh – or Eddie, it's his gun after all. He's the vet. Oh – hang on!"

"What?

"I just thought. I didn't bring any spare darts. I didn't think you really needed it. But there's a full box at the sanctuary." She stood up, then sat down again. "I'm so tired. I need to sleep for a week. But I'll get you those darts."

"I'll come with you," Carys said. "I'm only in the way here. I think Mum will be glad to be rid of me."

"Well, I'll be glad of the company," Janey said.

It was later than Carys had realised. She wished she'd waited to grab some breakfast before setting off. But Janey was obviously keen to get home – where she could get some sleep and pretend the events of the previous night never happened.

But Carys couldn't get them out of her head. Couldn't stop blaming herself. She'd got Peter into this, and now... She just hoped and prayed he would be all right.

She stared out of the car window, barely listening to Janey. They passed the turning to the Wolfstone Circle, and the entrance to the abandoned housing development. The diggers and earth-movers were stark silhouettes against the grey morning sky. With Forrest dead, Carys thought, they'd probably never be used now.

On the other side of the road, they drove past the overgrown drive that led to Wolfstone Manor. The house itself was just out of sight, over the brow of the hill. But Carys thought she caught a glimpse of another car disappearing down the driveway.

"There have been a few cars down there the last couple of days," Janey said, glancing out of the window to follow Carys's gaze. "Maybe they're finally starting to renovate the old place."

"Maybe," Carys said. She doubted it.

They pulled up next to a mud-spattered Audi outside the sanctuary.

"Looks like Josh is here," Janey said. "I'll tell him I'm bunking off for the day. He won't mind – I've covered for him often enough."

Carys waited outside while Janey went to find the box of darts. She wondered what, if anything, she'd tell her boss. The wolves were pacing up and down in their enclosures, as if they sensed a tension in the air. From somewhere came a muffled howl that sent a shiver down Carys's spine.

The main doors opened at last. But it was Josh not Janey who emerged from the centre. He caught sight of Carys and frowned. She gave a wave, and he waved back.

Josh was younger than Janey, maybe in his early thirties and dressed for "management" rather than looking after animals. His dark hair was receding, but he tried to hide that by combing it forward.

"Janey didn't tell me you were here," Josh said. He had his hands stuffed into his pockets. The mud spattered down the front of his grey suit matched the state of his car.

"I'm not stopping."

He nodded. "Yeah – sounds like you've had quite a night of it."

"Sorry?" What had Janey told him?

"It all sounds incredible. Wolf-men, silver arrows, crystal swords. Must have been quite a party."

He smiled indulgently, and Carys realised that whatever Janey had said, Josh didn't believe a word of it.

"Anyway," he went on, "I've got things to do. Can't hang around here." He turned to head off towards the enclosures.

"Where's Janey?" Carys called after him.

"I think she's making a cup of tea."

That didn't seem likely, but it might be what Janey had told Josh. Fed up with waiting, Carys headed into the building.

The lights were off and it was gloomy inside. Muddy footprints trailed across the floor to the door. Carys wiped her hands together – there was mud on the door handle too.

"Janey?"

No answer.

She called again, louder. "Janey – where are you? Do you need a hand?"

Still no answer. Outside the wolves were getting excited, calling to each other. She saw several of them run past the window. Instinctively, she felt for the light switch, and the hallway was bathed in stark white light.

The dark mess on the floor wasn't mud. It was bright red.

Carys took a startled step backwards, hands to her face.

Red hands. From the bloodied door handle.

She stifled a scream. "Janey?"

Somehow, she forced herself to walk through the centre, following the footsteps. There must have been an accident. Or maybe something had been spilled. Something red. Something that definitely wasn't blood and didn't make the air taste stale and metallic.

Janey was in the staff room. She was leaning back in one of the easy chairs.

"Oh thank God!" Carys hurried over to her. "I thought–"

Her voice caught, becoming a shuddering cry of horror. The woman's throat had been ripped away. Blood ran stickily down the remains of her neck and dripped into the growing pool on the floor.

CHAPTER 29

Carys edged backwards, away from the bloodied mess that was all that remained of Janey Donovan. Her foot caught on something and she cried out, spinning round. She slipped on the slick red floor, and almost fell. She'd knocked into a plastic box. Inside Carys saw small tranquiliser darts, their ends enclosed in clear covers. She grabbed it, trying to ignore the red spatter across the lid.

What now? She had to get away. But who could have done this? The wolves? They were in their enclosures outside. Except…

Except she'd seen several run past the window. And there were no enclosures on that side of the centre.

She looked round, hardly daring to breath. Whatever had been here was gone now. Leaving just a bloody trail to the main doors.

The main doors – where Josh had come from. Josh, with his hands in his pockets and mud down his suit.

Janey's keys were lying on the table beside her. Like she'd put them down while talking to someone – someone she hadn't expected to rip the life out of her moments later.

Carys snatched up the keys, and ran.

Not towards the main doors, but out to the back. There was a door that came out by the main enclosure. The top half of the door was a single glass panel, and through it she saw that the enclosure was empty. The heavy metal security gate was wide open – the wolves were out.

"Going somewhere?"

Carys spun round, clutching the box of darts to her chest. She didn't care that she was wiping blood down her top. All her attention was on Josh as he walked slowly towards her. His hands were out of his pockets now. He spread them out in front of him, perhaps to show he meant her no harm. Or perhaps to show her how stained with death they were.

"I only ask," he said, "because there's nowhere to go. Except to hell."

Or maybe he had his hands out like that to show her the ring he was wearing. Slowly, Josh flipped open the top of the ring, and the moonlight trapped in the sliver of crystal inside spilled out.

"Doesn't do to keep it open too long." His voice was already changing, deepening, becoming an inarticulate growl.

"Afraid you might use it up?" Carys tried to sound defiant, but even to her own ears she was just a frightened kid.

"Moonlight will never be used up," Josh snarled. "But it can use *you* up, if you don't respect it." He snapped the ring shut – no longer a man in a stained suit, but a wolf in man's clothing. The cuffs of the jacket tore under the strain as he reached out towards Carys. Buttons from his shirt scattered across the floor. Hungry saliva dripped on top of Janey's blood.

Carys turned and ran. He'd said there was nowhere to go, but he was wrong. She turned sideways, throwing her arms up in front of her face as she leaped. One hand gripped the box of darts, the other had Janie's keys held tight. Her shoulder crashed into the glass at the top of the door. It exploded outwards.

She tumbled through, catching her leg, hitting the ground hard. It knocked the breath out of her, but Carys didn't stop. She rolled to her feet and ran.

At any moment she expected a wolf to come at her. But no one and nothing seemed to be behind her. Why wasn't Josh following?

No time to worry about that. Carys sprinted along the side of the building, heading back round to the car park. She glanced through the window as she ran – and saw the upright wolf that was Josh running alongside her. Even though he was inside the building. He knew where she was heading, and he was taking the shortest route to Janey's car.

Lungs bursting, Carys forced herself to go even faster. She fumbled with the keys. The car was unlocked, but she had to get inside it.

There was an explosion of sound from behind her. A roar of anger and triumph as Josh crashed out of the main doors. Carys was ahead of him – just. She ripped open the driver's door and threw herself inside, pulling the door shut behind her.

There was a yelp of pain as the door closed on a massive hairy paw. Carys kept pulling, but the paw was trapped, so the door couldn't close. Instead, she opened the door, then slammed it as hard as she could.

She heard the crunch of breaking bones above the scream of pain. Opened the door again – just enough to let Josh instinctively pull out his injured paw before she slammed it shut properly and hit the central locking. She jammed the key into the ignition.

The windscreen crazed as the full weight of the creature smashed into it.

The engine roared into life as the creature roared at its fractured view of Carys. She reversed quickly, Josh rolling off the bonnet of the car. Then slammed the gears into first. Gravel spun out from the wheels as they got a grip.

The car shot forward – right into the Josh creature. The front bumper crunched into him, sending him flying.

Carys kept driving and hit him again as he rolled across the ground. This time, he didn't get up.

Carys reversed away, spinning the car round in the small car park before driving out and back onto the lane beyond. Across the fields, she could see dark shapes bounding across the grass, heading for the woods close to the manor.

Peter was sprawled out on a bench seat in the bar. His head was pounding and he was tired as hell. But the fever seemed to have abated and he was definitely feeling better. A poultice of wolf's blight and other herbs and remedies was strapped to his arm with surgical tape under his shirt. He could feel a gentle tugging sensation as though it was still drawing out the poison. The feeling was like a splinter gripped between tweezers.

"How are you feeling?" Dad asked for about the sixtieth time in the last hour.

Peter just nodded. He didn't have time to tell him that he was fine, because the door of the bar slammed open and Carys ran in.

"The wolves..." she gasped. "The wolves are running..."

A few minutes later, hands gripped tight round a mug of strong tea, Carys finished her story. They sat in silence, numbed with disbelief.

"Poor Janey," Abby murmured.

"It's my fault," Carys blurted. "I got her into this. I got her *killed*."

Her mother put an arm round her shoulders. "It isn't your fault. Don't you believe that for one moment. None of it is your fault. Janey was already caught up in all this, even if she didn't know it herself."

"But – she…"

"We can't help her now," Mike said gently.

"So where are the wolves going?" Professor Crichton asked. "To the manor?"

"And why?" Abby asked. "Why let the wolves out at all?"

"They must be needed for something," Mike said. "This Josh gave them a job to do."

"But why now?" Abby insisted.

Peter had struggled upright. He hauled himself to his feet and went over to join them.

"Hey," Carys said, smiling weakly.

"Hey." He managed to smile back. "You said Janey told Josh what happened last night. What she said must have scared him into action."

"Whatever happened, we need to know where the wolves are," Crichton said.

"Janey would know," Peter said.

Carys stared at him. "Of course she would."

"I'm sorry, I just meant…"

"No, no – you're right."

"But Janey's…" He couldn't bring himself to say it. He still couldn't believe it. Despite everything else he'd seen, Janey had seemed so *ordinary*. "We should tell someone. Call the police."

"Like they'd believe us," Mike said. He stuck a cigarette in his mouth and took out his lighter. "What?" he said round the cigarette as he caught Abby's expression. He sighed, and stuffed the lighter and cigarette back in his pocket.

"They'd probably arrest Carys just for being there," Crichton said.

Carys had taken out a bunch of keys. "Janey's laptop's still in the car."

There was a password on Janey's computer. But it was written on a Post-it note stuck inside the laptop bag.

"JANEY123," Peter said, typing it in. "Nothing like being obvious."

"We're lucky she wrote it down though," Dad said. "It's only obvious when you know."

"Can you find the software that maps where the wolves are?" Mike asked.

"This could be it..."

They all gathered round, staring at the small screen as a map appeared.

"Well, it knows where *we* are," Abby said. "There's the circle, look. And the main road through the village. The church."

Peter checked through the various menus. "This must be how you do it." He clicked on a choice that said, "Locate Targets".

"That's no good, it wants code numbers," Mike said. "We don't know them."

"Doesn't matter," Carys said. She pointed to a button further down the window. "Click on "Locate All"."

As soon as Peter clicked, a pattern of red blobs appeared on the map. They were moving slowly, in a pack – about ten of them. All heading the same way.

"So where's that?" Faye Seymour asked. "If this is the church..."

"And there's the crossroads," Carys said, reaching across to point again.

"Then they have to be about..." Peter's hand froze on the laptop's trackpad. "Oh my God. They're here." He looked up at the others" faces and saw his own fear reflected in them. "The wolves are coming *here*. They're right outside."

CHAPTER 30

"Lock the doors and windows," Faye ordered.

Her words were drowned out by the crash of breaking glass.

"Too late," Mike said. "They're in already."

"But where?" asked Abby. "Can you tell?"

Peter shook his head. "I don't know how accurate this software tracking is. It just gives a general area."

Professor Crichton slammed the main bar door shut. "No lock?"

"No," Faye told him, hurrying to close the door on the other side of the bar.

"But wolves can't do door handles," Abby said.

"Don't bet on it," Carys told her.

"Can't hear anything now," Mike said.

They all listened, but there was nothing.

"At least we have these," Peter said, pointing to the plastic box of tranquiliser darts on the table beside the laptop.

Listening by the door, Carys swore.

Her mother gave her an admonishing stare.

"The gun," Carys said. "I left it down in the cellar

when... When we were sorting out Peter."

"We need that gun," Crichton said.

"So we need to get down to the cellar," Faye agreed.

"We need to get to the restaurant too," Peter said.

"Why?" Abby asked.

But Carys had realised. "Of course – the crystal sword. Janey told Josh it was here. That's why he sent the wolves. They're after the sword."

"David Forrest was after it too," Peter said. "And I felt..." It was difficult to put into words – he didn't know quite what he had felt. "I was sort of drawn to it, last night..."

"Einzel needs that sword," Carys agreed. "So we have to stop him getting it."

There was only one door into the restaurant, and it was right outside the main door to the bar.

"So long as they're not waiting outside, or waiting in there," Mike said.

"Oh you're a bundle of laughs," Abby snapped.

"I was just saying."

"Well, don't talk about it – do it!"

Crichton was standing by the main door. He edged it open and peered out cautiously into the passageway outside.

"Looks all right," he said quietly.

"We should take it easy," Mike said.

"Oh come on." Carys strode across the room. "I'll go."

"Carys," her mother warned.

"It's right there – I can see the door."

"Just… be careful."

"I'll go with her," Crichton said. "Be ready to close the door if you see anything."

Peter wanted to help, he wanted to go too, but his dad raised his hand to stop him. He didn't need to say anything – Peter knew better than to argue right now.

Carys slipped out of the room and ran to the restaurant door, with Crichton close behind.

She felt such an idiot. They might all die, and it would be her fault. Why had she left the tranquiliser gun down in the cellar? She should have taken it to the sanctuary with Janey. Maybe she could have stopped Josh – saved Janey.

No, that was stupid. She had to stop thinking like that. Focus on the present. The past was done and she couldn't change it.

Carys stood by the restaurant door, torn between watching the passageway outside and seeing what Professor Crichton was doing.

"All clear so far," she whispered.

Crichton walked slowly and warily towards the glass-fronted bookcase at the end of the room. He glanced back over his shoulder and smiled at Carys to show he'd heard her. Not far now, and still nothing. Just the faint sound of the wind rippling the curtain that hung beside the windows. Carys could feel the breeze on her face.

Then the crunch of something breaking.

She held her breath. Crichton froze. Looked down.

"It's okay," he said quietly. "That was me treading on the broken glass."

Carys breathed again.

Crichton was at the bookcase. He reached up to open the glass door.

Broken glass… But – the bookcase door wasn't broken. Where had the glass come from? Carys looked round quickly. The only movement was Crichton on the other side of the room, and the gentle undulation of the curtain by the open window.

Except, the window wasn't open.

Carys remembered the sound of glass breaking. Broken glass under foot. Suddenly a dark shape was moving across the room. She yelled a warning. But it was too late.

The wolf was already in the air – hurling itself at Professor Crichton. He turned, his face etched with fear. Hand pulling back swiftly from the open door of the bookcase. The howl of pain drove into Carys's consciousness, numbing her. She could only stare in horror as the wolf seemed to twist in mid-air, right in front of Crichton, then fall to the floor, slumped in a bloody mess.

He had to put his foot on the animal's back to get enough purchase to pull out the sword. The crystal of the broken blade was stained and dripping.

Carys was still standing staring in horror when he ran to her.

"Come on. That won't be the only one."

He was right. Once through the door she heard the growl of the approaching wolves. Two of them slowly stalked down the passage. Their shoulders rose and fell as they padded forward. As soon as they saw Carys and Crichton, their heads dropped slightly and they charged.

Crichton pushed Carys in front of him into the bar. He turned to face the wolves, brandishing the broken sword. The wolves slowed, moving more cautiously. Perhaps they scented the blood of their fellow. It gave Crichton enough time to step back into the room.

As soon as he was inside, Peter slammed the door shut. A moment later, the wood shook as the animals butted into it. Again and again they hurled themselves at the door. It creaked and groaned under the attack.

Mike and Abby dragged the nearest table across. Carys and Peter ran to help, stacking tables and chairs against the door.

"Block the other door too," Crichton warned.

"And then what?" Faye demanded.

"Then we leave by the window," Mike said. "While they're busy trying to break the doors down."

"Good plan," Abby agreed.

Mike grinned nervously. But the next moment, a dark shape slammed against the main window. Several of the small panes shattered under the impact. Fur pressed hard against the others. A hungry snout slavered a sticky trail across the glass. Further along, another wolf leaped up, forepaws on the outside sill as it stared hungrily into the bar through rheumy eyes.

CHAPTER 31

"Maybe not the window," Mike decided. He grabbed the replica silver-tipped arrow.

"Like that's going to help," Abby told him.

"We've got the sword too," Peter pointed out.

"It won't be enough," Carys said. "We have to stop them getting in."

"Or we have to get out," Faye told her. She ran behind the bar, pushing crates of empty bottles aside.

There was hammering at both doors now. The lower panel of one disintegrated in a shower of splinters. A paw reached through, pushing at the piled-up furniture, testing the barricade.

"There *is* no way out," Abby said.

"This is my pub," Faye told her. "If I say there's a way out, then you'd better believe it."

"We *want* to believe it," Mike said. "But where?"

"Just come and help me clear this lot."

"We're going to fight them off with broken bottles?" Peter asked.

"No," Faye said with exaggerated patience. "We're going to move them, rip up the carpet underneath, and get out through the old trapdoor down to the cellar."

Carys ran to help. Behind her, the barricade collapsed. Chairs and tables spilled to the floor. Through the debris, the nose of a wolf emerged as it forced its way through the gaps in the toppled furniture.

Mike and Abby were ripping up the carpet. Faye bundled bottles and glasses over the bar to Peter who put them out of the way on the other side. He paused to throw a beer glass at the emerging wolf. It shattered nearby, and the wolf withdrew rapidly, its snout showered in broken glass. Peter grinned, and Carys was amazed at how calm he seemed – how well he had recovered.

Professor Crichton also seemed calm. He stood beside the bar, between everyone else and the shifting barricades, sword held ready.

"I had fencing lessons once," he told Carys.

"Were you any good?"

"Not really. Gave up after the third one."

The other barricade was looking precarious now. Another pane shattered in the window.

Mike heaved at the trapdoor. "It won't move!"

"Maybe it's locked," Abby suggested. "Do we need a key?"

"A key? You're joking!"

"It should just open," Faye said. "We used to stock the

bar straight from the cellar."

"Recently?" Mike asked as he struggled with the trapdoor, heaving on the metal ring that served as a handle.

"Twenty years ago maybe."

"Together," Abby said.

She reached round Mike to help him. They both heaved on the handle.

"This is cosy," Mike said as he strained.

"No it isn't," Abby told him.

Carys pushed past her mother. "I'll try to lever it up at the same time."

She grabbed the knife they used to cut slices of lemon, and jammed it into the narrow gap between the trapdoor and the surrounding floor. She couldn't get much leverage, but if she could work out where the wood was jammed…

The window exploded inwards. A mass of matted fur landed in the middle of the room. The huge wolf righted itself, snarling as Peter threw a glass at it. Professor Crichton stepped forward, sword raised.

At the same moment, two more wolves finally forced their way out from the fallen barricade by the main door.

The trapdoor shot upwards, knocking Carys off her feet. Abby and Mike collapsed backwards into the bar. Bottles and glasses crashed to the floor. Carys peered down into the dark pit that had opened up. There was no ladder, just a long drop into the cellar below.

"Go, go, go!" Crichton yelled. "We're right behind you."

The wolf that had come through the window leaped at the bar.

Carys caught a confused glimpse of Peter wielding a wine bottle like a club. She heard it shatter across the wolf's head. The snarl of anger. A shriek from Abby. But Carys was already dropping into the darkness.

She seemed to fall for ever. She bent her legs as she landed, but the impact jarred all the way up her body. The only light came from the trapdoor above, and that was blocked by the shapes of Faye and Abby as they hung on from the lip of the opening, struggling to descend.

Carys caught hold of her mum's legs, helping her down. "I've got you!"

Abby dropped beside them grunting with pain as she landed.

"Put the lights on."

"Yes, Mum." Like she hadn't thought of that. She scrabbled for the light switch.

Abby and Faye helped the others down. Mike first, then Peter and finally his father. Professor Crichton pulled down the trapdoor behind him. He jumped, letting the door fall.

But it didn't close. Something jammed in the way. The wolf howled as the heavy door slammed onto its back.

Its front paws scrabbled through the opening as slowly but surely it dragged itself through.

Crichton was sprawled on the floor, the wolf right above him. It inched its way forward, claws out, jaws snapping. Carys grabbed the tranquiliser gun from a shelf above the beer barrels. She spun round, bringing the gun up and – nothing.

It wasn't loaded.

"The darts!" she realised.

"Here – catch!"

Peter flung the plastic box across the cellar. Carys caught it in one hand, almost dropped it, managed to hold on. She put the gun down on a metal barrel as she prised open the box and took out one of the darts with trembling fingers. It seemed to take for ever to open the gun. She struggled to push the dart into place.

The wolf was through. The trapdoor clattered shut behind it as the animal fell towards Professor Crichton. He brought the sword up, but too late to connect with the wolf.

Carys snapped the gun closed, raised it and fired in one movement.

No effect.

The wolf landed across Crichton's chest. For a moment there was silence. Then a sound like a contented sigh.

Carys realised with relief that it was a snore.

"Someone get this thing off me," Crichton said, trying to heave it aside.

Carys reloaded the gun – why did it seem so much easier now everything wasn't so urgent?

"You're pretty good with that," Peter said.

"Just luck. Point and shoot."

"Let's hope our luck holds a bit longer," Faye said. "Till we're out of here at least."

They crept up the stairs. Carys and Faye listened at the door while everyone else waited behind them. They couldn't hear anything, so Faye carefully pulled the door open.

At once, a huge mass of matted fur exploded through the opening. Carys fired. But the shot went wide, the dart embedding itself in the doorframe. The wolf was coming right at her – how could she miss at such close range? She was near enough to smell its breath and see the veins in its eyes. She hammered the gun into the brute's face, and it fell away, sliding off the side of the staircase and crashing onto the stone floor below.

Professor Crichton, at the back of the group, turned at once, brandishing the broken crystal sword. The animal backed away, head down, watching warily.

As soon as they were all out, Peter closed the door. Even before it was shut they could hear scrabbling on the stairs.

Then the scraping of claws down the other side.

"Come on!" Mike whispered. "I've had enough fun for one day."

"It's not over yet," Carys told him.

The passageway was clear, and there was no sign or sound of the wolves in the car park outside.

"Now can we call the police?" Abby asked.

"And tell them what?" Faye said. "Okay, we could explain the escaped wolves, but everything else?"

"We might need all the help we can get," Peter said. "I may have lost track, but I think today's the twenty-eighth."

"So?" Mike asked.

"So it's the day of the meeting." Carys understood what Peter was getting at. "Remember the remains of that letter we found? And Janey and I saw a car heading for the manor. She said there had been lots of vehicles there. Even though Forrest is dead, Einzel's meeting must be going ahead. And it's happening tonight."

"So we don't know what he's up to, but we know it's tonight?" Abby said.

"And we know we have to stop him," Peter said. "Whatever the cost."

CHAPTER 32

Sitting crammed into Professor Crichton's Range Rover, they were parked between several huge diggers and a bulldozer. The whole area had been skimmed of grass and topsoil. Foundations for several houses were half dug, and there were even some walls and floors. But now the whole place was a vast grey ghost town that Peter knew would probably never be completed. Once again they were discussing going to the police.

"Anything we can tell the police is either meaningless or unbelievable," Faye said. "They won't want to know about werewolves. They'll think we're crazy."

"But what about this Einzel guy and his meeting?" Abby suggested. "We know that's happening."

"So, some people are having a meeting. There's no law against that," Professor Crichton pointed out. "It's not enough."

"We were attacked by the wolves," Mike said.

"Best case is they send someone out to round up the wolves and take them back to the sanctuary."

"And what about Janey?" Carys said. "Josh too – *if* he's dead." She turned away to look out of the car window.

"The wolves escaped," Faye said. "It's easier to believe they killed Janey than a werewolf did."

"But we know Forrest is dead," Mike added.

"In another country. With no body to prove it. And only a couple of teenagers as witnesses," Faye told him.

"The pilot won't say anything either," Carys added. "He probably broke all sorts of regulations bringing us back."

"So we can call the police," Peter said, "but anything we tell them they either won't believe, or it isn't enough to persuade them to do anything."

"Terrific. We're basically on our own," Crichton said. "Let's just accept that and get on with it."

"Get on with what?" Abby asked.

"Getting the hell out of here," Mike muttered.

"That would be the sensible course of action," Crichton agreed. But Peter could tell from his tone that it wasn't what he was going to suggest.

"So what's the plan?" Peter asked.

"In all probability we have until tonight, when the full moon rises."

"That makes sense," Faye agreed. "Whatever they are planning will happen by the light of the full moon."

"We need more information before we can theorise."

Peter smiled – typical Dad, reducing it all to an academic problem. But Mike and Abby were nodding. They could understand that.

"So how do we get more information?" Carys asked.

"We go for a walk. Not far – just to Wolfstone Manor. If we can sneak close enough to see who's there and what they're up to it might give us some clues. If we know what they're planning, maybe – just maybe – we can find a way to stop them."

"Into the lions" den," Mike said.

"If it was only lions we might stand a chance," Abby told him.

In contrast to the general mood, it was a bright, sunny afternoon. A chill breeze ruffled the trees as they made their cautious way through the woodland towards Wolfstone Manor.

The route took them close to the Wolfstone Circle. Peter caught a glimpse of it through the trees, standing silhouetted on the skyline. Several vehicles were parked close by. Figures moved among the stones.

"Hang on," he said. "Maybe the action's not at the manor at all."

They crept closer, right to the edge of the trees. Peter recognised where he had run from the wolves that first night when he saw Einzel arrive in his helicopter. In some ways it seemed like it had only just happened. In others it was a lifetime ago. Several lifetimes.

They crouched down, watching as the figures raised huge lamps into position at the edge of the circle. It was too far away to see if the figures were human or upright wolves.

"That looks like the equipment they had at the castle," Carys said.

"But they'll have a full moon tonight anyway," Peter said. "Why do they need their artificial moonlight as well?"

"On the principle that you can't have too much of a good thing?" Mike suggested.

"To enhance nature itself," Faye murmured. "Possibly."

"But why?" Abby said. "I mean, what's the point of it all?"

"Think about what we know already." Professor Crichton spoke in what Peter called his "lecture voice". He ticked off points on his fingers as he made them. "From what we've learned so far, it seems to me that the Wolfstone Circle – like the Vrolask Circle in Russia – was designed to focus the light, the *energy*, of the moon."

"Well that makes sense," Abby said. "The whole circle is laid out according to a lunar rather than a solar calendar."

Crichton nodded enthusiastically. "Quite right. And we've already likened the unusual parabolic shape of both circles to a lens. That's what Peter and Carys saw with the mirrors at the German castle."

"It ties in with the legend too," Peter said. "The stones

somehow focused the moonlight on the Crystal Room at Vrolask."

"But that can't have been the original intention," Carys pointed out. "The Crystal Room was made much later than the circle. I mean, the circle can't have been built for the same reason."

"So it focused the energy and light somewhere else," Professor Crichton said. He raised his eyebrows to encourage a reply. It was obvious to Peter that his father already had a theory. "The Vrolask Palace and Wolfstone Manor are both much more recent buildings. But we do know what was originally on their sites, don't we?"

"The Rogue Stone," Faye said. "I assume it's the same age as the circle. That's where it would have been focused."

"And the Rogue Stone is still there," Peter said. "Built into the wall of that cellar in the manor."

Crichton jabbed his finger in the air emphatically. "And the circle itself could also be a focus for the energy. Remember the high crystalline content in the structure of the stones is the very same crystal that my sword and the Crystal Room were made from."

Mike frowned. "Are you saying that the circles – here and at Vrolask – worked like the Crystal Room? That they forced werewolves into their wolf form?"

"That's why we found bodies of people running away

from the circle," Crichton told them. "They'd been force-changed in the circle, then tried to escape. They were shot with silver-tipped arrows, remember. The circle is a place of healing, in a sense – but it's more for diagnosis. And the cure is death."

"I'm not sure," Abby said.

"Oh?"

"We didn't find that many bodies. So what happened to the wolves that didn't manage to run away? From what you say, the circle just enhanced their condition. It's a pretty poor trap if it makes the wolves stronger so they can escape."

"Abby's right. It just aims more and more moonlight at them – either in the circle or ready to be sacrificed on the Rogue Stone or wherever," Mike added. "As I said before – you can't have too much of a good thing, right?"

"Maybe you can," Carys said. "I've just remembered something Josh said. When he opened his ring and sort of charged himself up with moonlight from the bit of crystal inside."

"Yes?" Faye prompted.

"Well, he said something about not wanting to overdo it. He closed the ring pretty sharpish."

"David Forrest did too when he changed," Peter remembered.

"You think they're worried about *over*-exposure?" Crichton asked.

"Too much of a good thing," Peter said. "Is that possible?"

"Well, too much of anything is a poison," Faye said. "We need water to live, but get too much of it and you drown. Perhaps they can overdose on moonlight."

They watched as the last of the lights was raised into position. Cables were being laid back to a large van, which Peter guessed housed a generator. But that just didn't make sense.

"If they can drown in too much moonlight," he said slowly, "then why are they setting up lights to produce even more of it?"

"They need it for something else?" Carys suggested. "Not to change, but for some other reason."

"Mr Seymour could feel the shard of crystal lodged in his leg," Faye said. "He told me it was like toothache. An itch he couldn't scratch. It was only the tiniest fragment – we had it X-rayed once. But he wouldn't have it removed. Said it was a part of him now."

"Like the broken sword in Einzel's shoulder," Peter said.

"Exactly. I used to wonder if the crystal was somehow responsible for my father-in-law's long life. If it somehow prolonged it."

"And Einzel is very old," Abby said. "Has to be."

"Einzel has crystal *and* silver in his shoulder," Peter's father said. "Would that make a difference?

"It might," Faye agreed. "They're opposites, pulling in different directions. The crystal perhaps gives life, but the silver is constantly working against that. Hence he suffers from relentless pain, and from argyria – silver poisoning."

"But silver has healing properties," Mike said. "Best thing there was before antibiotics came along. That's why the chalice in church is made from silver – all those people taking communion, it should be covered in germs, but the silver sort of suffocates bacteria and keeps the cup sterile."

"That's the point, though, isn't it?" Carys said. "It heals in small quantities, but too much is a poison. Plus we know that, traditionally, werewolves could be killed with silver bullets. Like Mum said, maybe the crystal prolongs his life, while the silver makes it agony."

"A combination of life and death," Professor Crichton said. "That's possible. But he's been picking away at the crystal, using it in those rings. Now the balance is turning in favour of the silver."

"So what's with all the moonlight lamps and everything then?" Mike asked. "Are we any the wiser?"

"We can theorise," Crichton said. "And I think maybe

Einzel plans to focus all that energy on the crystal in his shoulder. It will absorb the moonlight, like charging up a battery."

"But why come here to do it?" Mike said. "Why not use the Vrolask Circle?"

"Because most of the stones are missing," Carys told him. "It wouldn't work."

"So he's got to come to the complete circle, here, to – er, maybe it's to combat the effects of the silver..." Peter suggested.

"Perhaps it's more than that," Crichton said. "Perhaps it's to make him stronger; even to heal him – whatever that means."

"But whatever he is doing," Faye said, "it can't be good."

The best option seemed to be to split up. Faye was adamant that the villagers should be warned something was happening – even if they didn't know exactly what. She and Carys would head back to the village and warn people the wolves had escaped from the sanctuary. That would probably keep most people indoors. Carys was obviously not happy to be relegated to knocking on doors, but she reluctantly agreed.

Professor Crichton suggested Abby and Mike continue on towards Wolfstone Manor as planned, and keep watch.

"We need to know just how many people are involved. If you can get close enough to see or overhear anything useful that would be great. And take better notes than you usually do, Mike," he added.

"And what about you and Peter?" Carys asked.

"We'll stay here. It looks like they"ve almost finished setting up their lights. Once they're done I want to take a closer look."

"Maybe we can sabotage the systems somehow, unplug the cables or something," Peter suggested.

"Maybe." Crichton's tone suggested that he'd already thought of that. "Meet back here by sunset at the latest, okay?"

It was another hour before Einzel's men had all gone. Just the generator van was left, along with the huge lamps. There was no sign of anyone staying behind, but Peter and his father waited another fifteen minutes to be sure.

Then they made their way cautiously up to the circle. Peter was ready to turn and run back to the woods at the slightest movement. Professor Crichton rubbed his hands together like he did when he started on a new project or dig site. Like he couldn't wait to see what was going on.

"Let's just rip out some cables, take whatever we can, and get out of here," Peter said.

"Sounds like a plan. This is fascinating, but it probably wouldn't do to hang around."

"Oops – too late!" The voice came from behind them.

They spun round – to find David Forrest standing there. He was holding a pistol.

"Don't move," he said. His voice was firm, but the gun wavered nervously.

"You going to kill us, David?" Professor Crichton asked.

"Like you killed your own father?" Peter added. He was surprised how calm he sounded. He certainly didn't feel calm.

"Only if you force me to."

"Very comforting," Crichton told him. "Actually, you might be able to help us with something." He walked to the nearest of the lamps, for all the world as if this was a normal conversation about something mundane – like he was asking for directions.

"You think?" David jabbed the gun forward. "Just stand still!"

"We know the moonlight, both real and artificial, will be focused by the stones onto Wolfstone Manor."

"Onto the Rogue Stone in the cellar," Peter added.

"So you've worked it all out, then," David snapped.

"Everything except why," Crichton said.

David laughed, but it was forced and nervous. "That's

easy. This is the cure."

"Except that your *cure* is to become a wolf and throw off all your humanity," Peter said.

"Too right it is. And tonight Herr Einzel's long years of work will be fulfilled. Tonight he'll finally cure the wolves that are gathering, getting rid of their last vestiges of humanity. Whether they like it or not."

"You mean – you haven't told them that's what will happen?" Crichton said, appalled.

David shrugged. "They want a long life. Some of them know the cost. They don't care."

"What about your sister?" Peter said. "Would she care? What would she think? Your father certainly thought you were wrong."

"Well lucky for me, he can't tell me what to do any more, can he? And tonight, the moonlight will focus on the small pieces of crystal that each of us has. It will transform us permanently into the most savage and noble of creatures."

"Ready to work for Einzel?"

"Of course. He is our lord and master. He will use the Rogue Stone as a focus. The power will flow into him, making him all powerful. He will become Über-Wolf! No longer just the Old One. No longer the Lone Wolf – that is what "Einzel" means, of course – "alone"." David's expression twisted into a boyish smirk. "Or did you think it was actually his name?"

"So all this is just because he was lonely?" Peter sneered.

"Joke while you can. But Einzel wants you dealt with. So stop treating this like some sort of game."

"No one's playing games," Crichton said. "Just calm down."

David ignored him, aiming the gun right at Peter. "In fact, even though Einzel wants to tear you apart himself, why don't I just shoot you now?"

Peter felt like the life was already draining out of him. David's finger tightened on the trigger, and he grinned in anticipation.

CHAPTER 33

David had his back to the stone. So he couldn't see another figure rising up from behind it. Peter recognised his own coat before he realised who was wearing it.

Sensing movement, David spun round in surprise. "Annabelle?!"

She didn't answer, but regarded him warily. Beneath the coat, her bare legs and feet were muddy and scratched. Her face was streaked with dirt and her fair hair matted and filthy. She still wore the ring that she'd had when Peter first found her, trapped inside the cage in the cellar of Wolfstone Manor. Not a ring like David or the other wolves wore. This was more delicate, embossed with the engraved head of a wolf – the du Bois family crest.

David moved round, so he could keep Peter and Professor Crichton covered with the gun.

"Annabelle – thank God I've found you."

Her voice was all on one level. Devoid of emotion. "What are you doing to Peter?"

David frowned. "You know him?"

"He's my friend," she said. "He helped me."

"That's right," said Peter.

But David cut him off, jabbing the gun forward. "You shut up!" He turned back to his sister. "Where have you been? We were so worried."

"Then why didn't you look for me? Peter found me. I've been in the woods. Scavenging for food. Rabbits, rodents, anything I could find."

"You didn't have to stay in the woods."

"The woods are my home now," she said.

Peter tried to smile, to reassure the girl. She was confused and frightened, looking from Peter to her brother, and then to the gun.

"What did you mean?" she said at last. "Just now, when you spoke about father."

"I didn't mean anything."

"I heard you. I was here, listening. You said father can't tell you what to do any more. What did you mean?"

David stepped away from her, anxious. "Nothing. I didn't mean anything. Just that father's not here, that's all."

"Tell her the truth," Professor Crichton said sternly.

David turned sharply. "I'll kill you if you speak again!"

"Truth? What truth?"

"I'm sorry," Peter said. It would be a shock however she found out.

"Sorry?"

"I warned you!" David brought the gun up and fired.

But Annabelle moved lightning fast. She knocked her brother's arm and the shot went wide. She grabbed his wrist, holding it tight.

"What truth?" she demanded. "Tell me!"

David wrenched his hand free and staggered back. "There is no "truth". Dad's just… gone away, that's all."

There was no gentle way to do it. "He's dead, Annabelle," Peter told her. "He hasn't gone away, he's dead!"

"No!" Her legs buckled, and she dropped to her knees. "You were lying."

"Of course he was lying," David said. His face was a sneer of triumph.

"I don't mean him," Annabelle said. "I mean *you*."

David's expression changed. He suddenly seemed worried.

She stepped towards him. "Tell me what happened."

David brought the gun round to aim at his sister. "Nothing happened. There was… an accident, that's all."

"Father is dead," she said slowly.

"Yes. Yes, he's dead. But we don't need him, not any more."

"Your father is dead," Peter said. "I was there. I couldn't help him – in fact, he died helping me and my friend Carys."

"Don't listen to him!" David insisted.

"Why not?" she demanded, taking another step closer.

"He helped me. He tells the truth!"

"Don't move – stay there!" David shouted.

"Or what?" Peter yelled at him. "Or you'll kill your own sister? Like you killed your father?"

Annabelle stared at her brother, her face suddenly pale beneath the dirt.

"He's lying," David said. "You *know* he's lying."

"I know he's not," she said quietly. Then she ran straight at her brother.

A shot, but too late. Annabelle was already on David, knocking him backwards. The gun went flying – disappearing into the long grass. David managed to break free of his sister, pushing her away. But she came straight back at him.

"Look out!" Peter shouted.

David was reaching for his ring. Peter ran to help, but he was too late. Already the deadly moonlight was shining out from the tiny sliver of crystal. Already David was transforming into a snarling, savage creature.

But Annabelle launched herself at her brother again, wrapping her arms round him. The light from the ring played across her face as they struggled, illuminating her fury. Lighting up her features as they slowly changed into the face of a wolf. Her fingers were claws, ripping into his side. Her mouth clamped onto his neck in a deadly, brutal kiss – ripping and tearing into her brother's flesh.

"Too much," he gasped. "Close the ring – too much light." But his words were barely comprehensible. Blood coughed from his mouth and ran down his neck. His movements became weaker and he slumped in his sister's arms.

She held him for a moment, then let him fall backwards.

"I'm s-sorry," Peter stammered, staring into the bloodshot eyes of the wolf. "I'm sorry about your father. And about David. And about… *this*. I wish I could help."

A streak of lighter fur ran from the top of the wolf's head down its back, a grotesque echo of Annabelle's long, fair hair. Somewhere deep in the eyes he could still see Annabelle. Something about the creature's expression assured him she was in there somewhere.

For a moment the creature held Peter's gaze, and looked deep into him. He stood his ground, waiting for the claws to rip into his flesh, for the teeth to sink into his throat.

But instead, the wolf dropped down on all fours and bounded away towards the woods.

Peter's coat lay shredded on the blood-soaked ground. He picked it up. Feeling a weight on one side, he reached into the pocket and took out his torch. Then he tossed the coat into the long grass outside the circle. It landed close to where they had dragged David's body so it wouldn't be seen. He spared it a glance, then turned away.

"You okay?" Professor Crichton asked.

"Yes and no."

"Well, that's probably all we have time for." The professor pointed into the distance. "Someone's coming."

Two figures emerged from the woods, a little way from where the wolf had disappeared into the trees. They ran towards the circle.

Peter's first instinct was to head in the opposite direction. But the figures were waving at them urgently. He recognised them just as Crichton said, "It's Abby and Mike."

The two had stopped and were gesturing for Peter and Professor Crichton to head for the woods. From the other direction came the sound of an engine.

"Someone else is coming," Peter realised. "They're warning us we're about to have company."

They reached the safety of the wood just as a large black car crested the hill behind them and drew up next to the van.

"I wasn't sure you'd understood us," Mike said as Peter and his dad got their breath back.

"We overheard these guys saying they were heading back to the circle," Abby explained. "I think they're just the first. Everyone will be trooping up here soon."

"Everyone?" Peter said. "How many?"

"Must be thirty or more people at the manor," Mike said. "Just hanging around outside, chatting, like it's a cocktail party."

"People you wouldn't believe," Abby went on. "And they're just the ones we recognised."

"Like who?" Crichton asked.

"A couple of politicians – no one really famous. One's a junior minister, I think. The actress who just got axed from that soap opera."

"People in uniform," Mike added. "Army and police. So maybe it's as well we didn't just call 999."

He pulled a pack of cigarettes from his pocket, together with his lighter. Abby took them from him and put them in her own coat pocket.

"You're giving up," she told him. "Remember?"

"Any sign of Einzel?" Peter wondered.

"Not that we saw," Abby told him. "But he could have been there. Like Mike said, it was quite a party."

"And now the party's moving up here," Peter said.

"Not all of it," Crichton told them. "Remember what David Forrest just said about Einzel? He's going to be in that cellar at the manor, soaking up the focused moonlight."

"I'm not even going to ask," Abby said.

"So what now?" Mike asked. "It's starting to get dark. Once they're all up here for whatever it is they're going to do, our options will be rather limited."

While Crichton brought Abby and Mike up to date with what had happened and what they'd learned, Peter rang Carys. The signal kept breaking up, but he managed, eventually, to warn her to be careful coming back to the circle, and described where they were hiding.

It was almost dark by the time Carys and her mother joined Peter and the others. More people had been arriving steadily – by car, or walking across the fields from Wolfstone Manor. The most frightening thing about them, Peter thought, was how ordinary they looked. But then, Sebastian Forrest and his son had seemed so ordinary. And his daughter...

As evening turned to night, the people at the circle gathered closer together. Their voices were just a murmur of sound, and it was impossible to make out what they were saying. But now the conversations died away. The group stood quiet and still, within the semi-circle of stones and lamps.

"What are they waiting for?" Professor Crichton wondered.

"It's a cloudy night," Faye said. "The moon's hidden."

"They might need it to be at a particular angle or position," Carys said.

"But when they're ready, they'll turn those lights on, right?" Peter checked.

"Then the combined light of the moon and the lamps will focus on the manor," Crichton said.

"Which means we've got until the moon appears to sort things out," Peter said. "After that, they'll all be wolves and Einzel will be a super-wolf or whatever."

"But how do we stop them?" Abby asked.

"Same way people have always stopped them," Peter told her. "Right from the beginning, since the Stone Age." He looked round at their puzzled faces, barely more than smudges in the gathering night. "Isn't it obvious what we have to do?"

As he spoke, the clouds thinned. Streaks of moonlight filtered through, glinting on the stones. A howl of triumph split the air.

CHAPTER 34

Carys felt like she was racing the clouds. She watched them scud across the sky as she ran. Professor Crichton led the way through the fields as they looped back towards his car.

Occasional shafts of moonlight stabbed through the grey-black sky. Carys could only guess what was happening back at the circle. Peter would wait as long as he could for them, but if the others had to act before she and Crichton got back with the sword...

She concentrated on running, impressed that Peter's father was so fast and fit. Or maybe he was high on adrenaline and fear – every bit as scared as she was.

They were both out of breath by the time they reached the road; exhausted when they reached the car. Mud was spattered up Carys's jeans. She slipped and almost fell as they finally made it to the Range Rover. Professor Crichton caught her arm, and she gasped a thank you.

"The sensible thing to do would be to drive back," she said when she'd caught her breath enough to speak.

Crichton took the crystal sword from the back of the Range Rover. "The sensible thing would have been not to leave this here in the first place." He patted his jacket pockets with his free hand. He pulled a large bunch of keys from one pocket and stared at them. "Sebastian Forrest won't be needing these any more."

"We might though," Carys said, looking round the abandoned building site. "I've got an idea."

The ground was cold and hard under him as Peter crawled towards the circle. The night was filled with the growls and cries of the people gathered between the stones. Every time a shaft of moonlight escaped between clouds, they became gradually less human. Peter guessed they could use their shards of crystal to change completely, but were saving those to add to the force of the lunar energy when the moon emerged fully and the lamps came on.

He edged closer, inch by inch, afraid that at any moment one of the creatures would see him. But for now they were preoccupied with the process of transformation. A senior policeman ripped off his jacket and shirt, hair erupting from his chest. A woman kicked off her shoes to reveal the clawed feet beneath. A man stood staring up at the moon, his jaw elongating and splitting through his face as Peter watched.

All across the circle, the people were changing. Fur, teeth, claws…

Finally, he was there, crouched behind the stone,

praying he was out of sight. Peter risked a glance round the edge of the stone. A massive hairy face stared back at him. The creature reared up, raising a huge paw. Claws stabbed out from the fingertips, and slashed through the air.

Behind the wolf, others were turning. Peter was transfixed, too frightened to move. The creature's paw slammed into the stone beside his head, claws scraping across its glinting surface. The spell was broken, and Peter ducked back round the stone.

At the same moment, the clouds parted and the full moon was revealed. A perfect silver disc shining down on the stones, and the creatures between them. The lamps above and behind Peter snapped on, and suddenly it was as light as day. A rumbling sound was growing, approaching – like the growling of a hundred wolves.

Within the circle, the creatures opened their massive jaws and, as one, howled in triumph at the moon.

Peter ducked away from another tremendous blow. He felt the breeze from it, the claws were so close to his face. He rolled aside, as the creature leaped at him. More were following. Now or never – he couldn't wait for Dad and Carys.

He dived across, and grabbed the hidden mechanism buried beneath the stone's edge.

The centre of the circle slid away. The howls of triumph

became roars of surprise and anger as the creatures fell into the pit below.

But not all of them. The wolves that had come after Peter were outside the area of the pit. Others on the far side were turning to see what had happened.

More light shone as bundles of sticks flared outside the area of moonlight. The dry wood that Peter and the others had gathered earlier caught at once in the flame from Mike's lighter. Abby, Mike and Faye advanced on the wolves outside the pit, herding them backwards, waving the burning firebrands.

But they were on the opposite side of the circle. On his own, Peter backed away from the advancing creatures. Their howls of rage filled the air, echoing all round him.

That couldn't be right. He ducked under another blow. Dived to one side as a wolf leaped at him. How could their roars be coming from *behind* him? He risked a glance over his shoulder.

Two enormous glowing eyes loomed out of the night, heading straight for him. Roaring out of the darkness. Only when one of the moonlight lamps went flying did Peter realise what it was.

Another lamp toppled, sparking and flickering. Then it was crushed into the ground. The creatures attacking Peter backed away. He leaped out of the way of the bulldozer as it ploughed through another light, heading straight for the creatures.

Peter caught a confused glimpse of Carys at the controls. His father was leaning off the side of the bulldozer, hacking down with the broken crystal sword, sending one of the werewolves howling into the pit in front of them. The blade at the front of the vehicle connected hard with another, knocking the creature backwards. It tumbled into the dark opening with a howl of pain.

The last of the lights died, as Mike reached the generator. Only the moonlight remained, glinting on the stones and shining down on the creatures scrabbling to escape from the pit.

Carys jumped down from the bulldozer and ran to help Peter to his feet.

"You okay?" she yelled over the howls and roars from below.

"I'm fine." He couldn't help grinning with relief. "I wasn't expecting *that.*" He gestured at the bulldozer, engine idling and lights cutting across the circle.

"I've always wanted to drive one of those," Carys said. "Thought it'dbe more use than your dad's four-by-four."

"Don't stop, the job's not done yet," Peter's father shouted to them as he ran past.

One of the creatures was hauling itself out of the

darkness. Crichton swung the sword, connecting with a massive set of paws as they reached over the lip of the pit. The creature fell back with a roar of pain. Across the circle, Faye and Abby swung their firebrands, trying desperately to keep the nightmare creatures confined. Mike ran back from the van to help them.

Peter and Carys went too. A wolf-woman was struggling up onto the shoulders of a wolf that had recently been a man in army uniform. Peter kicked out as she struggled to drag herself out of the pit. She fell back into the angry melee below.

"We can't keep them in there for long," Carys said, shouldering another back over the edge.

"We may not have to," Peter yelled back to her.

The centre of the pit was in full moonlight, both from above and reflected off the glittering stones. The creatures caught there were howling louder now – in pain as well as rage. Smoke coiled up from their pelts. They tried to press to the shadows at the edge of the pit. One of them, unable to escape quickly enough, collapsed in a smoking heap. In a moment, flickers of fire burst from its fur.

"The moonlight's burning them," Peter said.

"Spontaneous lupine combustion," Carys agreed.

"Should I close the pit?"

"If you do, they'll just dig their way out," she said.

"And you'll cut off the moonlight that's destroying them. They'll survive longer if they keep to the shadows. But it will get them eventually," Crichton said. "Leave it open, but keep them in there." He turned away.

"Where are you going?" Peter demanded.

"To the manor. Einzel's down there. He's lost the lamps, but the energy of the moon will still be focused on the Rogue Stone. I have to stop him."

"*We* – *we* have to stop him," Peter told him. "I'm coming with you."

"We both are," Carys said. "Mum and the others can cope here." She turned to look down the slope towards where Wolfstone Manor nestled behind the woods. "This is easy, compared to what's down there."

CHAPTER 35

Wolfstone Manor was a dark silhouette against the gunmetal grey of the night sky. There were no signs of life – no lights, no movement.

"Einzel's here somewhere," Professor Crichton whispered as they approached. "There may be others too."

"Down in the cellars," Peter said. "With the Rogue Stone."

"I thought the moonlight was supposed to be reflecting down from the circle to the Rogue Stone," Carys said, looking back the way they had come. "But you can't even see the circle from here."

"It's energy more than light," Crichton told her. "It's channelled through the air, and through the trees and woods."

"You mean like magnetism, or something?" Peter said. "Like the way a magnet can hold metal even if there's a piece of paper or something in the way of it?"

Crichton nodded. "The same way you can't see ultraviolet rays from the sun. But sit outside long enough on a bright summer's day and you'll still get a tan."

"Or sunburn," Carys said. She looked at Peter. "How do you feel?" she asked.

"Nervous. Scared."

"That's not what I meant."

"Oh." He realised what she meant. "I'm okay. I mean, I'm not about to change into a wolf again if that's what you're asking."

"Of course it's what she's asking," Crichton said. "Now let's get on with this." He hefted the jagged crystal sword as he spoke. The broken blade was gleaming with inner light.

"You think Einzel knows what's happening up at the circle?" Carys whispered as they crossed the terrace.

"Perhaps. But I doubt if he cares."

"All those people..." Carys said.

"People are a cheap commodity," Crichton said. "It's himself he's worried about. And his precious process. Once he's perfected that he'll convert as many as he can."

They found the window where Peter had first broken in. It seemed ages ago. Peter had the torch he'd recovered from his coat. It cast a pale glow ahead of them, just enough to help them find their way along the main corridor.

Every creaking floorboard, every sigh of the wind outside, made Peter's heart jump. He stared into every shadow, looked twice at every window or alcove. Finally they reached the steps down to the cellars.

Peter's dad gave a thumbs-up and raised the sword, like

a talisman. It was glowing brighter than ever as it neared the point where the moon's energy was focused – the Rogue Stone.

There was another glow from the bottom of the stairs. As they descended, it grew in intensity until it rivalled the crystal sword. At the last turn of the stairs, Professor Crichton paused, hand in the air. He mouthed a count of "one – two – three".

Then they charged round the corner, and down the final few steps.

The whole cellar was bathed in the amber light of the crystal. The Rogue Stone glittered in the wall, light shining out from around its edges as if it was filtering through the crack under a door.

Peter expected Einzel to be standing by the stone, soaking up the energy that spilled out of it. But there was no sign of him. The cellar was empty.

Or almost empty. A low growl from behind made them turn abruptly. A man stepped out from behind the staircase. Not Einzel, but a tall, broad man wearing a dark suit. Except that above the white collar and plain, dark tie, emerged the head of a wolf.

The wolf-man regarded them through blood-red eyes that gleamed in the reflected glow. A trail of saliva dripped down the front of the otherwise immaculate jacket. Peter's father raised the sword and stepped forward.

But the wolf was too quick for him. It lunged forward, knocking Crichton's sword arm away. The sword spun off into the corner of the room. Shards of crystal splintered from its edges and lay glowing on the floor.

"Dad!" Peter yelled, running towards him.

The wolf was already bearing down on him. Crichton staggered back a pace, unbalanced by the first blow. The next connected with his shoulder and he dropped to his knees in front of the wolf. It gave a roar of triumph and reared up, claws glinting in the light from the stone and the base of the wall.

He was too far away. Peter wasn't going to get there in time. From behind him, Carys shouted, "Peter – duck!"

Instinctively, he did. When he looked up, the wolf seemed frozen in position, arms raised, poised to attack. Then it fell slowly backwards, and crashed down to the floor.

"What?!"

Peter and his father both turned – to see Carys standing with her legs slightly apart, both hands braced on the tranquiliser gun. She pushed it back into her jacket pocket.

"The only dart, unfortunately," she said, smiling at their surprised expressions. "Next wolf, someone else can deal with."

"If there are any more," Crichton said, retrieving the sword. "There's no one else here."

But as soon as he finished speaking, a distant rumble, like thunder, filtered through to them.

"Except for Einzel. He's here somewhere," Carys said.

"Are we too late?" Peter wondered.

Crichton shook his head. "I hope not. But where is he?"

"He can't be hiding down here," Peter said. "The light from round the stone…" His voice tailed off. The light was shining round the stone… like it was coming through the gap under a door.

"What is it?" Carys asked.

"It's not coming from the stone, is it? The light, I mean. The stone glitters, like the ones in the circle. But this is something else."

He ran over to the stone, the others close behind him.

"It's more concentrated. Like the glow from the sword," Carys said.

"Like it's shining round a door," Peter added. "But – it can't be…"

Carys gasped as she made the same connection. Her hand went to her mouth. "Oh no."

"Oh yes," Peter said. "There's a door, somewhere down here. We have to find it."

"A door to where?" Crichton asked. He realised as soon as he spoke. "Oh I see. The glow – yes, it's coming from another room. A room which, logically, would be through here…"

He stepped into an alcove just along from the Rogue Stone. There was a grinding of some ancient mechanism.

"Easy when you know how," Professor Crichton said, letting go of the iron ring set into the shadowy side of the alcove.

As he spoke, the back of the alcove swung open. Brilliant light spilled out, scorching their eyes.

"D'you think Sebastian Forrest knew what his father did?" Peter wondered. "That he was desperately searching for a cure too, using anything he could find. Einzel didn't – until now. An unexpected advantage for him."

"Maybe he tried to tell us," Carys said.

Whether he had or not, they both now knew that Lionel du Bois had not returned to Wolfenburg Castle to destroy the Crystal Room.

He hadn't broken it up. He'd dismantled it – and brought it back to Wolfstone.

They stepped over the threshold. Into the Crystal Room. The walls shone dazzlingly bright with the moonlight. Gradually they made out a shape in front of them – a dark figure standing in the middle of the room.

The triumphant roar of the lone wolf split the air as the enormous, savage creature turned towards them. Light seemed to pour into the matted fur and gleam in its eyes as it soaked up the energy of the moon.

CHAPTER 36

Peter watched in horror as his father walked slowly towards the huge creature rearing up in front of them. He looked tiny, pathetic, as he raised the sword. Its broken blade glowed as fiercely as the walls, silver glinting beneath the crystal.

As Peter and Carys followed Professor Crichton, another figure seemed to coalesce out of the light.

Heels clicked on the floor as the woman approached. She ignored Peter's father, striding towards Peter and Carys, blocking their view of the confrontation.

As she got closer, Peter recognised Irena – the blonde hair, ice-blue eyes and immaculate suit. She shrugged out of her suit jacket, letting it fall to the glowing floor behind her as she walked. Then she kicked off her shoes, padding towards them in bare feet.

"High heels are so impractical in these situations, don't you think?" she snarled.

Her face was already changing. The blonde hair became a mane of silver-white fur. Hair sprouted from her face as its shape altered, lupine features erupting from her immaculate skin. The sleeves of her blouse split apart as muscles knitted together. By the time she reached them, the transformation was almost complete.

Carys drew the tranquiliser gun, even though it wasn't loaded. But Irena lashed out, smashing the gun away. Her next blow was aimed at Peter.

He leaped back. Claws raked down his chest, shredding his shirt, missing his skin by a fraction.

Carys grabbed Peter and dragged him back. Irena was in front of them, so their only retreat was back through the door.

"We can't leave Dad!" Peter yelled.

"We don't have a choice."

Over Irena's shoulder, he saw his father standing in front of the Einzel creature, sword raised. His father looked back for a second – just long enough to nod at Peter. Then he turned away, hacking down with the sword.

Irena was coming at them again, blotting out Peter's view. Carys dragged him back, and together they fell out of the room.

"He'll be all right," Carys said, her face close to Peter's as they stumbled into the cellar room. "We have to get her out of here – deal with Irena first, or lose her. Then we can come back and help."

"If it's not too late," Peter muttered. But Carys was right, They had to tackle Irena first. Staying alive was their priority.

"At least he's got the sword," Carys said, backing further into the cellar.

Light shone round Irena, blurring the edges of her grotesque form. She stalked out of the Crystal Room, growling hungrily. Behind her, Peter saw his father swing the sword again. Saw the Einzel creature swatting aside the blade with ease. Heard the wolf's howl of triumph. But it was coupled with pain: the sword had bitten into the creature's flesh.

The view cut off as the door slammed shut behind Irena.

Peter looked round desperately for anything they could use as a weapon. The open cage. Burned out candles... Nothing. Carys had reached the same conclusion, and was running for the stairs.

"Come on!" she yelled.

The wolf was close behind him. Its breath was warm on the back of his neck. Its growls purred in Peter's ears. He took the steps two at a time, knowing the hideous creature was bounding up after him – would catch him at any moment.

He reached the top, ducked as Carys swung a piece of wood broken from an ancient piece of furniture. The wooden strut sliced over Peter's head, and connected with the creature behind him. He heard it cry out, fall backwards, stumble down the stairs.

But he didn't turn to look. No time. He grabbed Carys's hand and together they charged through the dusty house. Boards creaked and protested under their feet.

"Where are we going?" he asked.

"I don't know. Anywhere. Just keep running!"

Down the corridor and into the main hall. The front door?

Suddenly the wolf launched itself from behind them, skidding off the wall, landing on all fours. It stared back at them, blocking the way to the door.

Peter managed to turn aside, running up the main staircase. One step collapsed and his foot went right through it. He wrenched it free, feeling the splintered wood scrape along his shin and pierce the skin above his ankle. Ignoring the pain, he kept going. It was only when he reached the top landing that he realised Carys wasn't with him.

Above the hallway an enormous glass chandelier hung on a rusty chain. It was just below Peter as he looked back down. It swayed slightly, creaking, dripping dust like faint rain. Like everything else, it was ancient, decrepit, ready to collapse. Light from outside reflected off the less dusty glass drops, like a scattering of moonlight shining through the clouds.

Below it, Carys was sprawled across the floor where she

had fallen. The wolf-woman moved slowly towards her. It paused for a moment to look up at Peter. Its eyes gleamed red. Shreds of Irena's suit clung incongruously to its fur. Its jaw twitched open in a grotesque smile. Sharp teeth gleamed in the dusty moonlight.

Carys was struggling to get up, pushing herself backwards, away from the approaching wolf. The wolf paused again, savouring the moment. It tensed, back legs braced ready to leap.

Watching from above, Peter felt helpless. He looked down through a gap where the bannisters had broken away – horrified, numb, empty.

Carys looked up at him – her face pale and scared. Her eyes widened in a desperate plea. She was counting on him. She needed him. And he could do nothing but watch as she died.

"Peter!" she yelled.

The sound startled him into movement. He didn't think, it was just instinct. He jumped.

His body crashed into the chandelier three metres out and a metre below the landing. The impact jarred through his arms and chest. The unforgiving glass and sharp metal bit into him. The whole thing lurched sideways under his weight, and he almost slipped off. He struggled to hold on.

Then he was falling. The whole chandelier was falling,

crashing down into the hallway.

Through the dusty glass and tarnished metal, he saw the wolf turn again. It stared up at him, with sudden fear in its eyes. Very real, human fear as the chandelier crashed down with a crunch of glass, metal, bone, tissue.

Peter scrambled off the shattered mess, his whole body aching. He stumbled across to help Carys to her feet. A red stain edged out from under the broken frame of the chandelier and crept across the floor towards them.

CHAPTER 37

They stood by the door, well away from the smashed chandelier, holding each other tight.

Neither Carys nor Peter said anything for several moments. Then they both spoke together.

"I have to get back to Dad."

"We need help."

They stepped apart, Peter's hands on Carys's shoulders.

"*You* get help," he said.

"We both go."

He shook his head. "I can't abandon Dad."

"But what can you *do*?"

"Maybe nothing." Going back to the Crystal Room was futile, and they both knew it. "But I've got to try."

She bit her lower lip. "I'll come with you."

"No." Peter said it more sharply than he'd meant, but no way was he letting Carys risk her life again. He'd almost lost her just now. He could feel the emotion welling up inside him just at the thought of it. "You're right," he said. "We need help. I'll do what I can, but I'm relying on you – all right?"

She gave a quick nod. "All right."

"Be careful," Peter said as he turned away.

"You too."

He skirted round the spreading blood, and ran across the hall. On the other side, he turned back, hoping to see Carys watching him. Hoping to see her sad half-smile. Maybe for the last time.

But she had already gone.

Howls of pain echoed through the woods. Branches tugged at Carys's clothes. Leaves whipped across her face. She stumbled onwards, as fast as she could. She felt terrible leaving Peter, but what could the two of them do on their own? She'd never been so afraid as during the past few days. Never as frightened as when she faced the wolf in the hallway of Wolfstone Manor. She owed Peter her life, and now she was abandoning him.

No! She told herself, she wasn't running out. She was getting help. She'd be back. She'd save him.

Breathless, heart pounding, she staggered up the last of the incline to the edge of the circle. Mike, Abby and her mother stood looking down into the pit, their figures illuminated by the flickering remains of the firebrands they held. Their faces reflected the pale moonlight that splayed across the scene and glinted on the standing stones.

A wolf roared up out of the pit. Paws scrabbled on the

grassy edge. Claws bit into the ground as they tried to gain purchase.

Mike stepped forward, thrusting out his flaming brand. The wolf roared in pain, and fell back into the pit.

"It's taking too long," Carys realised. "Peter and his dad need help now."

"But we can't leave here until they're all dead," Abby said.

"It won't be long," Mike assured her, lunging at another of the horrific creatures. He forced it back into the turmoil of the pit. Steam rose up and blotted out the moon like clouds.

Faye put her free arm round her daughter's shoulders. "I'm sorry. You stay and help here – I'll go. I'll do what I can."

She held the firebrand out to Carys. But the girl didn't take it. "No. *I* have to do this. I owe Peter that."

But what could she do? She closed her eyes, forcing back tears. In the darkness behind her eyelids, she saw again the chandelier crashing down in an explosion of glass and metal. When she opened her eyes, her face was a mask of determination.

What if his father was already dead? Peter dreaded going back down to the cellar. What if he found Einzel standing triumphant over his dad's lacerated body? He thought about the blood staining the hallway, and imagined a similar crescent-shaped pool spilling across the crystal floor.

A roar from below – anger or pain? He clattered down the steps, fast as he could, not caring who or what heard him coming. In his hand he had the only weapon he could find – a broken length of metal from the chandelier. A makeshift sword of his own, for all the good it would do.

"Don't be long, Carys," he murmured as he stepped into the alcove. He knew she'd be back. She'd bring help. She'd do *something*. Knowing Carys, it would be something outrageous. He smiled grimly at the thought, and pulled the metal ring that opened the door to the Crystal Room.

Peter's father ducked aside as the creature lashed out at him. They were both slowing, both tired. Einzel's hirsute body was slick with blood. Professor Crichton seemed unharmed, but his clothes were torn and his face was smeared with sweat. It was only a matter of time before the wolf caught him. Caught him and ripped him apart.

Peter ran to help, hammering the metal strut into the creature's knee. It howled with pain and staggered back. But it didn't fall. Instead, it turned its huge, bloodshot eyes towards him. Peter felt the full impact of the creature's anger and hatred. He saw in its eyes only triumph and victory. It knew this was the last battle, and it knew it was going to win.

The creature flexed its claws, drew itself up and let loose the most almighty roar. It charged across the Crystal

Room, claws skittering on the hard floor and launched itself at Peter. He twisted out of the way, but too late. The wolf slammed into him, knocking him backwards. The air thumped out of his lungs as he hit the wall.

Then his father was there, swinging the sword up at the wolf's belly. A killing blow.

It stopped short. The creature caught the sword hand as it drove upwards, twisting the weapon from Professor Crichton's grip. It dashed the sword to the ground. The broken blade splintered again, crystal shattering across the floor like crushed ice.

The creature's triumph was a low, rumbling purr that echoed round the room. It seemed to get closer and louder as Peter's father staggered back to join him. Their backs were against the wall, close to the door. Was there time to run from the room before the wolf got them? And how far would they get – the stairs, maybe? Probably not even that far.

Knowing they were already dead, the wolf reared up. It was so huge that its head looked close to the top of the chamber. It spread its massive arms and bellowed in victory. The low rumble grew louder still, counterpointing the roar of triumph.

"That noise," Crichton said, "it sounds like..."

His words were lost in the growing roar. But Peter knew

exactly what it sounded like.

The Einzel creature seemed oblivious. It scented victory and nothing else mattered. At the very last moment, the rumble became a thunderous crash from above. And the creature looked up.

At the same moment, Peter grabbed his father's arm and pulled him down. They dived across the floor, keeping low, sliding into the safety of the doorway as the ceiling caved in.

The sound of the bulldozer filled the chamber. The whole front of the vehicle ploughed through the roof and it plunged downwards. Crystal fragmented around it. The weight crushed down on the end wall, bowing it inwards, until the whole structure broke under the pressure and exploded inwards.

The crystal shattered into millions of slivers, each as sharp as a silver arrow. It rained down from the roof and exploded out from the walls. Glowing, sharp and lethal – shards of crystal thundered like hailstones across the chamber, shredding anything in their path.

Standing in the middle of the room, Einzel was caught full in the storm. Flesh was ripped from the bones in a shotgun blast of crystal splinters. With a final howl of anger and agony, the creature crashed down amongst the glowing fragments.

When he dared to look, Peter saw the bulldozer halfway through the roof. Carys was slumped forward through the cabin window. She slowly lifted her head, smiling weakly down at him. And below her in the middle of the room lay the bloodied, lacerated corpse of the Lone Wolf. For a moment, its chest heaved in one rasping, final breath. Then it was still.

Above them, through the shattered roof and ruined walls of Wolfstone Manor, the full moon faded behind a cloud. And the glow of the crystal fragments strewn across the floor slowly died away.

CHAPTER 38

Apart from broken glass and wrecked furniture, the pub wasn't too damaged. The wolves were gone, rounded up by police, who tracked them by their embedded GPS chips. Peter had closed up the pit, and so, apart from the abandoned vehicles by the circle and at Wolfstone Manor, there was nothing to suggest Einzel and his associates had ever been there.

Carys felt like she could sleep for ever. But by lunchtime she was feeling hungry. She found Peter sitting in the remains of the bar eating a sandwich.

"Hey," he said by way of greeting.

"Hey," she answered.

They sat and ate in silence. They'd been through so much there didn't seem any point in talking. Not yet. Later they would have more than enough to say to each other.

The afternoon was cool but bright. They walked across the fields, past the abandoned vehicles and through the Wolfstone Circle, then on past the manor. They stood and looked at the wreckage of the end of the house. The tower was half collapsed, the side of the house smashed away. The bulldozer was wedged partway into the building, its back end tilted upwards.

There was a police incident van at the Lupine Sanctuary. Carys introduced Peter to Eddie, who was working his way through a mountain of paperwork. He was a middle-aged man with thinning, greying hair and glasses.

"I'm a vet, not an accountant," he protested.

"You got the wolves back then?" Peter said.

"Oh, you heard about that? They think Josh let them out, after..." He shook his head. "You think you know people and then... Anyway, yes they're back now. They even found one wolf that didn't have a tracking chip. Janey would know all about it. She'd have given it a name, probably." He took his glasses off and wiped his eyes.

Peter went back outside, but Carys stayed to talk to Eddie. The police were sure that Josh had killed Janey. She'd tried to fight him off – they'd found his blood outside. There was an alert out for him, but the man seemed to have disappeared. Carys guessed she'd only stunned him when she hit him with the car. But in any case, he'd be lying dead in the pit with the rest of Einzel's followers now.

Peter was by the gate to the main pen. The lock had gone, and it was secured with a simple chain with a peg through it. Carys watched as Peter crouched down in front of the gate.

One of the wolves was on the other side, so close its

muzzle was against the mesh of the gate. It stared intently at Peter, but he didn't back away. Instead he held his hand up to the mesh. The wolf didn't move.

"He said one of the wolves didn't have a microchip," Peter said, sensing Carys standing a little way behind him. "This one."

"How do you know?"

"I know."

Carys looked at the wolf. A streak of lighter fur ran from the top of its head down its back. Apart from that it looked just like all the rest as it continued to stare back at Peter.

Peter straightened up, taking the peg from the chain holding the gate shut. The heavy chain rattled through the clasp, and the gate swung open.

"What are you doing?"

Peter didn't answer. He was watching the wolf as it padded out of the pen. The wolf stared back at Peter for a moment. Then it leaped.

The weight of the creature knocked him onto his back. The wolf was on top of Peter, jaws close to his face. Staring into his eyes. He tried to sit up, to throw it off, but the wolf reached out a paw and pushed it down on his shoulder. He slumped back again.

Something glinted in the fur as the paw moved. A ring,

clasped round one of the clawed toes. Not like the ring David and Einzel's wolves had worn. A more delicate design, embossed with the engraved head of a wolf – the du Bois family crest.

Carys ran forward, ready to drag the wolf away. Ready to protect Peter from it – whatever the danger. She'd die for him if she had to.

He was aware of Carys running towards them. But Peter's attention was focused on the wolf. He stared into its eyes, and somewhere deep inside he saw what he was looking for.

The wolf's jaws opened. It stared down at him, through the eyes he knew so well. Then a long, pale tongue emerged, and gently licked Peter's cheek.

Peter got to his feet as the wolf rolled off him. She lay for a moment, looking up at Peter. Watching as Carys grabbed him and pulled him into a hug. She gave a slight nod of acceptance, then she turned and ran off across the fields.

Carys closed the gate. "She'll be all right."

"I know she will."

Peter took Carys's hand, and together they followed the wolf's path towards the wood and the ancient Wolfstone Circle.